PRIVATE
ROME

THE PRIVATE NOVELS

A list of more titles by James Patterson appears at the
back of this book

WHY EVERYONE LOVES JAMES PATTERSON AND THE PRIVATE SERIES

'Great action sequences…
breathtaking twists and turns'
ANTHONY HOROWITZ

'An **unmissable**, breakneck ride'
JAMES SWALLOW

'**Exhilarating**, high-stakes action'
LESLEY KARA

'An exhilarating and **totally
satisfying read**' NB MAGAZINE

'A **breakneck fast**, brutally
good page-turner' DAILY MAIL

'Hits the ground running and the
pace never misses a beat'
DAILY EXPRESS

'Yet another fine outing from the
master of thrillers' CITY A.M.

JAMES PATTERSON
& ADAM HAMDY

PRIVATE
ROME

CENTURY

1 3 5 7 9 10 8 6 4 2

Century
20 Vauxhall Bridge Road
London SW1V 2SA

Century is part of the Penguin Random House group of companies
whose addresses can be found at global.penguinrandomhouse.com.

Penguin
Random House
UK

First published in the UK by Century in 2023

www.penguin.co.uk

A CIP catalogue record for this book is available from the British Library.

ISBN: 978–1–529–90286–0 (hardback)
ISBN: 978–1–529–90287–7 (trade paperback)

Typeset in 12.25/18.25pt ITC Berkeley Oldstyle Std by Jouve (UK), Milton Keynes
Printed and bound in Great Britain by Clays Ltd, Elcograf S.p.A.

The authorised representative in the EEA is Penguin Random House Ireland,
Morrison Chambers, 32 Nassau Street, Dublin D02 YH68

Penguin Random House is committed to a sustainable future
for our business, our readers and our planet. This book is
made from Forest Stewardship Council® certified paper.

For everyone who is seeking answers

CHAPTER 1

I WAS ALONE in a room full of strangers. They all knew who I was, but only a handful of them were familiar to me. I guess that's why I was there. A curiosity, a minor celebrity, someone to draw a crowd. Starting a new overseas office was always exciting and I'd never missed a launch, but there was more at stake now. My exploits in Delhi, Berlin, Moscow and elsewhere had given me a degree of notoriety in law-enforcement and intelligence circles and I felt I had a reputation to live up to. Matteo Ricci, the former City of Rome police inspector I'd hired to start the Private Rome office, had been busy promoting me and the detective agency to Rome's rich, powerful and influential citizens.

Matteo, a personable man in his mid-thirties with an impressive track record as a cop, had spent the entire evening at my side, introducing me to a succession of potential clients. Roman entrepreneurs, politicians, clergy, journalists, police officers, lawyers, bankers . . . a blur of faces atop interchangeable tuxedos or glamorous cocktail dresses. I would only be able to put a handful of names to faces, but that wasn't my job. Matteo knew who these people were and would follow up when the office was fully running.

"Mr. Morgan," he said, drawing my attention away from the small group I was talking to. It was his way of signaling they'd had their time. "I'd like you to meet Joseph Stadler, Chief Operating Officer of the Vatican Bank."

He nodded toward a tall, angular silver-haired man in a well-tailored tux.

"Pleased to meet you, Mr. Morgan," he said, in excellent English spoken with a strong Swiss accent. "This is my executive assistant, Christian Altmer."

The man beside him had a thick crop of blond hair and a tan that spoke of too much time wasted on the slopes or at the beach. Altmer oozed easy charm, flashing a smile of pure white, and I disliked him instantly.

"Nice to meet you," he said, offering me his hand.

"Likewise," I replied, shaking hands with both men.

"This is quite a party," Altmer remarked.

We were at La Posta Vecchia, a well-known hotel overlooking the Tyrrhenian Sea, some fifty kilometers from the center of Rome. The splendid converted palazzo evoked Renaissance Italy, a time when people studied the achievements of classical antiquity and strove to match or surpass them. The building itself was equal to anything the ancient Romans had left behind; heavy stone walls, grand terraces overlooking the sea, cobbled pathways running through ornate gardens, ancient beams, polished wooden flooring, painted plaster walls, and in some rooms sculpted reliefs on walls and ceilings.

"I just wanted to put out a sign saying we were open for business, but Matteo said Rome prefers a party," I told the bankers.

"Come on! When do I get to meet the hero of Moscow?" a woman standing behind Stadler and Altmer asked loudly.

She wore a figure-hugging black mini-dress and her blond hair was pulled back into a tight bun.

"Jack," Matteo said to me with a smile, "this is Esther Cavalli."

If Stadler was put out, he didn't show it, but Altmer did, eying Esther with a look of disdain.

"Perhaps we will get a chance to talk later?" Stadler observed to me.

"I hope so," I replied, and he and Altmer moved on, allowing the brash blonde to take center-stage.

"It's like waiting to meet a king," she scoffed. "I only tolerate it for Matteo's sake."

"He assured me lots of people would be interested in meeting me, and it seems he was right," I replied.

"Matteo knows Rome better than most."

"Not so well as you do, Esther," he countered. "Esther is one of Italy's best corporate lawyers," he told me. "A grand attorney," he added with a low bow.

He was charming without being a creep. Knew when to engage, press a conversation, back off, which suggested a high degree of empathy, one of the many qualities that had impressed me when I'd interviewed him a little over four months ago. We'd met each other three times before tonight. The first was a formal interview in the Hotel Hassler; the second for a coffee at a little place he knew near Vatican City where we'd bonded over our mutual passion for boxing and Formula One. Our third encounter had been for dinner in the Hassler's rooftop restaurant where I'd offered him the job of head of Private Rome, which, judging by the width of his smile for the remainder of the evening, had meant a great deal to him. His track record with Rome police was faultless and he was athletic and good-looking, which I had observed made him the target for flirtatious advances from several of the men and women he'd invited here to meet me.

"How long do we each get?" Esther asked, glancing over her shoulder at the line of people standing behind her.

It was a question I'd been pondering myself. How long would I be expected to continue to make small talk? The line extended through several groups of people I'd already been introduced to, across the large function hall, toward an antechamber by the main door. There must have been another fifty people waiting.

"There is no time limit for someone as special as you," Matteo assured Esther.

He was naturally smooth, which was another quality he'd need to draw on in his new position. Gearing up the Rome office had proved to be more of a challenge than I'd anticipated. We were still short of people, and were probably about a month away from being fully operational. Matteo still needed a second-in-command, and our principal investigators and support teams were currently going through their training and induction. The launch party was a little premature in my opinion, but Matteo had wanted it this way. It would take all his natural charm to keep potential customers interested in engaging us until we could actually fulfill their requirements.

Esther rolled her eyes and punched him playfully on the shoulder. She was about to reply but the words went unspoken when a commotion broke out by the doorway.

"Release me!" a man shouted.

His voice echoed against the stone walls of the antechamber. I noticed an American accent.

The two hundred or so guests in the main hall fell silent at the sounds of a scuffle breaking out. Moments later a priest in a black three-piece suit and clerical collar burst into the room, trailed by the private security personnel we'd hired for the party.

The priest was in his mid-fifties, with curly gray hair. His ruddy cheeks were marked with a map of burst blood vessels and other blemishes that suggested a history of drinking. He scanned the room, eyes wild with fear, and when he caught sight of Matteo, shook off the restraining hands of our security guards and ran over to us.

I stepped forward to put myself between Esther and the priest, but I needn't have worried. He wasn't a threat, at least not to any of us.

He stopped abruptly. Glancing around fearfully, taking in the sight of the partygoers, he cried, "The right hand of God will strike me down! Tonight, here in this place, I will die."

CHAPTER 2

MURMURS OF CONCERN rippled through the room as all our guests focused on the priest. Undeterred, he took hold of both Matteo's hands.

"I came to ask for your help," he said, glancing around nervously as though all the eyes fixed on him belonged to enemies, "but it's no good. I cannot be saved. I must pay for my sins and pray that God will forgive me when I stand before Him. Only He sees all, but the Devil sees almost as much."

The poor man seemed very distressed, quite possibly in the grip of a mental-health crisis.

"I've put you at risk," he said suddenly. "I'm a fool. I came here to talk, but by doing so I only endanger you."

Matteo shook his head and soothed the priest. "Father Brambilla, let's get you somewhere you'll feel safe and then you can tell me what's troubling you." He turned to me. "You don't mind, do you, Jack?"

"You do what you need to do," I replied.

"I'll look after Jack for you," Esther said, taking Matteo's place at my side.

He smiled. "You're in good hands then."

Matteo took the distressed priest by the arm and led him away. "Come with me, father."

The priest glanced back at me, raw fear visible in his eyes. For a moment I thought about following. There were few things in life that could make a man look so afraid. This had to be serious.

"Jack, I'd like to introduce Aldo Accardi and his wife, Sofia," Esther said, trying to get my attention.

I watched Matteo and the priest go through a service door at the far end of the large function room. Once they were out of sight there seemed to be a collective exhalation of breath and the party resumed its former momentum.

I turned to find a distinguished man in his late sixties and his glamorous, much younger wife waiting to greet me.

"Aldo is chief executive of Russo Bank," Esther went on. "And Sofia runs Happy Paws, a local charity that rehomes abandoned pets."

"Very pleased to meet you," Aldo said, offering me his hand.

"Thank you for coming," I replied, returning the gesture and then shaking Sofia's.

"I would not have missed it," Aldo responded. "I have a friend in Italian intelligence. He's told me about some of your exploits. Is it true you staged a rescue mission in the mountains of the Hindu Kush?"

I had resigned myself to the fact I would always be an object of curiosity to some people because of my history, but that didn't mean I enjoyed being treated like an exhibit. I had almost died numerous times while trying to rescue US Special Forces pilot Joshua Floyd, a traumatic experience that would forever be imprinted on me, but which for others was simply a thrilling anecdote. They would never understand the toll it took on me to cast my mind back to those events.

I nodded without saying anything.

"Those are some of the harshest conditions in the world," Sofia remarked. "It must have taken much inner strength to endure them, Mr. Morgan."

I didn't need the praise of strangers. I would much rather have been in my Los Angeles home, having dinner with Justine, but this was part of the job of running Private. Building a client base was the first step toward establishing a successful office in Italy.

"It's not something I'd want to do again," I conceded.

"What pushes you on in such circumstances?" Aldo asked. "Where do you find the will to survive?"

I knew the answer. The quest for truth, justice, the love of friends, family, Justine most of all, but I wasn't about to share those parts of myself with strangers.

"I don't know," I replied. "Until you're in a situation where your life depends on—"

A loud bang cut me off. While the sound startled everyone in the grand room, I recognized instantly what it was.

A gunshot.

I raced to the doorway on the other side of the hall, weaving through the startled guests. Behind me, a couple of guards sprang into action. I sensed a few people at my heels, but reached the door first and pulled it open to reveal a wide corridor with a number of rooms leading off it and a grand staircase rising to the upper floors.

One of the doors halfway along the corridor was ajar and I rushed toward it.

At the door I slowed down, taking the time to push it further open, alert for any danger inside. No sound or hint of movement came from within the room.

I stepped into a grand old library with stacked bookcases lining the walls, and two leather-covered couches and a gilded coffee table arranged on top of a huge red Persian rug.

The area nearest the door was now a crime scene. The priest Matteo had addressed as Father Brambilla lay face-down, blood soaking into the deep fibers of the rug beneath him as it flowed from a bullet wound in his temple. Standing over him, holding a smoking pistol, was my new manager for Italy, the former police inspector I'd hired to head up Private Rome.

Matteo Ricci.

CHAPTER 3

"AND YOU FOUND Signor Ricci holding the gun?" Chief Inspector Mia Esposito asked me.

I nodded.

"For the recording, please," she said, gesturing at her phone.

"Yes," I replied. "I found Signor Ricci with the gun."

It seemed Esposito was leading the investigation into the priest's death. There were several senior Polizia di Stato officers at the party, and more junior ranks outside, providing security, so measures had been taken promptly to secure the crime scene, prevent guests from leaving, and ensure Matteo was taken into custody. The situation hadn't come fully under control though until Esposito had arrived, striding into the grand function room in gray trousers and a blue shirt, her hair pulled back into a tight ponytail. She'd deployed her team to interview every single one of the guests, staff and security personnel, as well as the officers who'd been on duty outside and her superiors who had been inside with us. As the person who'd discovered Matteo with the victim, she interviewed me herself, and so far had made me recount my story twice.

I was familiar with the tactic. It was a fairly basic way of trying to get a witness to reveal inconsistencies or holes in their version of events by comparing one with another, but she could find none in mine as I stuck rigidly to the facts.

Matteo had said nothing while two uniformed officers from Esposito's team had cuffed him and taken him into custody. I wondered if he knew them as former colleagues. Maybe he couldn't quite believe the way his evening had turned from attending a mundane corporate launch party into a full-blown murder investigation, with himself as the prime suspect.

But why would Matteo kill a priest? And even if he'd wanted the man dead, why would a former police inspector with a reputation as a highly effective investigator choose to murder someone at a public event while surrounded by friends and colleagues? A crime of passion, perhaps? Matteo and Father Brambilla seemed to know one another. Matteo's resumé said he'd trained as a priest at a seminary for a time before joining the police force, but there was nothing in the background checks our Rome attorney had conducted to suggest he was in a relationship of any kind, and certainly not with a priest. And what about Father Brambilla's dramatic announcement? He'd prophesied his own death, but if he'd known it was coming, why would he choose to be alone with his killer? Was the priest mentally ill or had he genuinely known he was in mortal danger? Something here didn't add up.

"I think I have everything I need," Esposito said, switching off her phone's voice recorder.

She signaled the officer near the door that led to the main entrance, pointed at me and nodded. It was the sign all her colleagues were using to tell the man that an interviewee could be released. There were dozens of others currently being questioned and many more waiting for their turn.

"Thank you, Inspector," I replied, heading for the door.

"One more thing, Mr. Morgan," Esposito said, and I paused. "Why do you think he did it?"

"I'm not sure he did," I replied. "Doesn't fit with what I know of him."

She nodded. "I never worked with Inspector Ricci, but I know his reputation. Normally I would agree, based on what colleagues have said about his character, but the evidence in this case is overwhelming."

I couldn't argue with that and made for the door. The uniformed officer let me pass, and I walked through the empty stone antechamber to the open double doors where I caught the scent of the sea on the evening air. There were more police outside, some gathered near a side entrance, about a dozen others holding back journalists in a cordon on the lawn some fifty feet away. A handful of guests were waiting for their cars in a nearby semi-circular parking lot, while others were walking down the driveway leading to the main road. I guessed they were looking for their chauffeur-driven cars or taxis, moved on by the police whose own vehicles now surrounded the building.

It was a chaotic end to the evening and not at all the one I'd hoped for. I was about to call Justine Smith, my colleague and girlfriend, but the press pack suddenly became agitated and I saw movement at a side door not far from me. The group of police officers standing nearby expanded like a lung taking in air, and the door opened to reveal Matteo being frogmarched by a couple of cops in uniform.

I hurried over.

"Matteo," I said, but my voice didn't carry above the hubbub, and his attention was elsewhere.

"Luna!" he yelled. "Luna!"

His attention was fixed on a tall, dark-haired woman in a tight black cocktail dress and heels. She stood at the edge of the semi-circular driveway, staring at him with pity in her eyes.

"Luna!" he yelled to her one last time before she kicked off her heels and started across the lawn toward the police cordon.

Matteo was hustled toward a waiting police car, and the press pack pushed against the line of cops, shouting questions, taking pictures, calling his name.

He looked around fearfully as he was manhandled into the back of the vehicle.

"Jack," he said when his eyes met mine. "I'm innocent. I didn't do it!"

I tried to get closer but was held back by one of the officers in his dishonor guard.

"Talk to that woman," Matteo called to me. "Luna Colombo— my former police partner. Speak to her!"

An officer slid in beside him, slammed the door shut, and another cop thumped the roof. The car sped away.

I hurried around the squad of cops and ran for the lawn, to see the woman called Luna still jogging barefoot toward the police cordon. She produced an identity card from a small purse and showed it to one of the officers, who stood aside and allowed her to pass into the crowd of journalists.

I tried to follow, but when I raced over to him and pleaded for admission the same officer only replied in terse Italian and waved me toward the long driveway on the other side of the lawn. I stood on the tips of my toes and tried to pick out the fleeing Luna, but she had already vanished into the trees on the far side of the lawn. She was beyond my reach for now.

Matteo had brought me to the hotel and his keys would undoubtedly be in the back of the police car with him, so I joined the handful of bemused guests walking down the driveway, heading for the main road where they hoped to find transportation back to the city.

CHAPTER 4

I WAS ALMOST at the main gates opening on to Largo della Stazione di Palo, a service road that led to the Strada Statale 1 Via Aurelia highway back to Rome. La Posta Vecchia's manicured grounds lay behind me: half a mile of driveway flanked by lush vegetation. Parked automobiles lined the road near the ivy-covered stone archway that marked the entrance to the grounds, but none was available for hire. When I spoke to the drivers, I discovered they'd all been pre-booked by guests who were still being interviewed.

The lights of the hotel didn't reach this far so all I had to guide my way was a half-moon up above and the occasional passing vehicle leaving the estate. Beyond the stone archway, I could see the road wasn't the sort of place taxis touted for trade. It was a quiet country lane that connected the surrounding properties with the main artery into Rome. I resigned myself to ordering an

Uber, which would involve at least a forty-minute wait. I pulled my phone from my jacket pocket and was about to open the app when a figure stepped out of the shadows beneath a tree.

"Mr. Morgan?"

It was a woman, her silhouette slim, tall, graceful. As she drew nearer, I saw a warm, open face and eyes that were spirited and bright. This was someone who didn't miss much. She wore a long red dress that hugged her figure closely.

"Trying to find a ride?" she asked.

I nodded. She knew me, but I had no idea who she was. Her outfit suggested she was a guest from the party.

"Have we met?" I asked, certain I would have remembered her.

Her English was fluent, but there was the hint of an East African accent beneath a more noticeable Italian one. Ethiopia or Somalia maybe.

"No," she replied. "We haven't met. But I know who you are by reputation."

"And you are?" I said, driven to directness since my polite invitation for her to introduce herself had been deflected.

"I'd rather not say. Not until I know whether I can trust you."

She could be direct too it seemed.

"Trust me with what?" I asked.

"I have to trust you to tell you."

I wasn't in the mood for riddles. "If there's an investigation you'd like us to undertake, you can contact—"

"Your country manager?" she asked, cutting me off. "Because I'm pretty sure he passed me a few minutes ago, sitting in the back of a police car."

"The authorities will get to the bottom of this tragedy and Matteo will be exonerated. In the meantime, there are other members of my organization who can help you," I said. "If that's why you're here."

"Who?" she asked. "Who else do you have on the ground in Rome?"

I hesitated.

"Matteo Ricci did all the hiring. Once you'd recruited him. Do you even know who you have working for you?" she pressed me.

She'd got right to the heart of my concerns about the new business. I now had so many operations, I couldn't take the same level of interest in them as I had when there had just been the original office in Los Angeles. I increasingly relied on the country managers to do the right thing and follow Private's rigorous training program and corporate ethos, but no matter how tight a ship we ran, we couldn't plan ahead for every eventuality. In this particular case, no amount of training could ever compensate for what seemed to be a basic error of judgment on my part: hiring a killer to run the Rome office.

"Did Matteo invite you?" I asked the woman. "Are you a friend or a former colleague of his?"

"Neither," she replied. "I never made it inside your party, Mr. Morgan. I'm a gatecrasher."

I studied her more closely, wondering who she really was. She didn't seem dangerous, but she wasn't friendly either.

"I'm trying to discover the truth," she went on. "Following a lead."

"Not police. A rival detective? Or a journalist maybe?" I

suggested, and her eyes flashed. "Our publicity team would have arranged an invitation, Ms. . . ."

"Nobody. I'm Ms. Nobody. It's not the kind of lead a publicity team can help with. I'm more interested in why a decorated Rome police inspector leaves the force to work as a private investigator."

"I only hire the best people," I responded.

"Perhaps. But it still feels an odd choice for Inspector Ricci to make. And sudden, too."

"If you know something about what happened here tonight—"

"I don't," she interrupted. "That's why I came here. To find out. I wasn't expecting there to be a murder."

"Find out what?" I tried.

"Again, you are asking me to trust you without earning it."

"Why wouldn't you trust me?"

"Because you appear to hire killers, Mr. Morgan."

That stung.

"In my experience killers are more likely to lurk in the shadows," I replied pointedly.

She scoffed. "Me, a killer? The suggestion is beneath you. Besides, there were plenty of killers and villains at your party . . . crooked cops, spies, corrupt politicians, vicious gangsters in suits. Your guest list wasn't just the great and good of Rome. It also included some of the troubled and troublemakers. This is an ancient city, Mr. Morgan. One of the oldest there is. Corruption has flowed through its veins since before the days of Christ."

"What corruption? What do you know?" I asked.

A car turned onto the driveway and drove under the stone arch.

"This is my ride," my mysterious inquisitor said, checking her phone. "We'll speak again, Mr. Morgan."

She moved away from me and flagged down the approaching vehicle. Her red dress seemed to glow in its dazzling headlights.

"How? What's your number?"

"I'm not going to tell you who I am," she replied as the driver slowed to a halt. "Not yet, Mr. Morgan. Not until I know I can trust you."

She opened the rear door and slid onto the back seat. Once she was settled, she closed the door and the driver turned the car around and headed back the way he'd come. After the arch he turned left, toward Rome.

I could have kicked myself for failing to suggest to the mystery woman that she should take a chance on me and let me prove how trustworthy I could be on the ride back to the city. Instead, I ambled along the country road, using my phone to summon a car of my own.

CHAPTER 5

MY UBER ARRIVED forty minutes later, and I finally reached the Hotel Hassler on the Piazza della Trinità dei Monti at a little after 1 a.m. The Hassler is located at the top of the Spanish Steps and is one of Rome's most prestigious hotels, its grand white stone façade looming over a small cobbled square. Inside there are magnificent restaurants, and suites offering some of the finest views of the Eternal City. Alessandro Calla, Private's local corporate lawyer, had suggested the hotel because of its proximity to the *centro storico* of Rome, and it was no hardship to stay among the narrow streets, crooked alleyways and ancient buildings that were reminders of the city's glorious past.

The hotel itself was a strange mix of old and new, the solid seven-story imperial-style building housing wood-paneled lounges and glass-and-steel suites. Gilt, marble and fine leather mingled with contemporary furniture and abstract art, but somehow the clash between present and past seemed to work, linked by the common value of luxury that infused every aspect of the place, from the food to the service.

A uniformed doorman held the door open and welcomed me by name as I entered the lobby, where a chalk-white marble floor met a curved onyx wall. I headed for the elevators but paused when my phone rang. I was grateful to see it was Justine returning the calls I'd made while waiting for my car to arrive.

"Jus," I said, answering.

"Everything okay, Jack?" she immediately asked.

Local news had been told someone had been murdered at La Posta Vecchia but no further details had been released, so there was no way Justine could have had any idea what had happened. "There's been a death," I revealed, and she stayed quiet. "Matteo Ricci has been arrested for killing a priest at the Private launch party."

"Oh, Jack," she gasped. "That's terrible."

"It's not been good," I replied. "The poor priest was shot at close range and Matteo was found holding the gun, but he claims he's innocent."

"Do you believe him?"

It was a very good question.

"I don't know. I mean, how well can a person know someone they've only met four times? Our interview process is designed to gauge performance, not weed out potential killers. I found him standing over the victim, holding the murder weapon, but something about it doesn't add up. If he wanted the man dead, why shoot him at the party where there was no chance of avoiding capture?"

Justine murmured agreement.

"And there was a woman lurking around the hotel. She claimed to be a journalist but refused to give me her name."

Justine sighed. "So, you're not coming home?"

This was meant to be a quick in and out trip, five days to attend the launch, take care of the last of the paperwork involved in launching the business, and meet the investigators Matteo had chosen to form the core team as they started their training.

"I—" I began, but Justine didn't let me get any further.

"It's okay," she said. "I know you can't leave a situation like this."

I breathed out a sigh of relief. Justine and I had been together through some turbulent times, but as Private's chief forensic psychologist and profiler she knew the demands of the job.

"I don't know what I've done to deserve you," I remarked.

"You were an angel in a previous life," she replied.

I laughed. "If you say so. Listen, can you do me a favor and ask Mo-bot to check out someone called Luna Colombo?"

Maureen 'Mo-bot' Roth was Private's head of technology. She was a world leader in digital security and data collection and management. She was also a renowned white hat hacker, someone who used their understanding of technology for good, though I suspected she was also a notorious black or at least gray hat in her free time, crossing the line into criminality when necessary.

"Luna was Matteo's partner in Rome police. Before they took him away, he told me I had to talk to her."

"Sounds like you've got the beginnings of a case," Justine replied. "I'll get right on it. You know what I'm going to tell you?"

"Be careful?" I guessed.

"That's right."

"I will," I replied. "Love you."

"Love you too. Speak soon."

I hung up and continued toward the elevators. As I left the reception area and passed the lounge bar, I saw the distorted figure of a man reflected in one of the mirrors and turned to see Joseph Stadler. Like me, he still wore his tuxedo. I'd undone my bow tie in the Uber, but his was impeccably taut.

"Mr. Morgan," he said. "I'm sorry to intrude upon you at your hotel at this hour, but I felt it imperative I see you after tonight's terrible tragedy."

"What can I do for you, Mr. Stadler?"

"I wanted to speak to you at La Posta Vecchia, but the police kept us all separated and I was concerned you might leave Rome quickly after such a blow," he replied. "I know you by reputation, Mr. Morgan. You are the best private investigator there is."

He hesitated, perhaps expecting a response, but it was too late for me to pretend to be taken in by easy praise, which from a stranger is sometimes a sign of attempted manipulation.

"Anyway," he went on, "Father Brambilla worked for me for many years as part of the Church's oversight team. He was a good friend."

"Then I'm sorry for your loss," I remarked.

Stadler nodded slowly, tears welling in his eyes. "Thank you. I cannot believe your associate killed him, Mr. Morgan. If he did,

I would like to understand why. If he didn't, I want to know the name of the true murderer and bring him or her to justice. I hope this is not putting you in an awkward position, but I would like to hire you and your agency to investigate the death of Father Ignacio Brambilla."

My mind instinctively turned to potential conflicts although, in reality, I had already decided to get to the truth myself.

"Please," Stadler said. "Please help me find the person who killed my friend."

His eyes were full of pain, but even such open distress wasn't enough to compel me.

"I can't simply accept a commission like this," I replied. "Not without first conducting due diligence and considering any possible conflicts of interest."

I'd been stung before when an imposter had engaged me to track down a woman he'd claimed was his daughter. After discovering the ruse, I'd implemented stricter client engagement checks, and wasn't about to ignore them, even if Stadler's interests seemed to coincide with my own.

"I'll think about it, Mr. Stadler, and take care of the necessary background," I told him.

"You can reach me here," he said, handing me his card. "I would expect nothing less than the utmost professionalism from you, Mr. Morgan. And I could hope for no more. Not under such tragic circumstances. I will wait to hear from you. Have a good night."

"You too," I responded, and he bowed slightly and backed away.

As he left the hotel, I sent Justine a text message.

Ask Mo to give me background on Joseph Stadler, COO of the Vati-can Bank.

Justine replied instantly.

Will do. X.

Exhausted, my mind still churning with questions, I finally made it to one of the elevators and headed up to my suite.

CHAPTER 6

I WOKE EARLY the following morning. The first fingers of dawn reached between the heavy drapes at the windows of my sixth-floor suite. I could hear faint sounds from the waking city, but neither sound nor light had troubled me. I'd been woken by disjointed dreams of the previous night's events, the troubling memory of a dead man lying at my colleague's feet. It had been a long time since I've been to church, but I'd been raised a Catholic. Despite drifting away from the faith and all the trouble and scandal the institution had faced in recent years, I still had a special respect for the men and women who devoted their lives to God. Whether one was devout or faithless, it was hard not to be moved by a strength of belief that drove people to seek a higher, more profound connection with the divine.

I couldn't put my finger on why the Church had shrunk into the background of my own life. Maybe my wartime experiences as a pilot had exposed me to horrors that made me question why an omnipotent God was not more vengeful in the face of wrongdoing. Or perhaps I'd sinned so many times myself, killing in the name of necessity, that I was afraid of how I'd be received by the Almighty. Whatever the reason, my faith today felt far less real and immediate than it had as a child, but the sight of a dead priest had stirred it into life. Even someone as lapsed as I was knew it took a special level of evil to kill a man of the cloth.

After trying and failing to fall back to sleep, I rose, showered and put on the only suit I had brought with me; a light blue linen two-piece, which I wore with an open-collar white shirt. It was professional, but cool enough to cope with Rome's scorching July heat.

I had planned to grab breakfast and head for Private's empty new offices on Via Attilio Regolo, near Rome's historic shopping district, but my phone rang as I was putting on my shoes. It was Alessandro Calla, our Rome lawyer.

"Alessandro," I said. "You heard?"

"I have," he replied. "And arranged for a criminal defense lawyer to interview Signor Ricci. Her name is Gianna Bianchi, and she is one of the best in Rome. She's going to see him at eight . . . half an hour's time . . . at police headquarters on the Via di San Vitale. I thought I should let you know in case you want to sit in."

"Thank you," I said, cradling the phone against my shoulder as I tied my laces. "I'm on my way."

"Good luck," Alessandro responded. "Let me know if I can be of further assistance."

I took a cab from the rank in the square opposite the hotel, and the driver, a young Moroccan, drove me on a circuitous route that navigated the city's one-way system, passing the Villa Borghese Park and the National Gallery, among other landmarks. It was impossible not to be captivated by the beauty and history of Rome. Everywhere I looked, the past reached out and called to me. From the ancient stones and statues that adorned the streets to the historic buildings and churches still in use, it was hard not to picture all the past lives spent in this awe-inspiring place. People caught up in intrigue and drama in what had once been the most powerful city on earth, or ordinary folk just struggling to get by—all of them had felt the warmth of the same sun that shone down on the city today, making its terracotta roofs, stucco and sandstone buildings glow beneath a cloudless blue sky.

We arrived at Rome police headquarters on Via di San Vitale at 7:50 a.m. I paid the driver and went inside. Constructed of monumental white blocks of stone in the classical style, the grand four-story building took up almost an entire city block. A large archway cut through the outer façade to reveal the imposing structure was built around a courtyard used for parking. I walked under the arch to find a vaulted reception area to my left. It felt cool, almost chilly, in the early-morning shade. The lobby was quiet, but as I made my way to the reception desk, a voice called out, "Mr. Morgan."

I turned to see a woman in a light brown trouser suit rise from a chair in a waiting area off to one side. She had wild black hair barely restrained in a messy bun and couldn't have been more than five foot four in her three-inch heels.

"I'm Gianna Bianchi," she said, swinging a messenger bag over her shoulder as she approached.

I shook her hand. "Jack Morgan. Alessandro told me I'd find you here."

"I'm just waiting to be taken inside," she told me. "You were at the party, correct?"

I nodded. "I found Matteo and Father Brambilla, the victim."

"I've read the first reports," she said, tapping her bag.

"Matteo claims innocence."

She smiled. "That's good. It's hard to convince a judge if even the client doesn't believe he's innocent."

A reinforced security door beside the reception desk opened and a uniformed cop stepped through.

"Signora Bianchi," he said, signaling to my companion.

She walked over and I followed; they spoke together in Italian. He looked me up and down, before standing back to allow us to pass.

We followed him along a maze of corridors until we reached a run of interview rooms. He took us to one at the very end and used a key card to unlock the door.

When we stepped inside the whitewashed room, I saw Matteo sitting opposite the police inspector who had brought order to the crime scene the previous night. Mia Esposito, dressed in a black skirt and red blouse, didn't bother standing as we entered.

"Mr. Morgan shouldn't be here," she said to Gianna.

"Mr. Morgan is assisting me. If that's a problem, we can go before a judge."

The lawyer stared at Esposito, who caved and nodded at the

uniformed officer. He stepped out and closed the door, and Gianna crossed the small room and took a seat next to Matteo. He looked drained, haunted even, his eyes wide and ringed by shadows that looked deep enough to be bruises. Shock and exhaustion had left his handsome face looking drawn. He was still in his tux, but instead of glamor, it added an air of desperation.

I leant against the wall and nodded to Matteo, who barely registered my presence.

"We will conduct the interview in Italian," Esposito noted. "For the benefit of the court."

Gianna nodded and the inspector pressed a button on a desktop device. She was about to begin her preamble when Matteo looked at me and interrupted her.

"Before we get started, I want to speak in English so Mr. Morgan can understand. I want him to know I'm innocent. I did not kill Father Brambilla."

Maybe he could see doubt in my eyes.

"There is knowledge and then there is faith. Sometimes when all the evidence tells us something, faith compels us to a different truth. I know how it seems, but I did not shoot that man."

"What happened then?" I asked, ignoring an irritated tut from Esposito.

Matteo hesitated. "I don't know." He paused again. "I understand how that must sound, but I did not kill Father Brambilla. He was my mentor once, and a friend."

Matteo's voice broke; he looked as though he might cry.

"I could never hurt him."

"Faith is the preserve of the naïve," Esposito said. "Those more experienced in life know that truth is a case of compiling facts and evidence. If you are finished with your little drama, perhaps we can begin in earnest now. Please explain to me if you can, Signor Ricci, how a man came to be dead at your feet, shot by a bullet from the gun you were holding."

Matteo sagged back in his chair. After a few moments' silence, he nodded.

Esposito bent closer to him and began the interview preamble in Italian.

CHAPTER 7

I COULDN'T UNDERSTAND Matteo's statement, but Inspector Esposito's skepticism transcended language. I recognized Matteo's defensive tone and the irritation in Gianna Bianchi's frequent interruptions. Matteo's account of events clearly wasn't satisfying the abrasive inspector. After an hour, she brought the interview to a close and led us out.

"I didn't do it," Matteo called to us as we left the room. "You have to believe me, Jack."

He seemed so earnest, his tone pleading. If he was guilty, he was an excellent actor, but then years of police work would have exposed him to the most convincing criminals. Proving innocence was not about observing human emotion; it was about interpreting the evidence. Gianna and Esposito spoke together as the Inspector led us back through a maze of corridors to the imposing lobby.

"Have a good day, Mr. Morgan," Esposito said, as we stepped through the security door into the vaulted space. It was busier now, with people gathered around the reception desk and thronging the waiting area.

"You too," I replied, before she retreated into the building and the door swung shut behind her.

Gianna muttered a curse and I looked at her quizzically.

"Signor Ricci does not have a convincing explanation of events," she said. "He claims to have suffered a blackout—says he has no recollection of how he came to be holding the gun. He admits there was no one else in the room."

"Apart from Father Brambilla," I remarked.

"Exactly. How could the priest kill himself and still hand Signor Ricci the gun? Or is the more plausible explanation that Ricci shot Father Brambilla?"

She hesitated.

"Don't answer that," she advised. "I need to maintain a reasonable belief in his innocence."

"I think he *is* innocent," I responded.

"How did it happen then?"

"I don't know," I conceded. "That's what I need to figure out, but unless I've become a terrible judge of character, I believe Matteo's telling the truth."

"I will take heart from your belief, Mr. Morgan. It will help me do my job."

Of course, my instincts wouldn't keep Matteo out of prison. I didn't know the man particularly well and couldn't vouch for him, but I knew when someone was telling the truth and Matteo was either being honest or else he was utterly deluded, and I was pretty sure he wasn't the latter. But my hunches wouldn't cut it.

A court would require evidence, and if Esposito was convinced she had her killer, she wouldn't pull at any threads that might prove his innocence. But I could.

"Do you think you could see if Luna Colombo is on duty?" I asked Gianna. "She used to be Matteo's partner before he left the force. He told me to talk to her."

Gianna nodded and went to the reception desk where she pushed through a small crowd of people and spoke to one of the duty officers. She returned a few moments later.

"They don't normally give out information but I've made some friends here. Detective Colombo telephoned sick today."

Coincidence or evasion? I wondered.

"Thanks," I replied.

"You're going to work the case yourself?" Gianna asked, as we walked out through the lobby.

I nodded. "We don't have any local detectives who've completed their training yet. And something doesn't sit right with me. I can't leave Matteo like this."

"Then let me know what you find," she said.

"I will," I replied as we stepped into the shadow of the wide stone arch.

A warm breeze blew in from the street and carried with it the smell of traffic fumes.

"Good luck, Mr. Morgan," Gianna said, turning left.

I was about to turn right toward Via Piancenza, but caught sight of a face I recognized on the other side of the street. It was the mysterious woman who had been lurking in the grounds of La Posta Vecchia. I paused to allow a slow-moving car to pass by then crossed the road to join her.

"Waiting for me?" I asked.

"Waiting to see who goes to visit your man," she replied.

"We could compare notes," I suggested.

She was in jeans and a white T-shirt today, looking more like a Ralph Lauren model than a journalist.

"I work alone," she replied. "Besides you don't have anything to compare. You're new to Rome. I don't think you have anything worth trading."

I scoffed but her words hit home. I'd been an outsider in Beijing and Moscow and knew how a lack of local knowledge could hinder an investigation.

"Go to the Pleasure Hall. It's a brothel in Tor Bella Monaca. If you're as good as people say, you might find something there that's worth trading."

She eyed me closely as she walked away. It was clear she still didn't trust me, but she was prepared to test my competence. As she crossed the street, I took out my phone and used it to snap a few surreptitious pictures of her.

I'd inhabited the shadowy world of crime and mystery for longer than I cared to remember, and this stranger was making a mistake in calling into question my honesty and ability. But some people need to learn the hard way.

CHAPTER 8

TOR BELLA MONACA is a rundown neighborhood to the east of Rome. The creation of idealistic city planners who'd imagined a diverse population living there in crowded harmony, the place was packed with graffiti-covered tenement blocks that flanked litter-strewn streets peppered with discount liquor stores and cut-price markets. I could see the tenements start to loom into view as we approached the area along Via Casalina, an elevated highway that ran to the south of Tor Bella Monaca.

I was only half paying attention to my surroundings, using my time in the back of an old Mercedes E-Class taxi to run a reverse-image search on the photos I'd taken of the mysterious woman who'd been waiting for me outside police headquarters.

Most of them were unusable, but one yielded a match: a profile picture for an investigative journalist called Faduma Salah, who worked for *La Repubblica*, one of Italy's leading daily newspapers. I translated her bio, which revealed she was originally a refugee from Somalia, who had come to Italy as a child, undertaking the perilous journey across the Mediterranean with her family. She'd studied journalism at the University of Milan, where she'd been a prize-winning undergraduate and graduate student. She'd joined *La Repubblica* out of college and had worked her way up the paper's ranks by breaking difficult stories. She had tackled organized crime, political corruption and terrorism; from this resumé she struck me as tenacious and brave.

I checked the time: 9:42 a.m. Too early for a call Stateside. It would be approaching 1 a.m. in LA, so I sent Mo-bot a secure email, telling her what I'd learned and asking her to run a full background on Faduma Salah and was only mildly surprised when I received an almost immediate reply saying she'd get right on it. Maureen Roth rarely slept, and yet she somehow managed to outperform the hardened tech heads she had working for her, despite in many cases being almost double their age.

Thanks, I wrote in reply, and she sent me a smiley face emoji straight back.

"It is just along there," the cab driver said, nodding to a bright yellow tower block that stood on the corner of the intersection between Via Giovanni Battista Cigola and Viale Santa Rita da Cascia. "The fifth floor of the building."

"You bring many people here?" I asked, as he slowed to a halt by the park opposite the high-rise.

"It's a popular place," he replied. "Twenty-five euros, please."

I gave him thirty and stepped out of the cab into a quiet street.

The noise of distant traffic filled the warm air but there was little to hear nearby, just a couple of radios leaking music and chat through open apartment windows.

As the cab turned around, I crossed the road and walked toward the apartment block. I saw two drunks sitting on a bench on the other side of some trees that fronted the street. They muttered quietly as they eyed me over their half-empty liquor bottles. Beyond the trees lay a parking lot filled with old cars.

I walked along a cracked concrete path toward the entrance to the block, which was set down a run of steps. The glass doors and windows either side had been painted black, making it impossible to see inside, and the apartments that flanked the entrance looked as though they never caught any sunlight, their windows edged with damp.

A guy in his early twenties, a little overweight, bearded, wearing a T-shirt, shorts and trainers, stood in a tiny patch of sun near the bottom of the steps and watched me as I approached. He didn't say or do anything but I suspected he was a lookout, keeping an eye open for potential troublemakers or cops.

"The Pleasure Hall?" I asked, wondering why Faduma Salah had sent me to such a sleazy neighborhood.

The guy looked me up and down and nodded. "Five," he said.

I went through the main entrance and found the floor tiles and walls of the lobby had been painted bright red. Dirty footsteps covered the floor and damp stained the walls, making me feel I was inside a smoker's lung. The place stank of urine and neglect. As I hurried to the open elevator I was greeted by the stench of bleach.

I took the tiny car up to the fifth floor. I stepped out into the corridor and heard pounding music. The walls were painted black and peppered with inset LED lights that changed color in time to the beat. There were twenty doors, ten on each side of the corridor, but only one stood open. It lay to my right and the music seemed to originate there so I walked toward it. As I neared it, a big man in a black suit and shirt appeared and blocked the doorway. He sized me up before standing aside to let me pass.

I walked into an open-plan seating area where a dozen women in revealing outfits lounged around on couches, armchairs and oversized cushions. A slim woman in her forties sat behind a high counter. Her shaved head was bowed over an iPad; she was engrossed in a movie.

"*Signore?*" she said, noticing my approach.

I couldn't figure out why Faduma had sent me to a brothel until my eye was drawn to movement on the other side of the room. Someone was trying surreptitiously to ease a door closed with their foot. Through the crack I could see a small sitting room and, reflected in the black screen of a turned-off television, the face of Luna Colombo, Matteo Ricci's former police partner.

CHAPTER 9

I MOVED THROUGH the open-plan room as the door clicked shut. The woman with the shaved head stepped out from behind the counter and blocked my path.

"*Scusi, Signore,*" she said.

"I need to talk to that lady," I responded, trying to pass.

"This is not a place for talking, sir," she said. "Alonzo!"

The guy at the door lumbered toward me, his face twisting into a scowl.

"Help the Signore out. He has come to the wrong place," the woman said.

The mass of flesh that was Alonzo grabbed my shoulder, but I ducked and slipped clear of his grasp. I sidestepped the woman blocking my path and ran toward the closed door. Alonzo came after me, but I moved aside suddenly, caught his arm and used his momentum to accelerate him at it. He crashed into it, cracking the lock from the frame, falling into the room as the door swung open. He stumbled to his knees and the women behind me gasped and cried out as I rushed forward and punched Alonzo in the face, knocking him down.

He fell back, groaning, clutching his face, and I punched him again, knocking him out cold. The woman with the shaved head cursed, and when I glanced over my shoulder, I saw her moving toward the counter.

I looked around the grubby side room. A couch heaped with pillows and blankets, a television and some used dishes. It looked as though Luna had slept here, but what would a cop be doing in a place like this?

There was no sign of her, but the window on the other side of the room was open, the curtain flapping in the breeze.

I heard more cursing and glanced behind me to see the shaven-headed woman aiming a Taser directly at me. I stepped clear just in time and the wired barbs shot into the air beside me. Alonzo was stirring. He fumbled for my feet, but I didn't give either of my assailants a second chance. I ran across the room, yanked the curtain back and saw a fire escape on the other side of the window. I caught a flash of movement below and realized it was Luna, about two flights down, racing for the bottom.

I tried to jump through the window, but felt a hand grab my arm. I whirled round and saw a dazed Alonzo back on his feet, trying to hold me back. I kicked him in the shin, and as he buckled, swung a right cross that knocked him out again. He tumbled to the floor and I leapt through the window and raced down the metal steps.

The fire escape zigzagged down the rear of the building, connecting all the apartments on this side.

I raced down, taking the steps two or three at a time, and quickly closed the gap between me and Luna to a single story. She reached the ground and sprinted around the corner. I followed moments later, my legs aching, my lungs burning, heart thundering.

I heard an engine start and rounded the corner to see Luna behind the wheel of an old BMW 3-Series, parked in the small lot beside the building. The car shot forward and the tires screeched as Luna swung a hard turn to navigate her way along the snaking route that would take her out of the lot. Old rusty cars filled most of the spaces so her options for shortcuts were limited. I knew if she reached the road I would have no chance of catching her. I raced forward, aiming for the exit point. I stooped to grab a loose chunk of paving block from the edge of the cracked path. As Luna turned in my direction and sped toward the road, I hurled the missile at the car.

It hit the windshield, smashing the glass, turning it crushed-ice white. Luna swerved instinctively and crashed into a couple of parked cars.

As I ran over, I saw her roll onto the back seat and escape through one of the rear doors. She was unsteady on her feet and managed only a couple of faltering steps before I caught up. I grabbed her by the arm and pulled her back.

She spun round and tried to punch me in the mouth, but I blocked the blow and pushed her against the BMW.

"It's over," I told her. "Enough."

CHAPTER 10

FURY STILL BLAZED in her eyes, so I repeated myself.

"It's over."

Her heightened emotion dwindled and she slumped a little. Acknowledging defeat? Or an injury picked up in the car crash?

"Are you okay?" I asked.

Luna nodded. "We need to get off the street."

She glanced around nervously. The man who'd been keeping lookout by the main entrance to the tower block was crossing the courtyard toward us. Luna caught his eye and waved him back.

"*Va bene—è un vecchio amico,*" she yelled. And to me: "I told him you're an old friend."

I looked at the man and gave him a reassuring wave. He hesitated but backed away.

"Come on," Luna said. She took a step and faltered. "I think I hit my head."

"Sorry," I said. "It was the only way I could think of to stop you. Do you need a doctor?"

She shook her head. "No doctors."

"Why?" I asked. "What's going on?"

She steadied herself against the BMW and focused on the row of cars opposite us.

"The Fiat Coupé. We can take that."

There was a twenty-five-year-old black Fiat Coupé parked in a line of ancient mid-range performance cars.

"We can't just steal—" I began, but she cut me off.

"Not steal. Borrow," she said. "These all belong to the Pleasure Hall. You drive."

She walked to the car and opened the passenger door. I found the driver's door unlocked and slid behind the wheel. The black leather interior was trimmed with chrome, and the Pininfarina signature on the dash signaled that the small sports car had borrowed its interior styling from Ferrari.

"The key is in the visor," Luna said as she closed her door.

I lowered the driver's shade and the ignition key dropped into my hand.

"What about thieves?"

"Thieves?" she scoffed. "We don't worry about them here."

I puzzled over her reply as I started the engine. Fiats were notorious for poor electrics, but this one had been well cared for and the engine growled to life on the first try. I drove out of the space, wove around the wreckage of Luna's crashed BMW and pulled out of the lot.

"Sorry about your car."

"It's not mine," she replied. "It's like this one, and most of the others back there . . . borrowed."

"Who from? Who owns the Pleasure Hall?"

She didn't reply.

"Where am I going?" I asked.

She shrugged. "You spoilt my day."

"Your day spent hiding in a brothel?"

She remained impassive.

"What was a cop doing in a place like that?" I pressed her.

"I'm not allowed a personal life?"

"According to your colleagues, you called in sick. And you tried to escape. So this is about more than an unconventional personal life."

I took a left onto Via Acquaroni and joined the traffic heading south toward the highway. We were in the heart of Tor Bella Monaca now and our surroundings were noticeably rundown.

"Even the most generous mind would think you were hiding," I remarked.

She gave a hollow laugh. "Why would I be hiding?"

"That's exactly what I want to know," I said. "Matteo told me to talk to you. You used to be his partner, right?"

She pursed her lips and kept her eyes fixed on the road.

"Why? What did he want you to tell me?" I wondered.

She glared at me.

"Let me out," she said.

"I don't think so. I think I'm going to take you in. Sit you down with Mia Esposito, the detective in charge, and see if she can figure it out."

I sensed anger and frustration radiating from Luna, but her resolve crumbled.

"How do I know Matteo wants me to trust you?"

"You don't," I replied. "But I can take you to police headquarters if you want to ask him yourself."

She pondered the situation and reached a decision.

"Filippo Lombardi," she said. "He was a Rome prosecutor who died in a car crash a couple of months ago. Matteo and I were working the investigation together. I thought Lombardi had been driven off the road, but Matteo said it was an accident. He said he'd been visited by a man who'd convinced him there was no need to investigate Lombardi's death. A priest."

"A priest?" I asked, sensing a connection. "Brambilla?"

"I don't know," Luna replied. "Perhaps."

"And?" I asked.

"And?" she repeated. "That's all I know."

I studied her, trying to gauge if she was being truthful.

"I know that look," she said. "Why would I tell half the story? Filippo Lombardi died out near Poli, in the hills. I thought there was another vehicle involved. Matteo convinced me I was wrong."

"So someone might have killed Brambilla to cover up the earlier murder?" I suggested.

"Or else Matteo silenced him?" she responded.

"You think your former partner is capable of murder? And even if it was him, why are you running? He's in custody."

"I've been a police officer long enough to know we can all kill. Given a strong motive," she replied. "And you're the only one in this car who thinks I was running."

I couldn't disagree, but I also couldn't believe her former partner, my country manager, was a murderer. But detective work was about evidence not belief, and so far the evidence against Matteo was overwhelming.

"Have I earnt my freedom?" Luna asked. "Or do you intend to keep me hostage?"

"You're free," I replied. "But if you think this has something to do with your earlier investigation, you should inform your colleagues."

I pressed the brake pedal as we approached the intersection with Via Amaretta.

"Welcome to Rome, Mr. Morgan," Luna said. "Spend enough time here and you will learn how the city works."

Was she alluding to corruption? Almost certainly.

"Show me where Lombardi died," I said.

She sighed and nodded. "Meet me at La Rustica Mall at two tomorrow afternoon. The west entrance. I'll take you where you want to go." She opened her door. "*Ciao*," she said, stepping onto the sidewalk.

She swung the door closed, and I watched her head east along Via Amaretta, past the graffiti-scrawled shutters of a shop in the ground floor of an abandoned apartment block.

The toot of a horn focused my attention on the road. I noticed the traffic had moved on. I stepped on the accelerator and caught up to the slow line ahead, wondering why Matteo would have subverted an investigation into the death of a city prosecutor.

CHAPTER 11

LUNA WAS RIGHT, of course. I was a newcomer, an outsider, with no idea how Rome worked, but it was clear there were complex, deep networks here linking law with crime, politics with corruption, and the street with the corridors of ultimate power. Such networks could be found in every city, but Rome was so old I could easily imagine some of the links here going back hundreds of years.

And then there was the Church, standing in the very center of the city with such power it was its own state. The Holy Roman Church, the beating heart of Catholicism, preyed on my mind, not just because Father Brambilla was a priest or because I had been approached by a senior member of the Vatican Bank, but because my current proximity to the Holy See had reminded me how far I had strayed from the faith of my childhood.

I don't think I felt guilt, more disappointment that somewhere along the way my belief in something greater had faltered; that I had not only lost faith in my Church, but in the goodness of the world around me as I'd been exposed to more of its cruelties and evil.

My mind churning, I returned the Fiat Coupé to the parking lot outside the Pleasure Hall. There was a gang of men gathered around the crashed BMW who eyed me coldly while I parked the Fiat at the edge of the lot, but they made no attempt to approach me. Had Luna spoken to them? What was her connection to this place? And why did she have more faith in the criminal underworld than in her fellow cops? I regretted letting her go without getting answers to those questions, but our best thoughts often come to us after the opportunity to implement them has passed.

I walked along Via Giovanni Battista Cigola and finally reached Via di Tor Bella Monaca, where there was a steady flow of traffic heading for the highway to the south. I finally managed to hail a cab and told the drive to take me to the Hassler.

Once I was in my room, I checked my messages on Private's secure email server and found one from Mo-bot asking me to call her.

"Jack," she said when she picked up. "How are things over there?"

"Interesting," I replied. "Matteo Ricci swears he's innocent but can't explain what happened. You got anything on his former partner, Luna Colombo?"

"Not yet. I'm still working on it," Mo-bot said. "But I've got the background on Faduma Salah. I'll send you the full file, but she's vanilla. What you see is what you get. Child refugee who came to Italy with her family and built a life for herself as an investigative journalist. Brave, thorough, and, more importantly, honest. No red flags at all."

"Good to know," I replied.

"How long do you think you'll be out there?"

"Until this gets done," I said.

"We've been talking about coming over to help."

"Don't. I'm okay."

"But the Rome office isn't even up and running," she protested. "You're on your own."

"I'll let you know if I need help. There's no point disrupting our other operations. What's happened here is disruption enough. Stay focused on the day-to-day."

"Yes, boss," she snapped back.

"I didn't mean it like that."

"I know," she said, her tone softening. "You're too stubborn. But you're also right, which is infuriating. Keep in touch."

"Will do," I said, before hanging up.

Outside the bells of a nearby church were tolling, divine sound rising above the mundane noises of the city. It was beautiful, and I could understand why churches had seemed magical places in the days before recorded music. Where else would ordinary people have heard such beautiful sounds?

I crossed my room and picked up a card from my desk. I dialed the cell-phone number printed on the front, and my call was answered after a couple of rings.

"*Sì?*"

"Mr. Stadler? It's Jack Morgan."

"Mr. Morgan. Good to hear from you. Have you reached a decision?"

"Yes," I replied. I was going to be investigating the death of Father Brambilla anyway. I might as well be paid for my efforts, and I suspected the Chief Operating Officer of the Vatican Bank would be a useful client. With his political and business connections, Joseph Stadler could probably open many doors around the city that would remain closed to me if I went it alone. "I'll take the case," I told him. "I'll find out what really happened to Father Brambilla."

CHAPTER 12

JUSTINE AND I kept a video link open while she put together a profile of someone who was blackmailing one of our New York office's corporate clients. I spent the evening reviewing Faduma Salah's background and journalism, and every now and again Justine and I would break off from work to chat. It wasn't the same as being together physically, but it would have to suffice. Finally, when it got late and the world outside fell silent, I said goodnight.

The following morning, I dressed and had breakfast on the hotel terrace overlooking the city. It was a clear crisp morning and the promise of a scorching day ahead grew with each passing moment. Rome seemed alive, and was already humming with the buzz of scooters, vehicle horns and the rumble of traffic. The air around me was rich with the promise of fresh-brewed coffee and pastries.

When I finished my espresso, I caught a cab in front of the hotel and the driver took me to police headquarters on Via di San Vitale. We arrived shortly before 8:30 a.m. and Gianna Bianchi was already there. I'd requested the meeting the previous night after puzzling over my encounter with Luna Colombo.

"Thanks for coming, Ms. Bianchi," I said, approaching the lawyer who was dressed today in a thin knee-length orange shift dress. It wouldn't have looked out of place at the beach but was practical in the Roman summer.

"It's no problem," she replied. "And please call me Gianna."

The day was only getting started and I was already feeling the heat. I took off my light blue jacket and draped it over my arm.

"It's going to be as hot as an oven today," she remarked. "Why do you want to see Signor Ricci again?"

"I spoke to his former police partner and our conversation raised some questions."

"Shall we go inside?" Gianna asked.

I nodded and we headed into the building. Ten minutes after presenting ourselves at the reception desk, we were seated in an interview room, waiting for Matteo.

I'd been in many such rooms, but they never lost their ability to remind me of the precious nature of freedom and how easily it could be lost. I was able to walk out of this place, but one mistake, one simple error, and I might find myself on the wrong side of the table, trapped at the whim of a cop or judge. Any of us might, which was part of the reason I was in this business. Justice should concern us all because we can all be touched by injustice. It only takes some bad luck.

The sound of the door opening interrupted my reflection and I turned to see Matteo brought into the room by a uniformed officer, who led him to the chair opposite us and cuffed his wrists to an iron staple fixed to the tabletop.

"Morning, Signor Ricci," Giana said as the officer withdrew.

"I need to get out of here," Matteo said abruptly. Shadows ringed his eyes, which were bloodshot and watering. "The men they're holding me with know I used to be a cop."

"The circumstances of your arrest preclude bail," Gianna replied. "I'm sorry. The only way you'll be released is if we can clear your name."

Matteo cursed under his breath.

"We're working on getting you out," I assured him. "I found Luna. It wasn't easy, but I found her."

Matteo gave me his attention, but his face was a mask of hopelessness.

"Why would a cop go to ground?" I asked.

He said nothing.

"Was Brambilla the one who warned you off the investigation into Filippo Lombardi's death?"

His eyes dropped and he focused on the tabletop. Was he ashamed? Or just trying to protect a secret?

"The prosecutor Lombardi," Gianna took up the questioning. "He died in a car crash. You said it was an accident. Was it?"

Matteo did not meet her eye.

"Was it Brambilla who persuaded you to drop the case?" I pressed him.

He hesitated.

"Yes," he said at last.

"Why?" I asked.

"Lombardi had driven his car off a hillside near Poli. Father Brambilla told me there was nothing for anyone at the bottom of that ravine but pain. He said he was speaking as my old mentor and friend—looking out for me."

"And you didn't think it was odd?" I remarked. "A priest warning you off an official investigation?"

"Not if he was a friend," Matteo replied. "This is Rome, Mr. Morgan. There are many webs connecting us all."

"And is it possible Father Brambilla was caught up in a web of crime?"

Matteo didn't respond. I was about to press him for an answer when he suddenly looked me in the eye and said, "I think he might have been."

He slumped in his chair as though defeated.

"I shouldn't have let him talk me out of it," he said. "But I'd already decided to leave the police, and I didn't want to put myself or Luna in danger. I didn't think about his motives at the time. Father Brambilla was a priest, I couldn't believe he would do anything wrong."

"What about now?" I asked.

Matteo sighed. "Now I'm not so sure. He might have been an emissary sent by the people who killed Lombardi, because they knew I would listen to my old friend and mentor."

CHAPTER 13

AFTER WE LEFT police headquarters, Gianna and I went our separate ways and I took a taxi to Piazza Adriana, the grand star-shaped park surrounding Castel Sant'Angelo, an awe-inspiring second-century castle in the heart of Rome. I asked the cab driver to drop me off at the western edge of the park, where I walked along the magnificent Via della Conciliazione toward Vatican City. The wide cobbled street was flanked by sandstone buildings in the imperial style. Some had been plastered and painted terra-cotta red or pastel hues; others had been constructed with their imposing stonework visible. None of them could compete with the dome of the Basilica di San Pietro—St Peter's as it was known in the English-speaking world—which stood at the end of the street, perfectly centered to create a picture-postcard scene.

As I covered the four blocks from the park to St Peter's Square, the grand buildings to either side of the basilica came into view:

the bone-white, semi-circular colonnades that stood in front of the papal residence to the north and large papal audience hall to the south.

Some say the ancient Romans realized belief was more powerful than any army. That if you can convince a person you hold the keys to their redemption in the afterlife, they will subjugate themselves to your will without the need to resort to threats or further persuasion. And so, the Eternal City waxed ever-splendid and impregnable. Conquering without an army, imperious without empire, powerful without temporal responsibility. Vatican City isn't just an architectural marvel, it is the embodiment in marble, stone and gold of the importance people set on the preservation of their souls.

St Peter's Square was crowded with tourists and pilgrims, and here and there priests and nuns crossing the cobblestones from building to building. There was a time I would have felt awed to find myself in the Holy See, by my proximity to the heart of faith. Now, I was simply conflicted. I longed to believe all the things I'd been taught as a child, but afterward I'd experienced so much horror it was difficult for me to cling to abstract ideals like justice and goodness.

I crossed the gray setts that had been worn to a high shine by the passage of so many worshippers over the years, and headed for the Porta Angelica, a gate located behind the North Colonnade. I showed my passport to gain access through one of the lesser-used routes into Vatican City, away from the crowds. I was nodded through a metal detector by a uniformed member of the Vatican police force, who checked my credentials under the watchful gaze of four of his colleagues. These men were sartorially a far cry from the city state's more famous ceremonial Swiss Guard, dressed in blue trousers, dark T-shirts and baseball caps, holstered Berettas at their hips.

I found the headquarters of the Vatican Bank not far from the North Colonnade, in a semi-circular, red-brick building that protruded from the Apostolic Palace and fronted Via Sant'Anna, one of the sidestreets that connected Vatican City with Rome. It was an unassuming place for an institution that controlled hundreds of billions of dollars in assets around the world, but such anonymity was likely deliberate. The faithful did not need to be reminded of the temporal riches of the Church. It would only encourage dissatisfaction and disgruntlement.

Unremarkable from the outside, the three-story building that housed the bank sang its opulence the moment I stepped through the smoked-glass door into a lobby constructed from marble with hardwood trim and gilt fixtures. Oil paintings by Old Masters hung from the walls, and on the ceiling was a fresco depicting a heavenly scene that might have been a warm-up for the Sistine Chapel. A couple of security guards in tan-colored suits stood by barriers that blocked the way to the elevators, and a lone receptionist in a white blouse and black skirt sat behind a long hardwood counter.

"*Sì?*" she greeted me.

"I have an appointment with Joseph Stadler," I replied.

I'd arranged to come in at 11 a.m. during the call in which I'd accepted his commission to investigate Father Brambilla's death. I checked my watch: 10:57 a.m.

"Please have a seat," the receptionist replied, and I walked to a seating area near the windows. A huge oil painting of the Passion hung on a wall above a black leather corner unit. I didn't sit but instead eyed the artistry of the piece. Fine brushwork had captured a photo-realistic depiction of Christ's last moments, and the glee and horror of the onlooking crowd. It was a magnificent chronicle of a great crime, arguably the greatest of all.

"Mr. Morgan?" a man greeted me some minutes later.

I turned to see Christian Altmer, the executive assistant I'd met at the launch party. He flashed me his dazzling smile.

"Good to see you again," he said. "Mr. Stadler is ready for you."

I followed Altmer beyond the security gates, and we bypassed the elevators and went through another door that took us into a glass-walled walkway connecting the red-brick building with a much older white stone structure behind it.

"The Vatican is beautiful," Altmer noted, his Swiss accent clipping his flawless English. "But it wasn't designed with business in mind."

"The bank isn't a business in the strictest sense," I responded. "It only has one client, right?"

He shook his head. "The Vatican Bank handles funds and transactions for people all over the world, Mr. Morgan. It is most definitely a business. We pride ourselves on the diversity of our client base."

He used a key card to open a door at the end of the corridor.

We entered a small lobby that was unlike any business environment I'd ever seen. The walls and ceiling were covered in depictions of cherubs and heavenly scenes, and angels looked down on me from between puffball clouds.

"This way," Altmer said.

He stepped into a solitary elevator and I followed him inside to see him press the only button on the panel. The doors closed and we rose through the magnificent old building. A chime sounded and the doors opened to reveal a large open-plan office containing four desks. There were two women and a man seated at these.

"This is where I work," Altmer said, stepping out. He nodded toward the largest, unoccupied desk. "And these are my colleagues. Mr. Stadler is through here."

We walked past the desks toward open double doors and stepped into a huge private office decorated like one of the finest chapels in Rome.

Old Master paintings covered the walls and sculptures were positioned around an opulent seating area, small library and Stadler's huge desk. Large windows ran the length of the wall opposite offering a commanding view of Via del Telegrafo, one of Vatican City's elegant side streets. I wondered if the Pope's private office was quite so opulent.

"Mr. Morgan," Stadler said, rising from behind his desk. "Please have a seat."

He crossed the room, shook my hand, and ushered me to a trio of leather-covered Chesterfield couches. We sat opposite each other.

"Can I offer you a drink?" he asked as Altmer closed the doors.

I shook my head. "No, thank you."

The younger man rejoined us and took a seat beside his boss.

"I'm very glad you agreed to take on the investigation, Mr. Morgan," Stadler remarked.

"You said Father Brambilla was a friend. How did you get to know him?"

"He did some compliance work for the bank. He was a junior oversight officer for a while, one of the Church-appointed guardians, making sure we money men stay honest."

Altmer scoffed. "It is an unnecessary level of regulation. The prospect of reputational damage to the Vatican brand keeps us honest. And most times, the priests the Church sends to watch over us don't have the expertise to know right from wrong when it comes to banking."

"Did Father Brambilla have that expertise?" I asked.

"He was a good man," Stadler replied. Altmer's expression suggested he didn't agree, but he remained silent as his boss went on. "But I don't know how much he understood of the world of high finance."

"May I see what he worked on?" I asked.

"Of course, but these are old affairs," Stadler replied. "Father Brambilla left his compliance role three years ago. My connection to him is purely personal now. Or rather, it was. I'm sorry, this is so difficult to accept."

"I understand," I said. "I'd still like to take a look."

Stadler smiled sadly. "Christian will give you everything you need."

"Of course," Altmer added, though I sensed resentment at the imposition.

"Why did he leave?" I asked.

"Who can say?" Stadler replied. "The Church moves people around. One day the compliance officer at the bank, the next the shepherd of a flock in the Democratic Republic of Congo."

"Is that what happened to Father Brambilla?" I asked.

Stadler shook his head. "No. He was appointed one of the Holy Father's special envoys to South America. A high honor and a poorly defined role that gave him plenty of personal freedom."

"You think he might have run into difficulties as a result of that?" I suggested.

Stadler shrugged. "I don't know, Mr. Morgan. If he did, he never mentioned it to me. That's why I need you. I want to know why my friend was murdered."

CHAPTER 14

I DIDN'T LIKE Christian Altmer. There was something off about the guy, as though he wasn't comfortable in his own skin. The easy charm, good looks and winning smile couldn't conceal that, and I'd learnt not to ignore my first instincts. The moment I settled into the back seat of the cab I'd caught on the Via della Giuliana, I sent Mo-bot a secure email asking for background on Altmer.

Stadler seemed more straightforward: a conservative businessman of high standing within his profession, who was obviously motivated by concern for a friend. But a successful track record in business didn't make him incapable of errors of judgment when it came to the people he worked with—something that had been brought home to me by Matteo's arrest. It was possible that I'd been mistaken in appointing him head of Private Rome, though I still hoped to be able to prove otherwise.

I told the cab driver, a cheerful guy in his thirties who hummed along to the Italian ballads blaring from his radio, to take me to La Rustica Mall on the eastern edge of the city. The neighborhood around Vatican City was alive with tourists, and the hot air thick with fumes from the heavy traffic. Rome was busy this scorching July day, but as we drove through the city the crowds and traffic thinned until we reached a mall that could have been in any suburb in the world.

Luna was waiting by the main entrance and jumped in next to me the moment the cab stopped beside her. She seemed skittish and glanced around nervously as the driver complied with my instruction to head east. We joined the slow-moving traffic rolling out of the parking lot.

"Thanks for doing this," I said.

"You shouldn't be thanking me," she replied. "You should be getting on a plane and going back to America."

"What are you afraid of?" I asked.

"Rome is full of enemies, old and new."

"Who are your enemies?"

She smiled enigmatically, didn't answer.

She relaxed a little once we reached the Autostrada 24 Roma a' Teramo, a wide highway that stretched north-east of the city. The driver told me it was known locally as the Parks Motorway. We raced along it for about fifteen kilometers before taking a curling exit and joining the Via Polense, a narrow, single-lane road that snaked through countryside and up into the hills to the east of Rome.

"Where are we going?" I asked.

Luna leant forward and said, "*C'è una piccola strada a nord di Bullica-Ciavaccone.*"

The driver nodded and when we neared the town of Poli, took a right turn onto an even narrower road that climbed higher into the hills. Leaves and branches whipped at the car, but when they cleared, I looked to my right and saw a magnificent view of the San Pietro Valley, a disorganized patchwork of forest, olive and citrus groves, farmhouses and small villages, all shining under the midday sun.

Luna's nerves eased the further we traveled from Rome and the higher we went into the hills. I tried to strike up a couple of conversations with her; the first about what a police officer would be doing in a notorious brothel, and the second about who could scare a detective. She didn't respond to either but continued to smile at me, eyes concealed behind a pair of opaque sunglasses with green tortoiseshell frames that matched her short voile dress.

The taxi reached a tiny hillside road, which according to a sun-bleached sign ran between Bullica and Ciavaccone. The earth around us was tinder-dry, but the leaves on the trees were green and gave the arid land a sense of vitality that would otherwise have been absent in the brutal heat.

"Hasn't been much rain," I remarked.

"We are into the fourth week of a drought," Luna replied, speaking for the first time since we'd left the city. "It's difficult for the farmers."

We climbed higher still, above the patchwork of citrus and olive groves spread out across the hillside.

As we rounded a bend, approaching a particularly sudden drop, Luna leant forward and touched the driver on the shoulder.

"*Proprio qui, per favore*," she said, instructing him to stop.

He pulled into a narrow turning place on the hillside and I asked him to wait, but he spoke quickly to Luna.

"He wants to go to Poli for fuel," she translated. "He'll be back in twenty minutes."

I nodded and we got out, watching the man drive away, leaving us in the baking heat of the exposed hillside.

"This way," Luna said, heading east, but I didn't need her to guide me; the site of the accident was clear to see.

"Are those his tire marks?" I asked.

She nodded.

There was a pair of thick black lines veering toward the edge of a steep drop, and a gap where bushes and trees had been uprooted and the view to the valley below exposed.

"Looks like he tried to stop," I said. "Like he really didn't want to crash."

"Yes," she agreed. "What else do you see?"

I crouched down and studied the rubber residue on the road surface before standing up and looking around.

"Quiet road, good visibility all around."

There was a clear line of sight in both directions from the sweeping bend, and the elevation meant we could see the road winding up and down for long distances around us. Headlights would have been visible from a great distance at night.

"He's in the center of the road to begin with," I said, as we walked between the tire marks. I crouched down again and examined the nearest mark. "There's a kink here, and again further on, as though the car hit something."

"That's what I saw too," Luna said.

"Maybe he was being shunted from behind?" I suggested, and she nodded. "You think there was another vehicle?"

"I think he might have been forced off the road."

We walked to the place where the tire tracks ended, the edge of the steep drop, and I craned over and peered down at the valley floor some 200 feet below. My stomach lurched at the thought of Lombardi plummeting to his doom.

"I think you're right," I said.

Luna was about to respond when gunfire erupted all around us.

CHAPTER 15

THE SHOTS CAME from the hillside above. We were lucky we weren't targeted by a proficient marksman. A volley of bullets chewed the dirt near our feet. I grabbed Luna and pulled her toward a tree by the side of the road as the gunman corrected his flawed aim.

He must have been using an automatic rifle because as we ran he switched from fairly targeted semi-automatic fire to strafing. The rapid staccato of shots echoed around the wide valley.

I pushed Luna behind the trunk of an ancient stone pine, rooted at the very edge of the hillside, and she grabbed a branch to stop herself from tumbling over the steep drop. I joined her as bullets shredded the thick bark of the tree in front of us, and we crouched and moved along a narrow ledge to take cover behind a collapsed stone sheepfold directly beside the tree. A hail of bullets chipped the large boulders that protected us and filled the air with dust.

Luna cursed in Italian. "He must have followed you."

"Or you," I countered. "Who the heck is it?"

The gunfire stopped. There was a moment of stillness disturbed only by the ringing in my ears. I took the opportunity to glance over the stones and saw movement on a ridge about 150 feet above us. The rough hillside was covered in tufty grass dried to an earth brown and pocked with patches of gray stone. There was a rocky outcrop on the ridge edged by some bushes, which concealed the shooter. The slope to either side of the ridge was steep but looked scalable. I ducked back as the gunman snapped a magazine in place and open fire again.

As a hail of bullets struck the stones, I leant close to Luna and said, "When he runs out of ammo, let him see you."

She looked dismayed but nodded agreement. I crouched and swung my legs over the side of the cliff, starting to climb down the root system that stuck out of the hillside.

Earth and stones fell away as I clung to the gnarled roots. Above me the crack and snap of bullets continued. I was soon low enough to be concealed by the lip of the road, starting to traverse a tiny ledge, a vein of rock that stuck out of the hillside. I held on to roots, rock, and, where there was nothing else, earth, as I edged around the bend, inch by inch. There was a lull in the gunfire as our assailant reloaded, but it soon resumed.

I started sweating in the sweltering heat. My clothes grew damp and dirty as I hauled myself along the hillside. My breathing became labored; my arms and fingers ached from the effort of keeping my balance. When I finally thought I'd be shielded from view by the curve of the road, I clambered up the steep slope to the edge. There was an old metal barrier here. I used it to pull myself up and over. I could see Luna behind the boulders, which were being peppered by bullets, but the shooter was hidden from my sight by the curving terrain, which meant he couldn't see me either.

I ran across the road and scrambled up the steep slope on the far side. I covered the 150-foot incline in a minute or so and was gasping and sore by the time I was about level with the gunman.

I picked up a large stone and crept along the hillside until I saw the man lying prone behind the scrub that concealed him from the road. The sound of gunfire meant he didn't hear me approach, but when I was a few feet from him, he ran out of ammunition and paused to reload. I froze, but wasn't quick enough. He must have caught my movement because he turned and his eyes widened when he saw me.

He reached for a pistol on the ground beside him, but I leapt forward and swung the stone down onto his skull, knocking him away from the handgun. We grappled and rolled around the outcrop. I was punching him in the ribs while he groaned and tried to defend himself.

He got lucky and dazed me with an elbow to my nose. I rolled clear. We both stood and faced each other. The pistol was behind me. I saw him eye it greedily, but I was closer.

I ran for the gun, grabbed it and raised it at him as I swung back.

To my shock, he didn't freeze. Instead, he ran across the outcrop, pushed through the vegetation, and hurled himself off.

CHAPTER 16

HE CRIED OUT as he fell. The terrible sound was cut short by a sickening thud as he hit the ground far below. I ran to the edge and pushed through the surrounding scrub as far as I could until I saw Luna begin to ease her way hesitantly over the boulders. As I leant forward, I saw our assailant's twisted body on the road below, a pool of blood spreading from his head.

Movement caught my eye and I saw our taxi approaching, taking one of the bends further along the valley, about a mile away.

I stepped back from the outcrop, hurried along the ridge to the sloping hillside and scrambled down the steep incline, sending stones and dirt sliding ahead of me. I was gasping and drenched with sweat by the time I joined Luna beside the man's body. She had crouched down next to him, her fingers pressed against his neck.

"He's dead," she stated, though I'd been in doubt. "What happened up there?"

There was accusation in her eyes or maybe I was just projecting my own guilt? I hadn't done anything though. It was strictly self-defense. Maybe she couldn't suppress the cop in her.

"He jumped," I replied. "We were fighting, and when I got the upper hand, he threw himself over the edge."

Luna stood and eyed me skeptically, but her attention shifted to something behind me and I turned to see the cab approaching.

The driver's eyes widened as he halted close by.

"You take the taxi back to Rome," I said. "I'll call the cops. Keep your name out of it."

Luna hesitated.

"Go," I urged her. "I can handle this."

She nodded and pulled her identification from her purse as she walked toward the cab.

"*Polizia*," she said, holding up her ID.

She spoke to the driver through his window. After a brief exchange, she climbed in the back.

The cab crawled by the body, the driver unable to take his eyes off the broken corpse. He sped up once past the bloody mess, and I saw Luna give me a final glance before the vehicle disappeared around the bend.

I pulled out my phone and dialed emergency services on 112. When my call was answered, I said, "Do you speak English?"

"Yes," a man replied. "Of course. Please state the nature of your emergency?"

"My name is Jack Morgan. I'd like to report an accident."

The operator took details of my location and a brief account of what had happened before telling me the police were on their way.

With the call made, I approached the body and conducted a quick search. I didn't find any personal possessions other than a cell phone, which I slipped into my pocket. The shooter's left arm was in the pool of blood spreading out from his cracked skull, but his right lay limp against the asphalt. I lifted it and rolled up his shirt sleeve to discover a series of distinctive tattoos.

I pulled his sleeve all the way up to his shoulder and used my phone to take photographs of the body art. I could see religious and occult symbols, skulls, crosses, strange fleur-de-lys, but nothing immediately recognizable, so I sent the images to Mo-bot for analysis.

When I had everything I needed, I rolled down the man's sleeve, repositioned his arm and then took some photos of his body and close-ups of his face, which I also sent to Mo-bot.

I had a feeling the cops would search me, so as I stepped away from the body, I removed the SIM card from his phone and put it in the second slot in my own.

I walked to the patch of shade beneath the stone pine next to the sheepfold that had saved our lives and stayed clear of the trunk and neighboring boulders, which had become a mine of forensic evidence. There were dozens of bullets buried in the pockmarked bark and embedded in the stones. I turned away from the body and gazed at the beautiful Technicolor countryside shining under the glorious Italian sun and waited for the police to arrive.

CHAPTER 17

TWO HOURS LATER, I found myself in the very same interview room where I'd met Matteo earlier that day, only this time I was on the wrong side of the table being held as a suspect, interviewed by Mia Esposito. A uniformed colleague lolled against the wall near the door, while an electronic recorder captured our conversation. I was aware my filthy suit smelt of churned earth and sweat, and desperately wanted to take a shower.

"And you say he jumped?" Esposito asked. There was no chance of me leaving any time soon. It seemed she was intent on going over my story one more time. I'd already told her what had happened, leaving out Luna's presence as promised, but otherwise offering the truth: that I'd visited the location to look into the accident that had led to city prosecutor Filippo Lombardi's death, and when I'd arrived a man had opened fire. I told

Esposito I had been able to climb to the outcrop, had fought the man, and had watched him jump to his death.

"And you didn't push him?" she asked.

I shook my head. "He jumped when he realized I'd got his gun."

"But there was no witness," Esposito countered. "Who can say what really happened?"

"You can see the state of the tree," I replied. "And the number of shots fired. There's no doubting what really happened."

"And how did you get there? Remind me."

"I took a taxi," I replied. "He didn't want to wait, and I don't remember his number."

I didn't want her interviewing the driver and learning Luna had been with me. "I paid cash and let him go because I wasn't sure how long I would be."

"I see. And you planned to walk back to Rome?"

"Uber," I said. "Or a phone call."

Esposito grunted and smiled. "I don't know who this dead man is, but he should have taught you a valuable lesson, Mr. Morgan. Rome is no place for innocents. And it is even worse for the guilty. You are shining a light into the shadows, revealing things other people want hidden. My advice would be to forget whatever it is you are doing here and go home."

I nodded slowly. "Does that mean I'm free to leave?"

She hesitated and glanced at her colleague.

"Yes," she said at last. "I see no reason to doubt your account. You're free to go."

Twenty minutes later, I walked out of police headquarters,

reunited with my possessions, and breathed in warm evening air scented with rich aromas of food coming from restaurant kitchens dotted around the neighborhood. I was glad to be out. I walked away from the imposing building, took out my phone and dialed a number while looking for a cab.

"Jack," Justine said when she answered. "Where have you been? I must have left half a dozen messages."

My phone vibrated as notifications arrived.

"I'm just getting them now," I replied. "My phone's been off. I was arrested."

She gasped.

"It's okay. I'm out now. Some guy tried to shoot me and Luna Colombo, Matteo's former partner."

"Jeez, Jack. Are you alright?"

"Nothing a shower and an Old Fashioned won't fix," I told her. "I've sent Mo-bot some photos of the shooter's tattoos. I need to know straight away if she identifies them. And I'm going to need the details of someone local who can analyze a SIM."

"You're borderline obsessive, Jack Morgan," she responded. "You get shot at and your mind is still locked on the case."

"The detective in charge thinks I should go home."

"I think you should too," Justine said. "Come back to me, Jack. Let someone else take care of this."

"I can't," I replied. "I've taken on the Chief Operating Officer at the Vatican Bank as a client. He wants to know the truth about Father Brambilla's death."

"Don't we have someone in Rome who can handle it?" she countered.

"Matteo was still in the process of staffing up. The people he's hired haven't started properly yet or had their Private training. I'm all there is."

She sighed. "I don't like you getting shot at."

"Me neither. I don't know what Matteo was into, but I might have made a mistake hiring him. I feel a little responsible for this mess and want to fix it. I underestimated the extent of corruption in Rome. Innocent or guilty, I have to find out the truth about him," I said. "I will come home as soon as it's done."

"Be—"

"Careful," I interrupted. "I know. I will. And I'll call you later. Love you."

"Love you, you infuriating obsessive," she replied, before hanging up.

I pocketed my phone and made a beeline for a cab that had responded to my hail.

"Hassler Hotel," I said, jumping in the back.

CHAPTER 18

THE TAXI TOOK me to Via Bocca di Leone and I walked two blocks though the luxury shopping district, passing busy sidewalk cafés, to the Spanish Steps where tourists thronged in the evening sun. Its glow caught the tops of the old buildings and shadows gathered in the narrow alleyways beside them as the day neared its end. I climbed the ancient stone steps, picking my way past people taking selfies and photos of the church at the top, the city laid out at the base.

The doorman at the Hassler nodded a greeting as I went inside. I saw his eyes flick up and down my filthy suit, but his training meant he knew better than to remark on my dishevelment. Hotel staff saw all sorts of oddities, and a higher star rating often correlated with more outrageous guests. My dirty clothing would not be the strangest thing this man had ever seen.

I walked into the cool marble-lined lobby, looking forward

to a shower, but the moment I stepped inside I knew such simple pleasures would have to wait. Faduma was seated on a chair from which she could see everyone who entered. She saw me the moment I came in. Her impassive expression gave nothing away. I still had no idea whether she was friend or foe but at least my background check had established she was probably honest.

I walked over to her. As I drew nearer, she got to her feet.

"You look like you could use a drink," she said, leading me into the lobby bar.

She didn't seem fazed by my appearance, and we took our seats at a table in the quiet room. A waiter came over immediately.

"Iced water, please," I told him.

"Orange juice," Faduma added. "You've had quite the day," she said to me while the waiter walked away.

She produced an iPad from a satchel she had slung over her shoulder and put the device on the circular table between us. She switched it on and flicked through a series of photographs of Luna and me at the spot where Filippo Lombardi had driven off the road, or more likely been forced off. The photos had been taken with a long lens and showed the gunman attacking us, my ascent, our fight and his death. Faduma paused at the photo of Luna getting into the cab.

"Why did you conceal her involvement?" she asked, tapping the image of the detective being driven away.

"How did you get these?"

"I followed you, Mr. Morgan."

I wondered just how badly I was slipping not to have noticed a tail.

"Why?" I asked. "Why are you following me?"

"You're stirring a hornets' nest," Faduma replied. "That makes you interesting."

"For a story?" I countered. "I know who you are."

She smiled. "It took you longer than I thought it would. Maybe your reputation isn't justified? Or perhaps you're losing your touch. The passing years haven't been easy for you, have they?"

I had no idea whether she was trying to goad me or if she was just upset I'd discovered her identity, but either way I didn't rise to the bait.

"I think you know a lot more about what's going on here," I said. "If you've got information, you should share it, but if you're mixed up in whatever this is, you need to know I will hold you to account."

"I'm not mixed up in this," Faduma assured me. "And I want to believe you're a good man. I want to trust you, but you keep doing questionable things, like letting a corrupt cop leave a crime scene."

"What makes you think she's corrupt?" I asked.

Faduma smiled again. "You need to do more digging, Mr. Morgan. Find out who your new partner really is."

"She's not my partner."

"Your associate then."

"Why don't you just tell me?" I asked.

"Like I said, I want to believe I can trust you," Faduma replied, getting to her feet. "Call it a test."

She walked away as the waiter came over with my iced water and her orange juice.

"I'll take them both," I told him. "It's been a hot day."

"Shall I charge them to your room, sir?" he asked, arranging the drinks on the table in front of me.

"Yes, please," I replied, watching the journalist leave the bar, wondering just how much she knew and what exactly I'd have to do to get her to trust me.

CHAPTER 19

AFTER I'D HAD a revitalizing and refreshing shower and changed into jeans and a black T-shirt, I ordered some pesto linguine from the hotel bistro and ate in the small dining area in my suite during a video call with Justine, Sci and Mo-bot, who were in the conference room in Private's LA headquarters.

"That looks good," Mo-bot remarked, nodding in my direction as I took another forkful.

I'd opted for a simple meal, but the Hassler bistro was known for making the simple magnificent. The sauce was rich and flavorsome and the linguine perfectly cooked.

"It is good," I replied. "I'll bring some back."

Mo-bot scoffed.

"So, we've got a prosecutor dead in a murder made to look like an accident?" Sci observed. Seymour 'Sci' Kloppenberg was the embodiment of an aging biker, but he was also one of the world's leading experts in forensic analysis and had examined the photos I'd taken of the hillside road where Lombardi had died.

"And the cop investigating the death, our new colleague Matteo, tells his partner to back off the case," Justine remarked.

I nodded. "Looks that way."

"He is then found holding a smoking gun, standing over the body of the priest he claims told him to back off the investigation, and his ex-partner goes into hiding while a reporter stakes you out," Mo-bot added. "And when you check out the scene of the earlier crime, some guy tries to punch holes in you with a machine gun."

"You take a look at the guy yet?" I asked, referring to the dead assassin.

"Yeah," Mo-bot replied. "The ink reeks of organized crime, but there's a bunch of other stuff there. Religious symbolism. I don't recognize any of the designs, but I'm running analysis against image libraries."

"And the phone SIM?" I asked.

"I have a friend in Rome, a gray hat called Valentina who I've collaborated with a couple of times," Mo-bot revealed.

"Gray hat?" I asked. Mo-bot was referring to the kind of hacker who did legal *and* illegal work. "How gray?"

"Pretty dark gray," Mo-bot replied. "But her heart is in the right place."

I frowned. She didn't like it.

"How long have you known me, Jack Morgan?" she asked. "You think I would send you to someone you couldn't trust? I'll message you her details. Stop worrying and focus on getting answers off that SIM."

I nodded. "Okay. No need to take it personally. I'm just a little wary of strangers right now."

"Because you've been shot at?" Mo-bot asked.

I smiled. "That might have something to do with it. Can you give me and Justine a minute?"

Mo-bot and Sci exchanged knowing looks.

"So you can do some smooching?" Mo-bot teased.

"So we can talk," I replied.

"Good to catch up, Jack," Sci said, rising. "Speak soon."

He and Mo-bot left the conference room and Justine drew closer to the camera.

"How are you doing, honey?" I asked.

"I'd be better if you were here."

"I know. Me too, but someone shot at me today, which makes this personal. It also tells me there's probably something to my suspicion that Matteo's innocent. I don't think he murdered that priest."

"Me neither," Justine replied. "It doesn't fit his profile. Speaking of which, Mo-bot ran background on Christian Altmer, and he isn't as squeaky clean as you might expect of one of God's bankers. I'll send you the file and my psych workup, but keep an eye on him, Jack: he has many of the hallmarks of a sociopath. Trouble in school, jail time for minor offences in his late teens and early twenties."

"Anything recent?"

She shook her head. "He cleaned up his act ten years ago.

Finished an economics degree in London, joined the graduate program at an investment bank and climbed the greasy corporate pole."

"You think people don't change?" I asked.

"Do you?"

In my experience it was rare for people to undergo genuine transformation, but it could happen.

"I'll keep an eye on him," I replied.

There was a moment's silence, and I knew she was building up the courage to say something else.

"I don't like you being shot at," she confessed at last. "It's becoming a habit, Jack."

"So is surviving," I replied. "I'm being careful. I'll come back to you in one piece."

"You'd better," she said.

"I will. I promise."

CHAPTER 20

I WOKE TO find a message from Mo-bot telling me she'd arranged a meeting with the hacker named Valentina at Ostia, an outlying district of Rome, at midday. I took the opportunity of a free morning to visit the local boutiques that lined the ancient narrow streets stretching out from the bottom of the Spanish Steps. I desperately wanted to be home with Justine, but I'd made a commitment to Matteo and our new client Joseph Stadler and would have to see it through. I added to the small selection of clothes I'd brought with me for a short trip and by 10:30 a.m. was back in my room with enough shirts, trousers and suits for an extended stay.

I opted for a new navy blue linen suit, a white shirt and brown shoes, and caught a cab outside the hotel.

The driver, a scowling woman in her early fifties, wasn't keen on visiting Ostia and while we drove through Rome to the coast told me it was not a good neighborhood. The sun was high and the foreshortened shadows harsh and stark against the dazzling light. Some of the buildings seemed to sparkle, their white marble shining beneath the bright sky, heightening the beauty of the ancient city. We drove with the windows open and the car filled with the smells of the city; coffee, pastries, sickly-sweet scents of over-ripe fruit and garbage, and every now and then the aroma of food being prepared for the lunchtime rush. Rome was not a peaceful place. Music blared from open vehicle windows and horns sounded anytime there was a delay in the smooth progress of the traffic, which was often.

Ostia was a rundown coastal town, nowadays almost linked to Rome by urban sprawl and regarded by many as one of the city's suburbs. It had been developed at a time when function had trumped form, the buildings mostly practical but ugly. Uniform blocks of flats; drab modern storefronts; office buildings with mundane and unimaginative façades. The area was characterized in all the wrong ways by graffiti, grime, trash, abandoned vehicles. All spoke to the soul of Ostia, but it probably wasn't the image most locals wanted to promote.

We made it to the seafront and stopped outside Caffè Babe, one of the area's few upmarket haunts, shortly after noon. I paid the driver, crossed the busy boardwalk and went inside.

Caffè Babe was the kind of distressed-wood, exposed-wrought-ironwork, filament-lightbulbs joint I could easily imagine visiting in Greenwich Village, New York City, or Clerkenwell in London, but it seemed out of place in this part of Italy. The incongruity didn't seem to bother its clientele and all thirty tables were occupied by groups of people busily eating and drinking, many of them while also working on laptops.

I approached the counter, which featured a glass cabinet displaying perfectly baked pastries. Their sweet smell mingled enticingly with the aroma of coffee.

"*Sì?*" said the barista, a woman in her twenties.

"Double espresso, please," I replied. "And a chocolate twist."

"Of course," she said, setting to work on my order.

"I'm looking for Valentina," I remarked, as she prepared my coffee.

"You shouldn't snack between meals," a woman said as she sidled up next to me.

She had short brown hair, piercings in her ears, nose and eyebrows, and tattoos covering her arms. They curled up her neck out of the back of her black T-shirt, and down her legs exposed beneath a pair of red shorts.

"Valentina?" I guessed.

"Mo-bot told me to keep an eye out for a square," she replied, pointing to my suit. "At least it's not gray." She turned to the barista. "Isabella, bring his order back to us, *per favore.*"

She led me past the counter and through a door that took us further into the building.

"I bought the place five years ago," Valentina explained. "I got tired of giving my money to other café owners and thought I could do a better job."

She walked me along a corridor to a supply room. Here she stopped by a rack of sugar sacks and pressed a concealed button.

"The volume of Internet traffic among the customers provides great cover," she said as the rack and wall behind it slid aside to reveal a hidden room full of screens and computer gear.

Isabella entered the room with my coffee and pastry. She seemed unfazed by the sight of the secret computer facility.

"Everyone who works here is in training," Valentina remarked. "Magicians with coffee *and* computers. Thank you, Isabella."

The barista nodded and withdrew. I carried my coffee into the computer cave.

Valentina sealed the room behind us and took a seat at one of half a dozen terminals. All around us there were racks of servers in Faraday cages, shelves laden with sensors, devices I couldn't identify, and stacks of data drives.

"I looked you up, Mr. Morgan," Valentina said as she woke her computer from sleep mode. "You're a saint. One of the good guys."

"I wouldn't say that," I replied. "I snack between meals."

She chuckled.

"Maureen says you have a SIM card to investigate."

I nodded and produced the dead gunman's SIM.

Valentina placed it in a reader and opened a program on her computer.

"This isn't much of a challenge," she remarked.

"I'll be sure to bring you something tougher next time," I responded, and she smiled.

"The suit conceals so much spirit," she said, before turning her attention to the screen. "There is one SMS message. The phone was never used for anything else."

She opened Google Maps. "Looks like GPS coordinates and a time—8 p.m."

She pointed at a little red marker on her screen that showed a location: a courtyard in the heart of Rome.

"It's in the Vatican," she noted, and I looked at the screen and the overhead view of St Peter's and wondered why an assassin would be given a location inside the spiritual center of the Eternal City.

CHAPTER 21

I HAD A time but no date, and it was impossible to tell whether the appointed hour referred to something that had already happened or something that was yet to take place. I didn't have any immediate leads. After a day spent at my hotel reviewing the background files Mo-bot had sent me on Joseph Stadler, Christian Altmer and Luna Colombo, I took an evening walk to Vatican City.

It's impossible not to picture the history of Rome. Its humble beginnings as a farming community, its emergence as a territorial power, unbounded riches flowing into the capital of an empire and leading to a grandeur that became the stuff of legend. The tiny alleyways threading between bars and cafés were once used to run details of intrigues or shield plotters on their way to clandestine meetings. The old churches witnessing countless confessions, the hidden sins of the city long lost within their thick stone walls. The old mansions and villas, monuments to commerce and conquest, and the modern infill in gaps created by World War Two. Unsightly post-war office blocks and apartment buildings dotted here and there, evidence of corruption in the city, the infamous nexus of construction, politics and organized crime that took hold of Rome during the 1970s and 1980s.

I walked the streets intrigued by the history of the place, each corner a detective's dream, full of stories, every building a trove of clues for the inquisitive investigator. All around me were the sounds and smells of a city winding up for the evening.

Tourists ambled, photographing the sites, and locals sought out their favorite eateries and bars. The tourists became more numerous as I neared Vatican City and I joined a steady stream of people heading for a late-evening service. Instead of following them toward the dome of St Peter's, I walked along the North Colonnade until I reached the pedestrian checkpoint that would allow me into Vatican City.

Joseph Stadler had put my name on a list of visitors who could pass as they pleased. Once I was through security, I walked round the back of St Peter's, past the beautiful gardens in front of St Mary's Chapel, to the Campo Santo Teutonico, the courtyard garden that occupied the coordinates Valentina had discovered in the dead man's phone.

I went to the center of a small bone-dry lawn and looked around. To the north lay the great basilica, to the east the chapel dedicated to St Mary, to the south a red-brick building with high arched windows. It looked institutional, like a school or hospital. To the west was the Museum of St Peter. I couldn't see any reason for an assassin to come here, other than the fact it was a relatively secluded location.

I waited until 8 p.m. to see if there was some temporal reason for this hour being specified, something that happened only at that time, but apart from the sound of bells near and far chiming the passing of the hour, the courtyard remained undisturbed.

I lingered a while longer and at 8:15 p.m. a figure came through the arched entrance to one side of me. As he passed from shadow to light, I saw a priest dressed in a black cassock. He was tall and slim, with salt-and-pepper hair and the dark eyes and olive complexion that marked him out as southern Mediterranean. From his hair and lined face, I put his age in the late forties.

He smiled warmly when he saw me.

"*Mi scusi, mi dispiace disturbarla,*" he said.

"I'm sorry," I responded. "I don't speak Italian."

"American," he said. "I love America. I spent many happy years there in Boston. I was apologizing for disturbing you and intruding on your meditation."

"I wasn't meditating. Just sightseeing."

"One doesn't need to be of the faith to recognize a person seeking answers," he said gently.

I thought about that. "Maybe," I conceded. "But I wouldn't call my quest for answers meditation. That sounds way too peaceful."

"Meditation can be active," he replied. "It need not be passive. My name is Vito."

He offered me his hand.

"Jack."

"Nice to meet you, Jack. Are you Catholic?"

"I was." I hesitated. "Am still, I suppose. In some ways."

"Faith is like a tide. The ocean is never constant, is she? She comes in and goes out, and in our lives faith does the same thing but is always there. Sometimes high, sometimes low, but always giving us what we need."

"And the ocean never runs dry?" I asked.

"Never," Father Vito replied. "It is ever-present."

"What brings you here?" I asked. "What is this place?"

"I like quiet. Vatican City is full of hidden places like this where one can find solitude even while surrounded by millions of souls, but there are few places exactly like this one," Father Vito confided. "The building behind you is a dormitory for visiting priests, and legend has it that long ago this courtyard was where they came to confess sins so grave they had to be hidden from the sight of God. Its official name is Campo Santo Teutonico, the Teutonic Holy Field, but unofficially it is known as *il giardino della confessione segreta*, the Garden of Secret Confession."

He gestured at the cherubs and saints in the stained-glass windows of the adjacent chapel.

"If you look, you will see all the good and holy have their eyes closed so they do not see what transpires here."

I looked up and saw he was right.

"But such superstitions run counter to the true word of the Lord, which is that all sins can be atoned for. So now this is just a place of quiet meditation."

"In that case it is I who should apologize for disturbing you, Father Vito," I said.

"It has been a pleasure to talk to you, Jack."

"Thank you for your guidance," I said, turning to leave.

"I hope you find what you are looking for," Father Vito called after me.

I hoped so too, but even if I learnt the truth about Father Brambilla, there would always be another case, another investigation to consume me, so in one sense I felt I was doomed never to find peace.

I didn't quite know what to make of that troubling realization as I passed under the shadow of the archway and left the Garden of Secret Confession.

CHAPTER 22

I WALKED BACK to the Hassler, passing through a city in full pursuit of its night-time pleasures. The bars and restaurants were packed with people who had no idea of the darkness that stalked this world, or if they had any inkling kept up a strong pretense of ignorance—laughing, chatting, drinking and making merry. The smells of coffee and pastries had given way to the rich aroma of baking pizzas, roasting meats, alcohol, and the occasional plume of fruity vapor or cigarette smoke.

I hadn't found any answers in the Garden of Secret Confession, but the priest had been right: I had been meditating, or at least musing, trying to feel my way to the truth. It now seemed almost certain Father Brambilla had been killed by Matteo, but though light on explanation, he was adamant he was innocent, which meant I had to find another plausible alternative. There were only two: Brambilla killed himself, or someone else had entered the room and been able to kill the priest without Matteo noticing then leave him holding the murder weapon. If that was the case, I was looking for a murderer who was also a magician.

I approached the Spanish Steps lost in thought, trying to puzzle my way through the disparate facts placed in my path thus far, when someone stepped from behind the corner of the building on Piazza di Spagna and grabbed me. I wheeled round, ready to fight, but saw Luna.

"I've been watching your hotel," she said, nodding up the Spanish Steps toward the Hassler, beautifully lit against the night sky. "I was waiting for you to come back so we could talk."

"Okay," I replied. "We can go to the bar."

"No," she said. "Not your hotel. Somewhere else. This way."

She pulled me along the cobbled square toward the Column of the Immaculate Conception, but before we reached it, took me right into Via Borgognona, a narrow street that was little more than an alleyway.

"Thank you for keeping my name out of things," she said.

"I don't understand why a police detective is so scared. Tell me what's going on."

"I can't," she replied.

"We should be on the same side of the law, Inspector Colombo. Why won't you trust me?" I pressed.

She didn't answer.

"At least tell me whether the shooter was after you or me?"

"I don't know," she said, as we hurried past luxury clothes stores and cafés. "This way."

She turned left onto Via Mario de' Fiori, another narrow, claustrophobic street cutting through this ancient part of the city, and headed toward a bar called Il Pellicano, which had smoked-glass windows. Through the open doorway I saw a large, low-lit space with booths, long shelves behind the counter stocked with liquor from all over the world. Il Pellicano was crowded with locals and tourists, but Luna pushed through and managed to grab a booth from a group that was going.

"What do you want to drink?" I asked, but we didn't get a moment to settle.

"We need to leave," she said urgently, drawing my attention to three men who'd followed us in.

They looked out of place; rough brawlers, the kind of men who were friends with the devil.

"They must have been watching your hotel," she said.

"Who are they?" I asked, sliding out of the booth.

"We need to go now," Luna replied. "Run!"

CHAPTER 23

WE PUSHED OUR way through the crowd, heading for the corridor linking the main saloon with the back rooms. I glanced over my shoulder to see the fierce-looking trio—all muscles beneath tightly fitting T-shirts, scowls and tattoos—barge their way after us.

I cleared the way for Luna, ignoring the irritated looks and hostile remarks we received, until we reached the corridor.

We ran along the dimly lit, narrow space, the restrooms to our left, a small catering counter to our right with next to it a storeroom and office. I glanced back to see the trio shoving people out of their way. One man made the mistake of trying to resist and was punched by the lead pursuer, knocking him backwards into the crowd as he fell.

The trio reached the mouth of the corridor as Luna and I made it to the fire door. I pushed the bar and barged the door open with my shoulder. An alarm sounded, panicking the already disturbed crowd, and I looked over my shoulder to see people moving as one toward the main entrance, away from the three men, who were close to us now.

I slammed the door shut behind us and scanned the gloomy alleyway for a makeshift barricade, but the dumpsters were all gathered fifty feet away where the alley met Via Frattina, and there was nothing else to hand.

Luna ran ahead of me, racing toward the road. The fire door burst open behind us and I turned to face the three fearsome fighters who spilt out. The first, a ferocious skinhead with a nose that had been broken long ago, swung at me. I ducked the punch and delivered a heavy fist to his gut, then caught him with an uppercut as he doubled over. I drove the heel of my palm into the ridge of his nose, breaking it anew, and he went down, his face a bloody mess.

His two comrades came at me. I lashed out, delivering a heel kick to the shin of the man on my right. The guy on my left was huge but moved slowly. As he threw a punch, I sidestepped, grabbed his arm and pulled it, so he lost his balance and took some compensating steps forward. I drove my knee into his groin and clapped his ears as he crumpled. The other man came at me, grabbing my shoulders, attempting to hurl me to the ground. I used his momentum and spun myself clear. We faced each other for a moment, while one of his comrades was on his knees clutching his bloody nose and the other had one hand pressed to his ear and the other to his groin.

I seized the advantage and rushed the standing man, charging him with my shoulder. I caught him with a savage tackle and felt the wind knocked from my lungs as he brought his fist down on my back. I ignored the pain and drove him into the fire door. He slammed into it bodily and I stood tall and swung a flurry of punches at him, which he tried to block ineffectually. I landed a right cross and his eyes swam, so I followed it up quickly with a couple of jabs and a hook that knocked him down.

Luna was at the mouth of the alley now, looking back at me.

"Come on!" she yelled.

I sprinted away from the incapacitated men, but as I neared Luna, my heart sank. A van pulled up behind her and she cried out as the panel door slid open to reveal two men in ski masks. They grabbed her before she could run and hauled her inside.

"No!" she shouted.

I sprinted as fast as I could, driving my heels into the cobblestones, but the van door slammed shut and the vehicle roared away. I managed to pound the bodywork impotently as it raced off.

I took out my phone and activated the camera to grab a series of photos of the speeding van, making sure I got its license plate.

When the vehicle finally turned left onto Via Mario de' Fiori, I became very aware of the three injured men behind me, now stirring.

I hurried away and dialed 112.

"I'd like to report an abduction," I said when the operator answered.

CHAPTER 24

"WHAT'S HAPPENED?" JUSTINE asked.

My first instinct had been to call her as soon as I was clear of danger.

To me she represented safety. Calm amid the storm.

"Some men took Luna," I replied, hurrying along Via della Croce.

I couldn't go back to my hotel for fear it was being watched, so I was wandering aimlessly, taking a snaking route through the city to minimize the risk of being followed, and maximize the chance of spotting a tail.

"What do you mean 'took her'?" Justine asked, audibly shocked.

"I mean some men abducted her, put her in a van and drove away."

I burnt with frustration at the thought I could have done more to prevent the abduction.

"I've informed the cops," I said. "I got some photos of the van. Tell Mo-bot it needs to be her top priority."

"Let me loop her in," Justine replied. The line went silent and a few moments later she returned. "I've conferenced in Mo."

"Justine gave me the headlines," said Mo-bot. "I'll see what I can do about the van, but your best bet would be to go to Valentina. She'll have access to local databases, dealer records."

"That's a good idea," I replied. "Do you think she could help me with accommodation too? I don't think it's safe for me to go back to my hotel."

"You can ask," Mo-bot suggested. "She's well connected."

"Thanks," I said. "Justine, I'll call you as soon as I've found somewhere."

I knew she wouldn't rest until I was safe.

"I'll be here."

"Watch yourself," Mo-bot advised.

"Always," I said, hanging up.

I hurried to the end of the street and flagged a cab passing on Via del Corso.

The driver, a taciturn old man with spiky gray hair, grumbled when I asked him to take me to Ostia, but I silenced him with the promise of a fifty-euro bonus.

We covered the journey through the city in forty minutes and I had the silent old man drop me a couple blocks from Valentina's café.

I walked the short distance, aware how the neighborhood had changed with the coming of darkness. What had seemed rundown before now had an air of menace. A gang of a dozen youths gathered outside a kebab shop, pushing and shoving each other. An emaciated woman hassled the customers going into a discount liquor store, asking for change or food. I could see why the cab driver hadn't reacted well to coming here. It was definitely the sort of place you could be mugged, and I stuck out in my fine suit.

But I made it to the café without incident. It too was different at night. The remote workers were gone, replaced by groups of young men and women talking animatedly over beers.

Valentina was with one such group. She excused herself and came over when she saw me.

"Mr. Morgan," she said, looking me up and down. "You run into trouble?"

I followed her gaze and realized my suit was flecked with someone else's blood.

I nodded. "I could use a friend."

"What kind of friend?"

"Someone with a place for me to crash. A safe place. Low-profile," I replied. "For a price, of course."

"Of course. You should meet my friend Amr."

Valentina led me to the table she'd just left. There were two women and a couple men seated there, all in their late twenties, looking as though they'd stepped off a Milan catwalk, oozing an air of wealth and success that was hardly in keeping with the neighborhood.

"Amr," Valentina said to the man closest to us. He was Syrian or Egyptian, with wide eyes and a warm smile. "This is Jack Morgan. He needs a place to stay." She turned to me. "Amr is one of Rome's most successful young entrepreneurs."

"I don't need to brag when Valentina is around," he said, getting to his feet and taking my hand. "*Marhaba!* Welcome, Mr. Morgan. I think I can help you. I have an apartment above one of my businesses not far from here. It needs to be redecorated, but it should be more than acceptable for someone who does not want the inconvenience of staying at a hotel."

"How much?" I asked.

"A man in a suit like yours will know the right price to pay," he replied.

I realized he was wearing the same style in black. He smiled as he registered this dawning on me.

"One favor delivered," Valentina said.

"I need another," I told her, pulling my phone from my pocket. I showed her the photo of the van that had spirited Luna away. "I need to know who owns this vehicle."

She took a good look at the image. "I'll see what I can do."

CHAPTER 25

ONCE HE'D FINISHED his beer, Amr Badawi suggested I follow him to my new accommodation. We moved through the rough nighttime streets of Ostia, but weren't troubled by any of the gangs, sex workers or drug addicts we passed. A few nodded greetings to Amr, and I got the impression he was at least respected if not feared in the neighborhood.

He told me how he'd immigrated to Italy with his family as a child; how he'd always dreamt of returning to Cairo but had been kept in Rome by circumstance and opportunity.

"The people in my home country are very similar to people here," Amr said. "Friendly, expressive, and family always comes first."

I nodded but couldn't comment. My knowledge of Egypt was limited to the due diligence I had done when considering whether to set up a Middle East regional head office there. The people I'd dealt with had certainly been friendly and helpful, but I'd decided not to proceed and had parked the idea for now.

"That's your place," Amr said, gesturing at an apartment above a brightly lit, gaudy cell-phone store on the corner of Via della Paranzella and Via Orazio dello Sbirro.

His business stood opposite an open square dotted with vacant market stalls. It wasn't a branded dealership and sold new and reconditioned phones, which might explain why Amr was known to so many of the people we'd passed. Old or stolen phones could be traded for cash in this man's shop, and I wondered how many questions he or his staff asked about provenance. Signs in English, Italian and Arabic proclaimed the store also did repairs and offered an array of accessories, vapes, shisha pipes and electronic paraphernalia. Products seemed to spill from the entrance like an overflowing laundry basket, and racks and displays clung to the walls and windows of the storefront.

"This way," Amr said, walking me to an archway two stores beyond his place.

The arch led to an alleyway that ran between two terraces. We walked in heavy shadow to a long yard behind the buildings. We climbed exterior metal stairs that took us to a wooden door. He opened both locks and handed me the keys.

"Don't lose them," he instructed. "And don't leave anything of value inside. There's no alarm, and the neighborhood is . . . well, let's just say, private property is a shades-of-gray concept around here."

"Got it," I replied, following him inside.

We entered a small hallway and he switched on the light.

"Kitchen, sitting room, two bedrooms and a bathroom," Amr told me. "It needs remodeling, but that will have to wait."

Everything was worn but looked perfectly usable and the place was better than I could have hoped for at such short notice.

"The shop is open twenty-four-seven, so just ask them to call me if you need anything."

I could hear the vague thump of dance music rising from below. Amr's store sounded like a lively place.

"Thank you," I said. "I owe you."

"This is a business transaction, Mr. Morgan. There is no need for thanks," he replied. "If you're all set here, I'm going back to my beer."

"I'm good," I assured him, and he shook my hand and left.

I closed the door after him and pulled my phone from my pocket.

Justine answered after a single ring. "Are you okay?"

"I'm fine," I assured her. "I've got a new place thanks to Mo-bot's hacker friend."

"I hate it when you're away like this. I feel so helpless."

"I'm okay."

"This isn't about you," she told me in a tone I recognized. It was meant to remind me she was an expert profiler. "This is about me needing to be there for you. I'm not and I can't be. Not all the time. I just have to accept that."

"I'm sorry," I responded. "I can understand—"

I was cut off by the hum of an incoming call and checked my phone to see who it was.

"It's Mo-bot. Let me patch her in."

"Sure," Justine replied.

I connected Mo-bot to our call. "Mo, you're on with me and Justine."

"I don't want to intrude, but you need to hear this, Jack. Sci and I have identified the tattoos on the shooter who took his own life. He's a member of Destini Oscuri, the Dark Fates. It's a brutal criminal gang that's engaged in just about everything you can imagine. They operate throughout Rome, but the real power base is in Esquilino, one of the oldest neighborhoods in the city, near the Colosseum. Sci's here with me."

"Hey, Jack," he said. "Three of his tattoos appeared to have religious significance. We've identified two as articles of faith, but we can't find anything on the third, a Jerusalem Cross which is the traditional symbol of a knight crusader. This one has three inset fleur-de-lys in each point of the cross."

"I'll check it out," I said. "I'm in the right place to find answers on questions about religion."

"We've got more," Mo-bot revealed. "Your friend Luna Colombo has gone to great lengths to conceal her true identity. Outwardly, she's an honest cop who lives alone in a tiny apartment not far from the Colosseum and devotes her life to her job. But there have been name changes, sealed records, the kinds of things you can only do with connections to power. Fortunately for you, even the darkest shadows can't resist my light."

"Don't boast," Sci cut in.

"Why not? It's part of the fun," Mo-bot countered. "And it's no surprise she's been able to do things other people can't," she told me. "Luna Colombo's father is Elia Antonelli, one of Rome's most powerful and notorious mobsters."

I reeled at the revelation, but as surprising as it was to learn a respected police inspector had an organized crime boss for a father, things suddenly started to make sense. The Pleasure Hall was likely one of her father's joints, and her secrecy and unwillingness to trust me or her police colleagues was probably rooted in fear of the truth emerging—or, worse, that it had already emerged and marked her out as a target. Had the assassin Mo-bot and Sci identified as a member of the Dark Fates been trying to kill Luna?

"Wow," I responded.

"Yeah," Sci said. "A cop with Rome's kingpin for a dad."

"Either this wasn't picked up during vetting, or they're not strict about family connections here," I suggested.

"Or dad used his influence to get her on the force," Justine suggested. "Be very helpful to have a cop you can always count on."

"I wonder if Matteo knows," I pondered.

"Hard to say," Mo-bot responded. "It wasn't easy to find out. I had to pull copies of old birth records. My guess is he'd only know if she had confided in him."

"So, she's connected," I remarked. "But the question is whether that has any bearing on Brambilla's murder."

"You're going to have to dig," Sci said.

"First I've got to find her," I replied. "Was she taken because of our investigation? Or because her father is in a beef with someone?"

I was puzzling the angles, trying to figure out how to answer all these questions. Mo-bot's and Sci's revelation had added a whole new layer of complexity.

"Let me know if you find anything else," I said.

"Likewise," Mo-bot responded. "You have a good night, Jack."

"Great work. Both of you," I replied.

"Night," Sci said, and they hung up.

"I really don't like how this is going," Justine observed when we were alone.

"I know. I'll be careful, and if the going gets too heavy, I'll ask for the right help."

She hesitated. I knew she wasn't happy, but there wasn't much either of us could do except play the cards we had been dealt.

"I'll call you as soon as I have news," I said.

"I love you," she responded.

"Love you too," I said, before hanging up.

CHAPTER 26

THE THUMPING TECHNO music was turned up just after midnight and its rapid rhythm seemed to rise through the wooden frame of my double bed and set every spring in the mattress dancing. I didn't mind. I was just grateful to have a safe place to stay. Somewhere I could crash without fear of attack. I checked local TV and Internet news for stories of Luna's abduction. I'd reported the incident to the police and couldn't imagine the loss of an inspector would go unremarked, but there was nothing. As far as the world was concerned, Luna Colombo wasn't worth worrying about. Either that or someone had spiked the report. Given the myriad connections of the key players in this investigation, the possibility wasn't far-fetched. Brambilla was linked to the highest levels of Vatican authority, and Matteo and Luna had ties to organized crime—Matteo through the Filippo Lombardi investigation and Luna thanks to her father. Any of these interest groups could apply pressure to the police to get them to sit on a missing persons report.

I fell into a restless sleep shortly after 1 a.m. Dreams and reality seemed to merge and fragmentary, disjointed recollections of the past few days filled my mind to a dance-beat soundtrack.

The thumping grew louder, although I woke to silence. Morning light edged the drapes and filled the room with a warm glow. There was more thumping, and I realized someone was knocking at the door. Groggy and slow, I staggered from bed fully clothed. I peered through the peephole to see a young man with a shaved head. He was casually dressed in shorts, a T-shirt and slides.

I opened the door slowly and kept one foot behind it.

"*Buongiorno*," the man said. "Valentina asked me to give you this."

He handed me a cell phone.

"*Ciao*," he said, hurrying away down the stairs.

"*Grazie*," I called after him, before shutting the door.

The phone was on and fully charged. As I made my way into the living room, it rang.

"Hello?" I said.

"Mr. Morgan," Valentina replied. "It seems we will have to be even more careful than I imagined. Meet me at Ponte Sant'Angelo at eleven."

She didn't wait for a reply but hung up. Her increased precautions could only mean she had learnt something worrying about Luna's abduction, and I was eager to know what it was. I checked my watch to find it was almost 9 a.m.

I showered and caught a cab into the center of Rome, where

I picked up new clothes. I wore a pair of black jeans, a black T-shirt and matching sneakers out of the boutique, and left my dirty, bloody blue suit in the changing room. I walked out of the store carrying a couple of replacement suits and some casual clothes in a large bag.

I reached Ponte Sant'Angelo ten minutes early and scanned my surroundings before setting foot on the historic bridge linking the north and south banks of the Tiber, just before a bend in the river. Constructed of stone and marble, the ancient crossing displayed statues of angels above its five arches,

When I was finally satisfied there was no obvious danger, I walked across and saw Valentina coming the other way. She wore a beautiful yellow shift dress and, to untrained eyes, we might have looked like lovers meeting for a date. When we finally reached the center of the bridge we were surrounded by crowds of tourists.

"I found out who owns the van used to take the cop," she told me. "It belongs to an orange-juice manufacturer located in Poli that is a subsidiary of a chain of companies ultimately owned by Elia Antonelli."

"Why would he abduct his own daughter?" I asked.

Valentina was surprised by the revelation. "His daughter?"

"Yes," I replied. "Mo-bot told me last night."

"Wow," Valentina remarked. "That I wasn't expecting. I have no idea why he would take his own family, but I do know this is a very dangerous man and his people are not to be toyed with."

I nodded. "I understand. Where can I find him?"

"Antonelli lives on a big estate near San Vittorino to the east of Rome," she said, handing me a piece of paper. "Here's the address."

"Thank you," I responded.

"You have my number if you need anything," she said. "Only use the phone I sent you. Everything else must be considered compromised."

She turned abruptly and walked away. I watched her go before unfolding the piece of paper she'd given me. As I gazed at the unfamiliar address, I wondered what dangers I would encounter there.

CHAPTER 27

THE AFTERNOON SUN made everything look perfect. The leaves on the olive trees were a deep green-gray, the sky sapphire blue, even the brown grass growing long in fallow fields took on an eye-catching golden hue. My taxi was on a quiet single-lane road winding its way up the valley that led to Casape, the nearest village to Antonelli's vast estate.

According to local tourism websites, the village had a population of less than a thousand people and was close to a number of World Heritage Sites. It had a rich history that wove legend with fact, drawing on stories of past kings and princes of Italy and popes of Rome. This was a place with a strong identity and an ancient connection to power. I could understand why a man like Antonelli would choose it as his base.

I had the taxi driver cruise by the main entrance, which featured a sandstone guard house beside two high cast-iron gates.

Ten-foot-tall stone walls stretched in either direction and were topped with serrated metal fangs designed to discourage all but the most determined intruders. As we drove on, heading east along the valley, I saw security cameras mounted on posts to either side of the wall, some pointing into the estate, others facing the road. This was a tight operation.

I asked the driver, a young Syrian who'd spent the journey telling me in broken English how much he loved Italy, to turn onto a narrow track that wound down the hillside opposite the estate. When we were out of sight of the road, I instructed him to stop, and offered him a 100-euro bonus if he'd wait thirty minutes. He accepted gratefully. As I stepped into the afternoon heat and started up the hill, I glanced back to see him recline his seat and turn his radio up.

I crossed the deserted road and went through some dry scrub. The estate wall was further back from the road here, hidden by parched trees and bushes. There were cameras, but I didn't care; I wanted them to see me.

I walked the line of the wall until I found a gnarly old syca-more tree with a branch that curled over the top. I scaled the tree, climbed along the branch until I'd cleared the wall, and jumped onto the hard earth on the other side.

There were more trees and bushes, but I could see them peter out about a hundred yards away, so I jogged toward the thinning treeline. As I picked my way over roots, through dappled sun and shade, I saw long rows of olive trees planted on the other side of the forest. The trees' crooked branches, outlined against the crystal-clear sky, looked so old they might have stood there for centuries. It seemed Antonelli owned an ancient piece of heaven.

When I reached a break in the trees, I saw his home high above the olive groves, a massive sandstone farmhouse with a red-tile roof. I started toward it, but only managed to get halfway across the strip of grass separating the shelter belt from the olive trees when an open-topped Jeep roared over a rise to my left, and a man standing on the rear seat wielding an assault rifle yelled something at me before taking aim. I didn't need a translator to know I was meant to freeze.

I complied and raised my hands. The off-roader rumbled to a halt beside me. There were three other men in the vehicle. Two of them jumped out and manhandled me onto the flatbed, where I was forced onto a bench seat with one of them either side of me.

The guy with the gun spoke to the driver and the Jeep swung a U-turn before heading up the hill toward the farmhouse. I looked at my captors, all hard men in matching gray camo T-shirts and khaki pants. My bold intrusion had given me an insight into Antonelli's security. These were clearly ex-military, well trained and professional. There was no chest-beating or bravado, just a calm, quiet assertion of their power over me.

We stopped in a graveled yard that was full of luxury cars. A couple of Range Rovers, a Ferrari, a Mercedes SLS and a Lamborghini were all parked in front of a large garage.

I was pulled from the Jeep and marched around onto a broad terrace running behind the huge old house. The view of the valley, dotted with ancient villas and covered by olive and citrus groves, was magnificent, but my eyes didn't linger on the vista.

Instead they were drawn to Elia Antonelli, a middle-aged man with neatly trimmed gray hair. He wore a white tailored shirt and beige slacks. He studied me, calmly and confidently, while I tried to conceal my surprise on recognizing his companion.

Seated next to him, informally dressed in a short green summer shift, was Rome police inspector Luna Colombo. His daughter.

She had the decency to look sheepish as she met my gaze.

"*Benvenuto*, Mr. Morgan," Antonelli said. "We're just about to eat. Won't you join us?"

CHAPTER 28

LUNA SPOKE SOME angry words in Italian to him and Antonelli shrugged.

"My daughter refused to accept my offer of protection, so I was forced to take direct action to bring her here," he explained. "She says I must apologize to you, and of course she is right. I should not have involved you in our family squabble."

Antonelli spoke to my captors. They backed away to take sentry positions in the shade of the terrace, standing close by the wide French doors.

"Please, Mr. Morgan, have a seat."

Antonelli gestured to the chair opposite his. The table was laden with antipasti, artisan breads, bottles of water and one of rosé wine in a cooler. Solid silver cutlery gleamed against the pressed, starched tablecloth, and crystal glassware sparkled in the sunshine. A manservant in a white shirt and matching trousers moved a huge parasol to cast the table into shade.

"Please do join us, Jack," Luna said. "My father isn't entirely monstrous."

I took the chair being offered and settled into my seat.

"Bread? Olives?" Antonelli said. "The flour is milled here on the estate and the olives are from the trees you can see on the hillside. You will not find finer anywhere in the world."

He didn't wait for an answer but spooned huge green olives and their oil onto my porcelain plate.

I poured some balsamic vinegar around them and took a crust of bread from the basket.

"You will doubtless have done your research," Antonelli went on, "and reached an opinion of me and my nature. Your research will be incomplete and your opinions improperly formed."

I soaked up some oil and vinegar with the bread and took a bite.

"For example, do you think a villain could make such beautiful olive oil?" he asked. "It is the finest you have tasted, is it not?"

"It's very good," I replied, following the mouthful with an olive. "These too."

"Very good? This is what you would say to an artist?" Antonelli scoffed. "It is excellent, Mr. Morgan. Perfection even."

"My father is very proud of his produce," Luna said.

"Of course," Antonelli interjected. "It comes from the earth and good earth is tended by good people. It cannot be otherwise. The fruits of evil taste as such."

"My research would suggest bitter fruit in that case," I replied.

"Which is why I said your research would be incomplete," Antonelli responded. "A caricature. Take my daughter, for example. You will most likely have assumed she keeps our connection secret to advance my interests."

Luna shook her head slowly.

"In truth, she is ashamed of me," Antonelli revealed. "She hides our connection so it does not hinder her advancement. She does not approve of who I am or what I do."

I glanced at Luna, who gave me a sheepish nod.

"Of course, she is not so stupid that she does not know my places of business are the safest locations for her to hide."

Antonelli confirmed what I'd suspected, that the brothel in the tower block was one of his.

"But she is stubborn like her father and will not listen when I say there are things happening that require greater security."

"What things?" I asked.

"Rome is a city built on power," Antonelli replied. "The pursuit of it awakens an addiction that can drive people crazy, and every so often someone has—how do you say?—an overdose that makes them crave more and more. Their hunger for power becomes insatiable and they try to take too much. More than is good for them."

"Who is trying to take it this time?" I asked, biting another mouthful of bread.

"We don't know," Luna replied. "But we're sure it has something to do with the Lombardi murder and Father Brambilla's death."

"Whoever it is, they made a grave mistake," Antonelli said. "Luna is the youngest of my children. Her mother was not my wife. She was my last love, taken from me ten years ago in the most recent power struggle. One of my rivals tried to kill me, but only succeeded in taking Luna's mother from us. He paid, of course, but I will not see my daughter suffer the same fate as her mother."

"You think this has something to do with you?" I asked.

"In Rome all things are connected," Antonelli said. "The people who have targeted you and Luna obviously consider you a threat. Perhaps they think you both know something."

"About what?" I asked.

"About the reason Filippo Lombardi was killed."

CHAPTER 29

"DID YOU KNOW him?" I asked.

Antonelli tilted his head and studied me. "Is that what you really mean to find out?"

He was sharp, but I guess one didn't rise to the height of power in Rome without an ability to read people.

"Was he corrupt?" I asked.

"I didn't know the man, but from what I understand, he was the opposite of corrupt," Antonelli replied, ignoring his plateful of mozzarella and soft ripe tomatoes, which he'd spread on estate bread. "Perhaps that was his problem. The stick that won't bend is sometimes broken."

"We found nothing," Luna nodded. "In the time we were looking into Lombardi, we didn't turn up anything to suggest he was dishonest. And I asked around. People said he was a decent man."

"A jewel," Antonelli remarked. "An honest prosecutor is a diamond to be cherished."

I gave him a surprised look.

"Not by people like me, of course," he added. "But by the public. How would the world be if everyone was dishonest? My daughter might be surprised to hear me talk like this. We don't often discuss our work."

"Because you know what I think of what you call work," she responded.

"Our lives are kept separate, for her protection and mine," Antonelli said. "If Lombardi was an honest prosecutor that might have been enough to get him killed."

"So, someone had him driven off the road because of what he knew?" I suggested.

Antonelli shrugged. "Perhaps."

"And now they're worried your daughter and I might know it too?"

He shrugged again.

"And Brambilla?" I pressed. "What about him? How is Matteo Ricci involved?"

"Who knows?" Antonelli said. "Your job is to find out answers, Mr. Morgan. Mine is to grow olives. But if the priest knew a secret, that might explain his death. And my daughter's former partner could be discredited so that no one would believe anything he said. Or perhaps made into an easier target. People die in jail all the time."

I shuddered, and the sweet tomato and mozzarella in my mouth turned sour at the thought Matteo might be in imminent danger. I'd assumed incarceration was the worst he'd face, but Elia Antonelli had opened my eyes to a new dimension of danger.

Luna said something in Italian.

"You can protect him, surely?" she added for my benefit.

"I will do what I can for you, my dear Luna, but even my protection is not infallible," Antonelli replied. "Perfection is the sole preserve of God."

"Or artisan olive growers," I quipped, and Antonelli smiled.

I wondered how a mobster could talk of perfection in such an imperfect world. How could he, an instrument of evil, still hold faith in a religion rooted in the concepts of virtue and sin?

Sitting in the man's company, eating the fruits of his land, seeing the way he looked lovingly at his daughter, it was clear he did not consider himself a bad guy.

"I trade in power," Antonelli said. "The things I do to retain or grow that power are as necessary as war waged by government or state-sanctioned execution for capital crimes. Power does not concern itself with right or wrong. Morality is not the issue here—only the individual's standing in the sphere of influence."

So Antonelli's world view was amoral at best. My business was justice, and without some appreciation of the difference between right and wrong, I could not function. At least, not happily.

"What else can you tell me about Lombardi?" I asked.

Antonelli shook his head. "You now know as much as I do."

"And Father Brambilla?"

"I don't know anything about the priest. I've given you all I can. My advice would be to stay out of the game. Leave Rome to the Romans and go home, Mr. Morgan."

"I can't do that," I told him. "I don't believe in the legitimacy of power for its own sake. I believe in good, in right and wrong, and I gave my word I'd learn the truth about what happened here."

Antonelli looked thoughtful. "Maintaining a sense of personal honor involves the use of power, Mr. Morgan. I admire you. I wouldn't want to be you, but I admire you."

I stood. "Thank you for lunch, Signor Antonelli."

"One of my men will drive you back to the city."

"That's okay," I replied. "Hopefully, I still have a cab waiting."

"We sent him on his way," Antonelli advised. "Politely, of course, and with a generous tip."

"I'll walk you to the car," Luna said, rising.

"Remember what I told you, Mr. Morgan," Antonelli added. "Someone in this city is overdosing on power, throwing the balance of Rome into turmoil. Like all addicts, power-seekers are dangerous. They will stop at nothing to secure their fix. And they will let nothing stand against them. Not even an honorable man."

"I'll bear that in mind, Signor Antonelli," I said, walking away.

CHAPTER 30

LUNA AND I walked side by side along the terrace to the end of the house.

"I'm sorry I couldn't tell you the truth," she said, "but I have spent a lifetime hiding this secret. My father imagines he is some kind of hero, a Robin Hood, when in fact he is a gangster who is bad news for Italy and for Rome."

I was surprised to hear her talk in such unequivocal terms.

"What?" she asked belligerently. "Tell me I'm wrong."

"I don't think you're wrong. It's just that those closest to us often lose the ability to see things clearly."

"As detectives we have to remain clear-sighted, no?"

I nodded my head. "Yes, we do."

"Matteo grew confused. Wasn't clear about the focus of his job. He was supposed to pursue the truth above all else," she told me as we followed a path beside the house.

I could see the driveway full of cars ahead of us.

"I know he works for you now, and I should probably be more discreet, but he had no business pulling us off the Lombardi investigation."

"I agree," I said, wondering what that meant for Matteo's long-term prospects with Private.

But that wasn't the issue I had to worry about right now. His contract included a termination clause for arrest and prosecution on any criminal matter. If he was found guilty, the clause would trigger automatically, but if innocent I would have to think about what to do with him and whether he could remain as head of the Rome office.

We reached the front of the house and I saw two heavy-set guys in suits standing beside a Mercedes GLA that hadn't been in the driveway when I'd been brought in.

"They will take you back to the city," Luna said. "They're good men. Some of my father's best."

"Good?" I asked.

"Proficient then. If 'good' carries too many moral implications," Luna said.

I paused as we reached the edge of the white-gravel driveway. "What about you? Are you good?"

She held my gaze and glared with suppressed fury.

"Will you help your partner?" I pressed.

"I'm a prisoner here," she replied. "My father's men are under strict instructions not to let me leave."

"There are other ways to help," I remarked, producing my phone. "These tattoos were concealed under the dead man's sleeves."

I found the photos of the shooter who'd attacked us by the scene of Lombardi's death. She studied the intricate occult tattoos.

"I didn't show these to your father in case it was one of his men who died, but I'm showing you now." I presented her with the photos of the tattoos. "If you know what these are and what they represent, now is your chance to do good."

I knew what the tattoos symbolized but wasn't going to reveal anything so I could see just how deeply she believed in doing the right thing.

"These belong to a gang known as Destini Oscuri, the Dark Fates," she said. "It's a street gang. Vicious and brutal. They operate from a bar called the Inferno in Esquilino, one of Rome's oldest and toughest neighborhoods. It is owned by a man called Milan Verde. They say he is the leader of the Dark Fates. There isn't a police officer in Rome who would dare touch him."

"What about police inspectors?" I asked.

"Not many of us either. He is known for his brutality."

"Can you tell me the significance of this?" I asked, swiping to a photo of the tattoo of the fleur-de-lys inside the Jerusalem Cross.

Luna shook her head.

"That's not one I've seen before. It might be new or signify some special rank in the gang maybe."

"Thank you," I told her. "You've restored a little of my faith."

"In humanity?" she asked.

"In my own judgment. I thought you were a good person. You haven't disappointed me."

"A good person wouldn't be here with these men." She indicated her father's thugs, who shifted impatiently.

"We can't choose our family," I said, suddenly thinking about my own fractured relationships with my father and brother.

Luna nodded. I was about to walk away when she took my hand. "Please do not go against the Fates. They are dangerous, and Milan Verde is a monster."

"I go where the truth leads me," I replied. Looking wistful, she nodded.

"I understand."

She let go of my hand and I joined the villainous men who would take me back to Rome.

CHAPTER 31

SILENCE SOMEHOW SEEMS deeper in certain cars. The sound-proofing of the Mercedes was exceptional and my two companions, captors perhaps, didn't utter a word as we drove toward the city. There was no radio, nothing but the muffled rumble of tires on road and the steady hum of the engine, cruising easily as we wound along deserted hillsides. The soft leather upholstery seemed to deaden everything.

I couldn't risk holding a conversation in such circumstances, so I used my phone to text Faduma, the journalist who had been so eager for me to learn about Luna's background:

I know about the cop.

There was a pause, followed by the dots that showed someone was responding. Then:

And?

We should meet, I replied.

OK.

Where? I asked.

Quadriportico Verano Cemetery. 7 p.m.

OK.

I pocketed my phone.

It took us an hour to reach the outskirts of Rome, and the traffic grew heavier with each passing mile until, by the time we were on Via Tiburtina, which curled into the center of Rome behind the main train station, the Mercedes was at a crawl, and my two companions were showing fidgety signs of impatience.

"You can let me out at the next intersection," I suggested.

The driver looked at the man next to him, who shrugged and then nodded at me.

We ended up getting caught in an unbreakable stream of traffic. It wasn't until we reached the intersection with Via Nola, to the south of the ancient Castrense amphitheater, that the driver was able to pull to the side of the road and let me out.

The Mercedes continued south while I headed in the opposite direction toward the old red-brick wall that delineated the amphitheater grounds. The heavy traffic limited the prospect of a car tailing me, but I was mindful of the scooters and bikes weaving through the crowded streets, and the pedestrians on the sidewalk. It would have been foolish not to assume Elia Antonelli would try to have me watched.

I walked a couple of blocks, along the wide avenue flanked by elegant terracotta-brick apartment blocks constructed in the classical style. When I neared the amphitheater, I passed a large motorcycle showroom set on the ground floor of one of the blocks, and the glare of the sun against the picture windows created a mirror that allowed me to see if anyone was tailing me. I saw nothing.

I circled round the amphitheater and walked along Via di Santa Croce in Gerusalemme, a broad street with more of the terracotta apartment blocks to either side. I found a street café and took a seat at one of the exterior tables, where I ordered a double espresso and watched the people passing by. When I'd finished my drink, I paid, made use of the café's restroom and left the place via the staff entrance near the kitchen to the rear of the building. It took me into a courtyard parking lot flanked by apartment blocks on three sides. I walked through the entrance to the courtyard and joined Via Eleniana, a busy road that ran north to south.

Satisfied I wasn't being followed and that I'd been in the café long enough to exhaust the batteries of a drone, I gave my surroundings one last check before concluding that if Elia Antonelli had assigned anyone to follow me, they had either given up or been thwarted by my precautions.

I hurried along the street and found a cab sitting in a line of vehicles waiting at the next set of lights. The driver, a slim middle-aged man with the worry lines of the perpetually stressed, grimaced when I asked him to take me to Quadriportico Verano Cemetery, but he eventually nodded and I jumped in the back.

I realized why he'd grimaced when I got to experience the full weight of Rome's evening traffic on the journey to the cemetery. We crawled through a city choking on the sheer volume of people it hadn't been designed to accommodate.

The driver finally pulled over by Piazza San Lorenzo, a square surrounded by the makeshift booths of florists serving the streams of mourners visiting the huge cemetery. I settled the fare and climbed out.

I found Faduma waiting for me on the cobblestones near the main gates. When she saw me, she started walking, but rather than heading through the arched gateway into the cemetery, we followed the perimeter wall north, toward the column of San Lorenzo, a tall monument that stood in front of a church of the same name.

"I know who Luna Colombo's father is," I said. "I understand why you didn't trust me. I've been consorting with the daughter of a gangster, but Luna says she has nothing to do with his activities."

"And you believe her?" Faduma asked.

"I'm starting to think I can't believe anyone."

"Now you're thinking like a Roman! Honesty and truthfulness are not absolutes here. They are cultural constructs. Rome, particularly in certain sections of society, has always maintained a flawed relationship with the truth, because this city is built on power, and sometimes truth is its enemy."

"Trust no one—is that it?" I asked, and she nodded.

"It's a good place to start, but you'll still find yourself trusting people. We like to think the best of others. It is both a strength and a weakness of our species."

She paused by the column of San Lorenzo, and I looked up at the statue of the martyr standing atop the red granite plinth.

"I might have brought you into an ambush," she said, and I was suddenly alert. But when I looked at those bright, keen eyes in her open, ingenuous face, I received no hint of danger. "I didn't, of course, but it's an example of how easily you can place your trust in people. Just as I'm going to trust you now."

She hesitated for a moment before producing a large envelope from the bag slung over her shoulder.

"These are reports of the deaths of eight priests." She handed me the envelope and I flipped through the contents to see photographs, newspaper articles and police reports. "You've earnt my trust by seeing Luna for what she really is."

"I don't knowingly collaborate with criminals," I assured her. "I'm honest. Maybe too honest."

She nodded. "Good. Let's hope it stays that way. This is what I've been investigating. I think someone has been murdering priests but I don't know why."

"Was Father Brambilla the most recent victim?" I asked.

"I think so."

"Anything that connects them?" I asked.

"Other than they're all priests?" She shook her head again. "But the only other person I went to with this dossier was Filippo Lombardi the prosecutor. Three days before he was killed."

My stomach churned.

"I think he started making inquiries into what happened to

these men of the Church," Faduma said. "I think the inquiry got him killed, which is sad because I know he was a good man."

"How?" I asked.

"If he had not been, he would have passed on my name and by now I would be dead too."

CHAPTER 32

I LEFT FADUMA at the cemetery and caught a cab to Ostia. I had the driver stop a few blocks from Amr's cell-phone store and covered the rest of the journey on foot.

The streets were full of people here to experience the nightlife—gangs of youths stalking for easy prey; hollow-eyed addicts lurking in the shadows. The summer night was buzzing with the sounds of busy bars and clubs, and ripe with the smells emanating from the fast-food joints.

I checked I wasn't being followed before I turned onto Via Orazio dello Sbirro, where I saw the phone shop blazing brightly with its gaudy signs and lights in the windows. I walked past, took out the keys Amr had given me and went through the archway that split the terrace. I hurried along the alleyway beyond, crossed the yard and climbed the metal steps to the front door. I made one last check that there were no hostile eyes on me and went inside.

The place was as I'd left it. I took out my phone as I went into the living area and moved one of the chairs to the window so I could keep an eye on the street outside while I made a video call to Justine.

"Jack," she said when she answered. She was in her office on the fifth floor of Private's Los Angeles headquarters and sitting in one of the armchairs by the window, so I could make out the sun-soaked city skyline behind her. I missed home, but I missed her more. "Are you okay?"

"I'm fine," I replied. "I'm in the thick of something here."

I shared what I'd learnt from Faduma about the dead priests, and what Luna had told me about the Dark Fates.

"I need you to check out a guy called Milan Verde. He's the leader of the gang. I'm also going to send you the details of the dead priests. Look for any connection between them and Milan Verde, or any of his associates."

Private didn't have the NSA's network analysis capabilities, which were so good they could tell whether you'd stayed at the same hotel as someone three years ago, but Mo-bot had developed some pretty sophisticated data-mining tools and, even more importantly, had the right contacts to get the information we needed if her own systems drew a blank. If the priests were linked outside the Church or were connected to Milan Verde or his gang, we would find out.

"We'll get right on it," Justine replied. "What are you doing now?"

"I'm going to read this file," I said, brandishing the envelope Faduma had given me. "Probably grab a bite to eat."

"Pizza?" she asked.

"Maybe. What else would a person eat in Rome?" I joked. "Maybe we'll come here for a trip one day? Do a tour of Europe."

"I'd like that," Justine replied. "I'd like that a lot."

She hesitated, and I felt the weight of her unspoken words tug at my heart. She missed me, but she knew this separation was the price of the job. I felt the same way.

"This will be over soon," I said. "And then I'll be back home."

"I can't wait," she replied. "I'm going to go brief Mo-bot. Send me the files. Love you."

"Love you too," I responded, before she hung up.

I used my phone to take photos of the dossier Faduma had given me, and once I'd sent everything over to Justine via Private's secure email server, I settled into my seat and started to read about the dead priests.

CHAPTER 33

EIGHT PRIESTS.

Eight good men.

At least that's what the dossier told me. I slept poorly that night. Dreams of the helicopter crash in Afghanistan that ended my military career morphed with the heart attacks and accidents that were supposed to have killed these priests. Apart from Brambilla, who had clearly not died from natural causes or by accident, the other men had met early, but seemingly not suspicious, ends. Only Faduma had picked up a connection: the men had all died in and around Rome in the last three months while on missions from their home dioceses overseas. They were travelers visiting the city on what one might reasonably assume was Church business or else pilgrimage.

I was still waiting for Mo-bot to report, but there didn't seem to be any other obvious link between the men, at least not according to the information Faduma had provided.

I woke many times in the night, haunted by the faces of the priests who merged into the memories of fallen comrades and victims of past crimes I'd investigated. I finally fell into a deep sleep as dawn broke, waking a couple of hours later as tired as if I'd never slept at all.

I gathered the photos and papers scattered across my bed and returned them to the envelope. After showering and getting dressed in one of my new lightweight suits, I went downstairs, walked a few blocks in the morning sunshine, and hailed a cab to Vatican City.

I picked my way through the crowds of pilgrims and tourists gathered in front of St Peter's and passed through the security checkpoint by the north colonnade.

I walked along Via Sant'Anna until I reached the Vatican Bank headquarters.

"I'd like to see Joseph Stadler," I said to the receptionist. "My name is Jack Morgan. I don't have an appointment."

I waited in the luxurious vaulted lobby, admiring the paintings, until Christian Altmer came through the lobby security gates. He wore a navy blue suit and a matching shirt and was as somber as an undertaker. When he saw me, he pinned a fake smile on his face.

"Mr. Morgan," he said, offering me his hand. "Mr. Stadler has a busy day, but he can give you ten minutes."

"I'm grateful," I replied.

I followed him through to the ancient building and there was no small talk this time.

We took the elevator and passed through the outer office where Stadler's executive team studiously ignored me while Altmer led me into his boss's suite.

Stadler was by the window, looking out over Via del Telegrafo, but he turned when we entered and greeted me with a warm smile.

"Mr. Morgan, this is a welcome surprise."

"I'm sorry to intrude, but I need your help with something."

"Please have a seat. Drink?"

"No, thank you. I won't be long," I replied, and stayed standing. "I have reason to believe Father Brambilla was one of eight priests murdered here in Rome."

Stadler's eyes widened, and Altmer's mouth gaped in shock.

"I believe Filippo Lombardi started looking into these murders," I said, taking care not to reveal Faduma's role in identifying the victims. "I think that may be why he was killed."

"Priests?" Stadler asked incredulously. "Eight priests?"

I nodded.

"Such a thing would be an outrage against God," he suggested.

"A great crime," Altmer agreed.

"If I give you their names, can you arrange for Church records to provide me with any details of how these men might be connected?" I asked.

Stadler nodded emphatically. "Of course. Christian will get you whatever you need."

Altmer nodded. "I am here to help you, Mr. Morgan," he said, with all the sincerity of a fairground barker.

I pulled a folded sheet of paper from my pocket and gave it to the younger man. "These are the priests. Beside each name is their diocese and the date of their death."

"I will get to work on this immediately," he said, before leaving the room.

Stadler walked slowly toward his desk and eased himself into his chair, clearly shaken. "I hope you're wrong, Mr. Morgan. I truly do."

"So do I," I replied. "So do I."

CHAPTER 34

I LEFT THE bank puzzling over the fate of the priests. Altmer said he would phone me if he found anything, and Stadler assured me the Vatican would take steps to protect its own if it discovered someone was targeting members of the clergy.

I walked east along Via Sant'Anna in the shade of the Pope's official residence and heard the sweet sound of a sung mass coming from one of the churches nearby. I didn't know whether it was a service or a choral rehearsal, and it didn't matter because the joy expressed in the harmonious chant lifted my spirits.

"We meet again," a man said, and I looked round to see Father Vito, the priest I'd met in the Garden of Secret Confession. He hurried along the street to catch up and fell in beside me. "I'm glad to see you again. I sought guidance after our last conversation. You seemed conflicted."

I curled my lip. Most people are conflicted. Was I any more

torn than the average person? It seemed to me as though this priest might be fishing for a vulnerable soul.

"Your faith once comforted you," Father Vito said. "It can be a safe haven for you again. If you embrace it."

"Do we deserve comfort if there is hard work to be done?" I asked. "Difficult work. Shouldn't we be troubled by leaving it undone? Shouldn't we feel conflicted, guilty even, about so much left undone in the world?"

He put his right hand on my shoulder and gently pulled me to a halt.

"Are you the Christ?" he asked, and the question surprised me. "Are you the one to carry all the world's burdens?"

The heresy of the suggestion was quite shocking.

"Yes. It is a ridiculous idea. You are not the Savior. You can take comfort in the faith of your forefathers, knowing all is as it is meant to be and that the great plan is unfolding as it should."

"And suffering? Injustice? Poverty? Pain?" I responded.

"Can you see the end of time? Can you peer into the beyond?" Father Vito asked. "Your conception of the world is limited. Only the Almighty sees and knows all. Only the Almighty can judge what should be and what is necessary for each of us, now and forever."

He held my gaze.

"Rest your troubled soul, Mr. Morgan. Find your way back to your faith."

He stepped back before heading west along Via Sant'Anna, returning the way he'd come.

I thought about what he had said and wondered how one

could find peace in a world full of injustice. I walked the other way toward the gate near the North Colonnade. As I passed by a small fountain set in a yard between two buildings draped in flags, a priest I didn't recognize came hurrying toward me.

A lean man in his late twenties, he had short black hair and Southern Mediterranean features. He held up his cassock as he jogged to intercept me.

"My name is Carlos Diaz," he whispered. "You are in grave danger. Meet me tonight—ten at the Basilica di Santa Maria in Montesanto. I will tell you everything."

He hurried away, taking the same route as Father Vito, but glanced back at me intermittently until he disappeared from sight around the corner of Via della Posta.

I had no idea whether he was friend or foe, wise man or lunatic, and the only way I would find out was by going to meet him.

CHAPTER 35

MY PHONE VIBRATED as I walked along the North Colonnade. I saw it was Justine calling.

"I have the background you wanted on Milan Verde," she said when I answered.

"No hello?" I asked.

"For now I'm trying to keep it professional," she replied. "Besides, we're beyond the small-talk phase. You know I love you."

"I know," I said. "What time is it there?"

"Two in the morning. But this is important. I'm sending you a file of everything Mo-bot has been able to pull on Milan Verde. He's bad news. Served with Col Moschin, the 9th Paratroopers Assault Regiment, Italian Special Forces. Saw action in Afghanistan and was rumored to be involved in hostage rescues in Iraq and Syria. Left under a cloud when his unit was accused of brutality toward residents of a Syrian village. He's had a couple arrests since then for gun running, but the charges never stick. AISI, the Italian Internal Information and Security Agency, has a file on him and flags him as a potential leader of the Dark Fates. It's a vicious outfit that's been implicated in gangland murders, political assassinations and organized crime at the highest level. These are very bad dudes."

"Luna told me they're based out of a bar in Esquilino," I replied.

"You're not thinking of going there?"

"It's a bar," I replied. I wasn't going to lie to Justine. "They won't kill me for having a drink."

"You have no idea what they're going to do," she countered, and I couldn't deny the truth of her words.

I did not know what their agenda was or how much they knew about me. It was clear a member of the Dark Fates had targeted either me or Luna, so going to the bar might be the equivalent of stepping into a lion enclosure.

"I'll be careful," I said.

"I know there's no point reminding you this is a police investigation and that you could just give the information you have to the detective in charge of the case," Justine responded coldly. "Or you could ask for help and have us fly out to support you."

"You could try if you like," I replied. "But it would just be a waste of breath."

"You're a stubborn man, Jack Morgan, but you're also a good man." Her tone softened. "And I wouldn't change that."

"I'll stay out of trouble," I assured her. "Love you."

"You too, even if you give me worry lines," she replied before hanging up.

I wandered through the crowds milling around St Peter's Square and left Vatican City, thinking about what lay ahead.

If the Dark Fates had targeted me, I would know the instant I set foot in their bar. If Luna had been the target, I might not be known to the other gang members and could possibly gather useful intelligence, maybe even confront Milan Verde himself.

I walked along Via dei Corridori, buzzing with traffic, and hailed a taxi. The driver was a cheerful lady who smiled and nodded happily when I asked her to take me to Esquilino.

CHAPTER 36

IF NEIGHBORHOODS WERE bands, Ostia, where I was staying, was an energetic grunge group. Esquilino, on the other hand, was a dangerous death metal band that had been around since the beginning of time.

The streets exuded menace: from the dark cross-hatching of graffiti on every surface to the gangs of angry-looking men gathered outside bars, discount liquor stores and pool halls, glasses in hand, their skin emblazoned with images of skulls and devils. There were bars on any windows within reach from the ground; modified cars and souped-up motorcycles, engines wailing, endlessly prowled the narrow streets of buildings with flaking stucco. Esquilino was not a safe place.

The Inferno, Milan Verde's bar, was the worst of all the low-down drinking joints we passed. Although it was only early afternoon, we arrived on Via Mamiani, a particularly rundown side street, to find the place already clouded by a fog of degeneracy. Groups of heavily inked men in biker vests and T-shirts jostled for space on the sidewalk outside the bar, bingeing heavily as they traded jokes and stories. It was a weekday, so these were men without regular jobs. And it was mostly men. I could see two women among the crowd of about fifty, and they were dressed similarly and tattooed in the same way.

The cab driver stopped further up the street. Once I had paid her, I walked back, passing a convenience store and boarded-up café before I reached the corner opposite the Inferno, which, in addition to the dull roar made by its rowdy customers, was filling the neighborhood with fast-paced thrash metal.

I crossed the road and pushed through the crowd gathered on the sidewalk, earning myself hostile looks, muttered curses and one threat I couldn't understand.

Inside, the bar lived up to its name. The walls were decorated with heavy metal-style images of hell: devils in biker jackets riding flaming motorcycles among tormented masses. The place was packed and the bar heaving with drinkers. I recognized Milan Verde from an intelligence photograph contained in the dossier Mo-bot had sent via secure email. He looked a couple years older than the photo, his dark close-cropped hair now flecked with gray. His piercing eyes were just as soulless, and his scowling face appeared to have picked up a few new scars, including one on the bridge of his nose where it had clearly been broken.

He was sitting with a group of four guys and two women, who looked like roadies for the devil's favorite band. I saw a flash of recognition when he caught sight of me and felt a pang of anxiety as he nudged the big man sitting next to him.

I thought he was coming for me, but it was even worse than that. The big man pushed his way through the crowd to the entrance and locked the front door. He folded his arms and became a sentinel guarding the only obvious way out.

The noise made by the patrons dropped slightly as they eyed me and made comments to their companions. They clearly knew who I was and had trapped me in the bar, so now I really had nothing to lose. I approached Verde's booth, and the crowd parted to allow me access to the man who'd likely tried to kill me.

He nodded to his companions and they eased out of their seats, leaving him alone and the bench opposite him unoccupied.

I slid onto it and held his gaze as I settled.

"You know who I am?" I said.

"You're brave and stupid coming here, Mr. Morgan," Milan replied.

"Why did one of your men try to kill me?"

"I don't have men." He smiled. "I own a bar. You have me confused with someone else."

I scoffed. "Those guys cleared a place for me because you asked them nicely, I guess?"

"That's what friends do," he said.

"So why did your friend try to kill me?" I pressed.

"My friends aren't criminals, Mr. Morgan." He held up his hands, palms facing me. "We're peaceful people here."

As he lowered his hands, he turned his wrists toward me and

I saw the same tattoo that the assassin had worn: the Jerusalem Cross with fleur-de-lys inside it.

"Nice ink," I said, gesturing to the mysterious pattern. "What does it mean?"

"It means this meeting is over," he replied, nodding to his companions waiting nearby. "Take Mr. Morgan into the back and teach him Italian manners."

"For a guy who owns a bar, you sure behave like a gangster," I remarked, and he smiled darkly.

"Goodbye, Mr. Morgan."

Large hands grabbed my arm and I was hauled out of my seat.

CHAPTER 37

WHAT MAKES A good fighter? It's a question I've often asked myself. I've seen one man defeat six, a small guy overcome someone twice his size, and I've come to the conclusion two things mark out a winner.

The first is spirit, an indefatigable sense that no matter how much punishment you take, you're going to keep getting up. The second is the ability to create advantages for yourself through surprise, shock or savagery.

I combined all three by grabbing Milan's beer bottle as I was hauled up. I smashed it over the head of the man to my right, shattering it with such force he staggered back, dazed. I turned and drove the jagged teeth of the remains of the bottle into the shoulder of the man to my left and he yelped and jumped clear.

I sensed movement behind me and heard a voice yell, "*Basta!* Stop!"

I wheeled round to see a grim-faced skinhead pulling a gun from beneath his T-shirt. I rushed him, clapped his ears, grabbed his wrist, twisted it until I felt something crunch, then pulled the gun from his limp fingers.

"Back!" I yelled, turning the weapon on the gangsters encircling me. "Get back!"

The crowd fell silent but bristled with menace. Milan looked at once enraged and humiliated, which made him doubly dangerous. I knew I didn't have long.

The way to the front door was blocked by the crowd. It would be too risky for me to try and push my way through. I didn't want to kill unless I absolutely had to, and I was pretty sure taking that way out would lead to someone's death, mine or an attacker's.

Instead, I moved toward the service door beside the bar, which led to the kitchen.

"Back!" I yelled, keeping those nearest me at bay.

Thrash metal blared from the speakers but there was no other sound. The roar of fast-paced music only added to the tension that gripped my stomach.

I pushed open the service door and saw a corridor lined with offices and restrooms that ended at a kitchen. On the other side of a long stainless-steel preparation counter was a fire exit.

I hurried down the corridor, aware that Milan was on his feet now, following me.

I moved faster. In the gloomy kitchen there was a smell of grease and stale fat that turned my stomach. I ran forward and sensed movement from close by my left side. I ducked just in time to avoid one of Milan's thugs, who slashed at me with a carving knife.

He overbalanced, and I sent him flying with a swing of the hand that was holding the gun. The weighty pistol cracked the man's skull and I saw his hate-filled eyes go blank as he fell.

The attack broke my rhythm and slowed me, allowing Milan and the others to close the gap between us.

I burst into the kitchen, leapt onto the preparation counter and slid to the other side. As I rolled off, I fired a couple of high and wide shots into the wall above the doorway.

Milan and his squad of thugs paused, and that gave me the space and time I needed to reach the fire door safely.

I pushed the bar. Nothing happened. The door remained firmly shut. I noticed a padlock and chain holding it in place and fired a brace of shots at the lock, which shattered.

Milan and his people were almost on me now.

I unwound the chain, pushed open the door and slammed it shut a second before Milan reached it. I wrapped the chain around the stem of the outer handle and threaded it through an old eyelet that would once have housed a bolt. I pulled the chain tight as the door was forced opened a crack and looped the links on themselves to hold it fast.

I turned to find myself in an alleyway behind the bar. There were footsteps approaching from left and right.

A fire ladder hung down to my left. With no desire to fight my way through Milan's people, I hauled myself onto the bottom rung. I clambered up the rusty old fire escape to the roof of the building. Once safely behind the balustrade, I craned over the edge to see one of Milan's men run down the alleyway and unwind the chain. He opened the fire door for his boss and the crew, who stormed out.

I watched them for a moment as Milan barked instructions. Satisfied they hadn't cottoned on to my escape route, I backed away from the balustrade and made my way across the rooftop to safety.

CHAPTER 38

AFTER CROSSING A city block over the rooftops, I found a safe place to climb down: a fire escape on Via Alfredo Cappellini. I jogged toward Termini station, went through the busy concourse and hurried east to Via Marsala on the other side of the grand terminus, where I caught a cab.

There was no sign of Milan or his people, but I sat low in the back and obscured my face with my hand until we were out of Esquilino. I was grateful to put the run-down neighborhood behind me, and if the cab driver thought there was anything unusual about my behavior, he didn't so much as bat an eyelid. People didn't work poorer neighborhoods like Esquilino without learning to take the rough with the smooth.

I instructed the driver to head to Ostia. We passed through the heart of Rome before reaching the colorful coastal neighborhood a little over an hour later. I asked the driver to drop me a couple blocks from the cell-phone store, and after checking I hadn't been followed, I hurried into the apartment where I showered and changed into a dark gray suit of lightweight cotton. I wore it with a white shirt, open at the collar.

Once I'd washed off the sweat and grime from my encounter with Milan Verde and his people, I called Justine.

She answered immediately, her face filling my phone screen.

"What's wrong?" she asked.

Was she really that perceptive?

"Nothing. Why?" I tried, chancing my luck.

"I know where you were going, and you've just cleaned yourself up, which means you probably ran into trouble," she replied.

Never try to outfox a profiler.

"It wasn't anything I couldn't handle."

"I don't like the thought of you being out there alone. I want to come to Rome. Mo-bot and Sci too," Justine said. "You need an experienced team around you. You shouldn't be facing this alone."

"I appreciate the sentiment, but you all have work to do in LA and I'm okay," I replied. "I really am. You're giving me everything I need from there. You're reacting to perceived danger, but I'm fine."

"Don't try to psych me, Jack Morgan," she replied. "You'd be more effective with us at your side."

Justine was probably right. I would benefit from having my team around me, and I wanted to be with her, to feel her in my arms . . . but Private was already devoting resources in the form of my time and energy to this unexpected situation. I didn't want to divert more unless absolutely necessary.

"Let's see how things go," I suggested.

"Okay," she conceded.

"Milan Verde is definitely the leader of the Dark Fates," I revealed. "He reacted super aggressively when I remarked on the Jerusalem Cross tattoo. Can you ask Mo-bot to focus on that image? See if she can find out anything about its meaning."

"Sure," Justine responded.

"I'll call you later. I've got a meeting with a priest and don't want to be late."

"A priest?"

"Yeah. I'll explain tonight, I promise. Love you," I said.

"Love you too," she replied with more than a hint of resignation in her voice. I knew she wanted us to be together. I did too.

I ended the call, grabbed my wallet, phone and keys, and left the apartment to meet Father Carlos, the mysterious priest who had accosted me earlier.

CHAPTER 39

I ARRIVED AT the Basilica di Santa Maria in Montesanto, which stands at the southern edge of Piazza del Popolo between Via del Corso and Via del Babuino. The seventeenth-century church has a twin on the opposite side of the Via del Corso. Together, the two domed houses of worship form a beautiful architectural pairing.

I had taken a taxi into the city and had dinner at Il Gabriello, a traditional restaurant famed for its wine and the display of art on its walls. The hubbub of the crowded dining room and the constant flow of serving staff and patrons gave the place a natural rhythm that made it easy for me to spot unwanted company. There was no scope for anyone to linger in the doorway or at the windows. They would have caught my attention like a dead fish floating amid a living shoal.

When I'd finished my braised ox cheek, I asked for the bill, paid and went to the men's room, checking the dining room constantly to see if I had a tail. No one came with me. I left the restaurant through a staff entrance by the kitchen and hurried along Via del Babuino toward the grand piazza.

The night-time city was illuminated by a kaleidoscope of colored lights, bright yellows, oranges and reds shining from storefronts and restaurant windows. I'd allowed myself time to loop around the streets surrounding the old church, to make sure there was no one lying in wait.

When I was finally satisfied there was no obvious danger, I walked the ancient cobblestones in front of the church. There were a handful of tourists strolling here and there, taking in the wonderful architecture around the square, but this late in the evening the area was pretty quiet. This historic neighborhood was at its best in daylight when the sun's rays picked out the stunning lines and magnificent colors of the buildings and illuminated the details of sculptures, carvings, statues and stained-glass windows in their full glory.

I could see why Father Carlos had chosen the location for our meeting. It was quiet, but not so deserted that two people would be noticed, and far enough away from the Vatican to avoid any chance encounters.

I walked up four broad stone steps and went through the huge doorway into the church. The devout had access to the interior at all times. I found myself in a large, domed chamber with a floor laid with black squares interspersed with white diamonds. The simple pews were modern and stretched away to either side, facing the altar. There was gilt everywhere, rich paintings of heavenly scenes, and carvings in wood and stone ornamenting the nave and the three side chapels to either side of it. The faint smell of incense hung in the air, like a spiritual spice.

I couldn't see anyone and moved slowly toward the altar. The sounds of the city barely penetrated the church's thick stone walls. I strained my ears against the quiet, listening for any movement.

I checked my watch; it was now after 10 p.m. I advanced, creeping so my footsteps didn't disturb the stillness. I was afraid of what I would find in the gap between the pews—the body of Father Carlos, murdered to prevent him talking to me?

I continued, eyes scanning to left and right, holding my breath, heart thumping, fearing the worst.

A sudden movement startled me and I looked ahead to see Father Carlos, hunched over in fear, emerge cautiously from behind the altar.

"Were you followed?" he asked.

I shook my head.

"Are you sure?"

I nodded.

"These are dangerous times," he told me, drawing near.

"What do you want to talk to me about?" I asked.

"I know who is behind the deaths of the priests and the murder of the prosecutor," Father Carlos said. Fear radiated from the young man. His eyes were restless as a gazelle's keeping watch for lions. "It was Elia Antonelli the Mafia king. He had all of them killed."

"Why?" I asked, regretting the ease with which I had let Antonelli explain away his involvement in recent events.

How could I have misjudged the man so badly? What did this mean for Matteo and his protestations of innocence?

But Father Carlos didn't get the chance to answer. There was a commotion at the main entrance and something slammed against the stone wall nearby, making a sound like a thunder-crack. A gang of masked men streamed through the open doorway, brandishing guns as they raced toward us.

"They must be Antonelli's men!" cried Father Carlos. "Run!"

CHAPTER 40

THE PRIEST MOVED surprisingly fast, leading me behind the altar as the masked men yelled at us in Italian. The first shot chipped the stone as we sprinted past it.

Father Carlos nodded and urged me on. We sprinted across the floor toward an open door as gunfire chewed the surrounding timber.

The priest slammed the door shut behind us and pulled a bookshelf in front of it, sending prayer books and bibles scattering as it fell on its side.

"This way," he said, as the door shook under the assault of our pursuers, who were trying to barge it down.

Father Carlos led me toward a line of robes hanging on hooks set in a wood-paneled wall. For a moment I thought he had made a mistake, but he grabbed one of the robes, felt for the hook beneath and pulled it down. There was a click and a section of paneling snapped open to reveal a dark tunnel beyond.

"Hurry!" Father Carlos said, illuminating the tunnel with the torch built into his phone.

Gray stone surrounded us and stretched ahead into the distance.

I went first and the priest followed, pausing to shut the secret panel, sealing us in.

"Rome is full of old tunnels from times of persecution and high politics," he explained. He was breathless and afraid but calmed slightly now we were hidden. "Come on. This will take us to the twin church across the street."

We moved further into the tunnel and the jittery priest jumped at the crash and splinter of the door being broken down behind us.

"Will they know about the secret passage?" I asked.

He shrugged. "Who can say?"

He picked up pace, his formal black shoes clip-clopping against the flagstones. The floor was worn in places, bowed by centuries of footsteps. I wondered when the tunnel had last been used because it was relatively clean and free from spider webs and dust.

"Are you sure you weren't followed?" the priest asked.

"As sure as I can be," I replied. "You?"

"I don't know," he said. "Why would anyone suspect me?"

"How do you know about Antonelli? Is he behind all this?" I asked.

"Shush," said the priest, slowing as we reached the end of the tunnel. He moved toward the panel that concealed the tunnel mouth and put his ear against it. I held my breath and was almost certain he held his as he listened carefully.

"Nothing," he whispered at last.

He reached for a catch located in a tiny cubby carved into the stone wall. When he pulled it there was a click and the paneling covering the tunnel mouth swung open. He pushed it wider and led me into a much smaller robing room. So small, in fact, we had to dance around each other awkwardly so he had space to close the secret panel.

"Carefully," he said, as I opened a heavy door that took us into a church that was an almost exact replica of the one we had just fled.

A couple safety lights were on, but most of the interior was shrouded in shadow, and I couldn't help feeling we were being watched from the darkness as we moved between the pews toward the exit. But there was only the silence and stillness of an empty building.

We hurried across the black and white tiles and soon reached the main entrance, where Father Carlos unlocked the door. It was huge: four inches thick, triple-height and width, studded with iron. It swung open ponderously on elaborate hinges.

"I know a place we will be safe," said the priest, stepping outside.

At that moment I heard the terrible and familiar crack of pistol fire and saw Father Carlos lurch back as a bullet hit him in the chest. He clutched at his black shirt as a stain began to spread across it. I grabbed him and pulled him inside just in time to avoid a volley of bullets.

We'd walked straight into an ambush.

CHAPTER 41

I SLAMMED THE door shut and crouched beside Father Carlos, who lay slumped against the wall beside the huge door, clutching his chest. The dim light inside the church exacerbated his loss of color, making him look ethereal, like someone who already belonged to another world. His breathing was rapid and shallow, and he wore the expression of anguish and regret that I'd seen on the faces of others during their last moments.

"Sir," he said, between hurried gasps. He clutched at me weakly. "*Proditio. Mendacium.*"

His body shook with the force of a convulsion. He was losing a lot of blood. I tried to help by pressing my hand against his wound, but I knew there was nothing I could do for the man. The injury was mortal, his fate was sealed.

"Signor Morgan," he rasped. "*Quia precium sanguinis est.*"

His last words were in Latin. The moment they passed his

lips, his eyes glazed and rolled back. It felt as though the effort of delivering a final message in the ancient tongue of the Church had cost him his spirit.

I'd drifted far from my faith but felt the death of a priest should be marked by proper religious ceremony, however simple. I made the Sign of the Cross over Father Carlos's body and said a Hail Mary for his soul. The Almighty wouldn't decide this man's fate based on my intercession, but at least the universe would know someone lamented his passing. And I truly did. This man had died while bringing me the truth, one of many innocent victims I'd seen cut down in my years as a detective.

If he was right, and Antonelli was responsible for these killings, the old Roman gangster would pay for what he'd done.

I couldn't do anything more for Father Carlos so I rose to my feet and stepped away from his body. I pressed my ear against the door and listened carefully, straining to hear any sound coming from beyond the ancient, heavy planks. There was nothing so I pulled the door open and peered round it, slowly and carefully.

The portico immediately beyond the door and the surrounding cobblestones were deserted. There was no sign of whoever had shot Father Carlos. They had clearly been under instructions to kill the priest but couldn't have known he'd already told me the most important piece of information he possessed.

There were a few passers-by on the other side of the piazza, but they showed no sign of having seen or heard anything out of the ordinary and paid me no attention as I eased my way out of the church. I was tensed ready for a sudden onslaught, but none came. By the time I reached the stone steps in front of the church I was moving fast. I hurried down them and sprinted right along Via del Corso, my footsteps echoing off the surrounding buildings as I ran into the night.

CHAPTER 42

I FINALLY STOPPED running when I reached the Via Tomacelli, which was eight blocks south of the church. It was approaching 11 p.m. and there were a few diners and revelers meandering along the sidewalks, laughing loudly at jokes, arguing animatedly, or in the case of lovers, holding hands or walking arm-in-arm. Many swayed with intoxication but gave me no trouble nor paid me much attention as I picked my way through the streets to a taxi stand on Piazza di San Silvestro, a beautiful cobbled square lined by luxury jewelry stores, offices and apartment blocks whose windows were lit like golden lanterns.

I took the first cab in line. The driver, a cheerful man in his late thirties, tried to talk in halting English, but soon picked up that I wasn't in the mood for conversation.

I was focused on my phone and spent the journey to Ostia trying to get hold of Justine, Mo-bot or Sci.

I had no luck reaching them. When I finally made it back to the apartment above the cell-phone store, I changed out of my suit, which was flecked with the blood of the fallen priest. I put on my black jeans and T-shirt and sat and waited impatiently for one of my colleagues to call.

Finally, almost two hours after the priest had died in my arms, my phone buzzed and the screen lit up with Justine's name.

"Jus!" I said, relieved.

"What's happened?" she asked.

"Another priest has been killed. I was with him at the time. I . . . I couldn't do anything for him."

"I'm so sorry, Jack."

"I'm fine," I replied, a little too emphatically.

"Jack, you're not fine," she said. "The death of another is always a shock, no matter how many times you've experienced it. Please don't downplay what just happened."

I nodded and stayed silent.

"And you're taking too many risks out there on your own."

"I know what I'm doing."

"No, Jack," she responded. "You're doing what you know. There's a difference. I've talked to Maureen and Seymour."

I always knew it was serious when she used their proper names.

"And we're coming to Rome. I'm not going to let you face this alone."

"Justine—" I tried, but she cut me off.

"Would *you* leave *me*? If I was the one in Rome, facing what you're facing, would you leave me to deal with it on my own?"

"That's diff—"

"If you're about to say it's different, you'd better have a good reason. One that doesn't ultimately rest on you being a man and me being a woman."

"Justine," I tried one last time.

"You said we'd review the situation. Well, consider it reviewed. I'm not going to let you face this alone," she reiterated. "Nor are Seymour and Maureen. We've made arrangements for our workloads to be covered here. We'll be on the first available flight."

I knew there was no point resisting any longer. I had zero chance of defeating the concentrated determination of three stubborn minds.

"Before he died, the priest told me Elia Antonelli is behind all of this," I revealed. "He said the men who shot him worked for Antonelli."

"Do you believe him?" Justine asked.

It hadn't occurred to me that the priest might have been lying.

"I think so," I replied. "I think Father Carlos—"

My response was cut short by the sound of a knock at the door.

I froze.

"Someone's here," I whispered to Justine.

"Get out, Jack," she replied.

"If it was bad guys, I don't think they'd have bothered knocking," I said, rising from my seat on the couch.

"Hello?" I called, approaching the door.

"Mr. Morgan, may I please come in?"

I recognized Faduma's voice immediately and opened the door

to find her standing at the top of the metal staircase. She was in black slacks and a green halterneck top and looked as though she was made up for a date.

"I have to go," I told Justine. "Let me know when you'll be arriving."

"Will do," she said, before I hung up.

"Have you been following me?" I asked my visitor.

"What? No," Faduma replied, stepping into the apartment and closing the door behind her. "Not tonight, anyway. I was out for dinner."

"What do you mean, not tonight?" I asked. "How did you know where to find me?"

"I followed you here after we met at the cemetery. I wanted to see what you did with the information I gave you."

I scoffed, but she waved away my disbelief.

"I came because there's something you need to see."

She reached into her purse for her phone, which she turned toward me. The screen was filled with a news website's piece covering Father Carlos's murder.

"There's been another priest murdered," she said.

"I know. I was there."

Her eyes widened in surprise.

"He said Antonelli is behind the killings, right before he was shot."

"That's terrible. Poor man."

I nodded. I couldn't shake the memory of the priest dying in front of me.

"But you were unhurt?" she asked.

"They didn't seem interested in me, thankfully," I said. "It's clear they wanted to silence Father Carlos, but they weren't quick enough."

"Do you think he was telling the truth?"

I nodded.

"Does that mean Matteo Ricci is a liar?" she asked.

"I have no idea," I replied. "But I do know I want to talk to him again."

"I want to come with you," she said. "We'll go first thing in the morning."

She turned for the door.

"Don't I get a say in that?" I asked.

"Of course not," she replied with a mischievous smile. "Meet me on the Via di San Vitale at eight tomorrow."

I nodded. "And I'll ask Gianna Bianchi to join us."

CHAPTER 43

I TRIED TO get hold of Justine again once Faduma had left, but there was no reply. After grabbing a gyro from one of the local Turkish takeout stands, I went to bed, exhausted.

I hardly slept and when I did drift off, I was troubled by dreams about the death of Father Carlos. I kept waking with a terrible feeling of guilt. I could and should have done more to protect him. Looking back on my career, I wondered how many more innocents might still be alive if I had just been that little bit faster, stronger or better.

I rose before dawn and went for a run along the coast, relishing the relative peace and quiet, the streets sparsely populated by other early risers, runners, people coming off their night shifts, and workers just beginning their day. I covered ten kilometers in forty minutes and returned to the apartment where I showered and dressed in the black T-shirt and jeans I'd worn briefly the previous night.

I took a cab from Ostia to police headquarters on the Via di San Vitale and arrived at 7:55 a.m.

Faduma was already waiting outside. She wore a dark green maxi summer dress.

"Good morning," she said.

"Morning," I replied.

It didn't feel like a good one to me.

"Any sign of Gianna?" I asked.

Faduma shook her head just as the lawyer emerged from the large archway that at the front of police headquarters. She looked distraught.

"Mr. Morgan, I have terrible news," she said. "According to the duty officer, Matteo Ricci tried to hang himself last night. He's in Ospedale Fatebenefratelli under armed guard."

CHAPTER 44

FATEBENEFRATELLI HOSPITAL WAS located on Isola Tiberina, a small island in the center of the Tiber near the Marcello Theater. Approached from the treelined southern bank of the river, across the cobbled Cestio bridge, the hospital looked like one of the classical terracotta apartment blocks found in the upmarket older parts of Rome. The windows of the three-story building were surmounted by white stone frames, beveled slightly, giving the building additional character.

Gianna had driven us to the hospital in her dark green Audi Q7, weaving skillfully through the city traffic so we covered the three-mile journey in under fifteen minutes. She spent most of the drive on the phone, speaking to Mia Esposito to ensure we had access to Matteo when we arrived at the hospital.

He was in a private room on the third floor and there were two uniformed Carabinieri posted outside. Gianna presented her identification and they allowed us into Matteo's room. There was a window overlooking the river. Matteo had a dressing around his neck and was dozing beneath a sky-blue sheet. He was surrounded by monitors and an IV feed. This shadow was a far cry from the confident, competent man I'd hired to run the Rome office, and I was struggling to understand how he'd unraveled so quickly and comprehensively.

He stirred when we approached the bed and his eyes flickered open. They were bloodshot and sunken, his skin gray. He seemed traumatized by whatever had happened to him.

"I . . ." he rasped.

More words followed, but his voice was too weak and strained for us to make sense of them.

I moved closer and put a reassuring hand on his shoulder.

"It's okay," I said. "You're going to be okay."

He strained against whatever damage had been done to his vocal cords. I looked at Faduma and Gianna, both wearing pained expressions as they felt Matteo's struggle and suffering from across the room.

"Jack," he said at length, his voice as raw and rough as a deep-scored graze. "I didn't do this."

He gestured to his neck.

"Was sleeping. Someone strangled me. Staged hanging."

He fell back exhausted from the effort of communicating, and I looked at Faduma and Gianna.

"Did you hear that?" I asked.

They shook their heads.

"He says someone tried to kill him. Made it look like he tried to kill himself." I turned to Matteo, somewhat relieved to have his explanation but not entirely sure I could trust it. "I'm glad they underestimated you. Do you know who it was?"

He shook his head slowly and covered his face with his hand.

"Mask?" I suggested, and he nodded.

"Do the police know this wasn't your doing?"

He shook his head again, wincing with pain.

"I know this is difficult, but it's important," I told him. "Why did you tell Luna not to investigate the prosecutor's death? Filippo Lombardi, the car wreck. Why did you listen to Brambilla when he told you to back off?"

Matteo shrugged.

"Did you know Luna is Elia Antonelli's daughter?"

His eyes darted to Gianna and Faduma before he nodded.

"Do you think Antonelli and Father Brambilla were connected?" I asked.

He hesitated then nodded again. "Ignacio . . . Father Brambilla . . . told me Antonelli had asked him to warn me off."

I looked at Faduma who very obviously understood the significance of this immediately. Antonelli was implicated in this whole affair. I felt very foolish for having taken the man at face value.

"Why didn't you tell me about the connection to Antonelli?"

Matteo's eyes welled up and he forced out a word.

"Shame."

I patted his shoulder. "You rest, Matteo. Get better. I will take care of this."

I turned to Gianna and said, "We don't have an operational

team yet. Do you have any security agencies you can recommend? I want to put a couple of close-protection specialists on this ward to boost the police guard."

It was standard operating procedure whenever a Private employee's life was in danger. Until I had evidence to the contrary, I had to take Matteo at his word.

She nodded. "I'll phone a company we use."

"I'm worried they'll make another attempt on his life," I said. "It seems Elia Antonelli is busy tying up loose ends."

CHAPTER 45

FADUMA AND I stayed at the hospital until Marcus and Pietro, two agents from Primo Security, arrived at Gianna's behest to stand watch over Matteo. Pietro, a short wiry man who looked as though he was pure sinew, posted himself by the ward entrance, while Marcus, a lumbering bear of a figure, sat opposite the cops outside Matteo's room. Gianna smoothed the cops' ruffled feathers, pointing out we had every right to provide our own security to a Private employee.

Satisfied with the arrangements, I left the hospital with Faduma and we took a taxi to her car, a silver Volkswagen Golf parked on the Via Piacenza a block north of police headquarters.

I climbed in the passenger seat and she slid behind the wheel, started the engine and pulled out of the tight space. She drove along narrow back streets, navigating the maze of one-way roads, and soon we were on Via Bari, heading out of the city.

"Do you believe him?" Faduma asked.

I was puzzled.

"About the attempt on his life," she explained. "Sometimes people feel embarrassed to tell the truth."

I got her meaning. "I think we have to take it at face value. There are multiple linked murders. It makes sense that someone might try to kill Matteo. He is a loose end."

She thought for a moment. "What about us? Are we loose ends?"

I didn't reply. I didn't need to. We both knew the answer.

Faduma concentrated on the road ahead, navigating the traffic. The sun was low over the suburbs, tinting everything with its pastel-pink light. Soon we were beyond the malls and industrial estates and in the hills and valleys on our way to Casape. The landscape was beautiful, but we made no comment on it and travelled in silence, each wrestling with the puzzle confronting us.

There was very little traffic out here as we headed into the hills, following the single-lane road as it wound through olive groves. I thought about Matteo and whether a disgraced cop accused of murder would be sufficiently ashamed to try and take his own life. He'd been caught red-handed, standing over Brambilla with the gun, and if he knew he would be found guilty, then ending things by his own hand might seem the only escape. And when the attempt failed, he might concoct a cover story about someone trying to murder him.

But there was also Antonelli and the dead priests. There was Father Carlos, the man of God who'd been murdered in front of me. Matteo was not responsible for his death, and, as far as we knew, for those of any of the other priests. He struck me as genuinely distressed but honest.

We rounded a bend and Faduma overtook a slow-moving tractor pulling a trailer. We drove through the cloud of dust being churned up by the clattering vehicle and she accelerated onto a clear stretch of road.

"Puzzles," she observed.

"Yeah," I scoffed.

"You can retreat in on yourself. Live in your head, trying to put the pieces together."

"Tell me about it," I remarked.

"The priests who died were all frequent travelers," she said. "They ministered to churches in trouble spots. Ukraine, the Philippines, Brazil."

"You think they were running money?"

"Or intel," she replied. "The Vatican has a long history of involvement in espionage. Organized crime too."

"Antonelli might have been using the priests to funnel money abroad," I suggested. "Or launder income from illegal activity through the bank."

Faduma nodded. "It's been done before. Propaganda Due in the 1970s. It was a secret society that infiltrated and corrupted the highest offices in Italy."

"Organized crime would connect Antonelli to the dead priests," I said. "But why would a gangster need to involve clergy in his activities?"

"We'll find out soon enough," she replied, turning off the country road onto the narrow lane that led to Antonelli's estate.

She slowed as we neared the property, both of us alert, watching for signs of danger. Antonelli wouldn't be so civil this time if he knew we were closing in on him, but I was confident he wouldn't harm us, not here. The disappearance of the head of the world's largest detective agency and one of Rome's most famous investigative journalists would be hard to explain, particularly as I'd let Justine know exactly where we were going. If Antonelli wanted to come after us, it wouldn't be on his home ground.

When we reached the gates to the estate, I was surprised to see they were open. Faduma didn't slow but followed the track into the property, past the olive groves until we came within sight of the large farmhouse where I'd had lunch with Luna and Antonelli.

There were no vehicles in the drive and the shutters were all closed. The property was still and silent and had the air of being deserted.

Faduma pulled to a halt and I saw an old man with a bolt-action rifle slung over his shoulder walk slowly from behind the house. He wore a flat cap and colorless threadbare clothes. Squinting into the dying sun, which was behind us, his weathered skin and crinkled features spoke of a lifetime spent outdoors.

Faduma talked to him in Italian. I caught the name "Antonelli," but not much else.

He replied, removing his cap and scratching his head. When he stopped talking, he turned and walked back the way he'd come.

"He says they've gone away. He doesn't know where and doesn't know when they will be back," she told me. "But he called Antonelli 'general', which I'm pretty sure means there's going to be trouble."

A mob boss in retreat, or on the defensive, preparing for war. Against whom? And why had he marked out all those priests for death? The answers seemed further away than ever, and I felt a sense of disappointment until Faduma spoke.

"I think I might know where they've gone," she said, turning the car around. She registered my surprise. "What can I say? I'm thorough. Don't worry, it's not far."

CHAPTER 46

"ANTONELLI'S FAMILY WERE farmers," Faduma explained as she rejoined the country road.

The announcement didn't surprise me, given the way he'd talked when we'd had lunch.

It was getting dark and twilight made the olive trees seem weirdly human, their gnarly branches reaching out like old men's fingers.

"His family owned a lot of land around here. That's why Antonelli has his estate in these hills. He feels an affinity to this place."

"How do you know?" I asked, marveling at her detective skills. I had operatives at Private who wouldn't be able to deliver such extensive background, and even Mo-bot's trawl of Antonelli hadn't yielded this level of information.

"I make it my business to learn everything I can about the key players in any investigation. You never know how the pieces will come together. I've interviewed dozens of police and underworld contacts about Antonelli, and they all say the same thing: he has a genuine love of the land of his childhood."

I nodded. He had spoken about the soil and its produce with such pride.

"While his love of the land round here might be common knowledge, what few people know is the location of the family's original farm," Faduma said. "Or the fact that Antonelli was born there and considers it his sanctuary."

"How did you—"

She cut me off. "That source is secret, Mr. Morgan. I hope you will appreciate the need to take proper precautions. To protect my source, not me."

"I understand."

"The farm is two valleys over. Antonelli lived there until he was twelve," Faduma said.

She steered us off the road onto another rough track, and we took a jarring ride, up and down, over a badly rutted surface. Faduma killed the lights as we continued our journey to Antonelli's childhood home. It seemed darker here in the folds of the hills, and the landscape more rugged.

The track had reached a vantage point overlooking the valley from which I could see the lights of a house below us in a sheltering fold of land. I could tell from the uneven lines of the walls that it was old and not as well cared for as Antonelli's principal residence, but even at a distance one sensed the building's grandeur. This was not the home of a poor farmer, and I wondered whether Antonelli was the family's worst villain or whether he was simply following a long tradition.

I was stirred from my thoughts by a sudden, jarring halt. Fatuma slammed on the brakes and veered off the track, and when I peered into the darkness ahead, I saw why.

The track was rising toward the crest of a hill, and there, silhouetted against the night sky, were five men milling around a low stone boundary wall, the outlines of their long assault rifles unmistakable.

CHAPTER 47

"WHAT DO WE do now?" Faduma asked.

My mind raced through a range of options and settled on a simple but bold course of action.

"Switch on the headlamps," I said, taking my phone from my pocket.

"Are you serious?" she asked, glancing nervously at the shapes of the armed men ahead.

"Trust me," I replied, activating the video recording app on my phone.

Faduma hesitated before switching on full-beam, lighting the track ahead, illuminating the men clustered against the wall. They were dazzled by the glare; a couple raised their weapons blind, while others shielded their eyes. I lowered my window and pointed my phone at them.

"You are being recorded and the footage is being streamed to a secure site on the Cloud," I yelled. The last part was a lie, but there was no way they would be able to tell that. "Our colleagues know where we are and that we've come to see Elia Antonelli. If anything happens to us, you will be held responsible."

Faduma lowered her window and shouted in Italian. I could tell she was giving the men her own version of my speech, and as their eyes adjusted, they edged back, keen to avoid being caught on camera.

"Drive on," I advised, and Faduma started the engine and moved slowly along the track.

One of the men was on his phone but we couldn't hear what he was saying. Soon we were past them and the car gathered speed as we headed toward the lights of the farmhouse a few hundred yards away. We bounced along the bumpy track, churning up dust that obscured the star-filled sky.

"That was brave of you," Faduma remarked.

"Both of us were brave," I said. "I took a calculated risk they would never shoot us on camera. Antonelli is too smart for that."

Faduma nodded, but I sensed she wasn't so sure.

She slowed as we entered a courtyard enclosed on two sides by a large barn and attached farmhouse. There were half a dozen cars in the yard, and a tall, skinny man in his mid-forties was making a dash for one of them: a gray Mercedes E-Class. When our headlights fell on him, he froze like a jackrabbit stunned by the dazzling glare. He turned away sheepishly, trying to hide his face before hurrying on to his car.

"That's Stefano Trotta," Faduma observed. "He's a junior finance minister."

I shouldn't have been surprised Antonelli had links to government, but I was thrown to have caught an Italian minister of state openly consorting with a man implicated in so many deaths.

Trotta jumped in his car and sped past us, heading for the track.

As Faduma parked, I saw Antonelli lumber out of the farmhouse with Luna a couple of paces behind him.

"Mr. Morgan, Ms. Salah, this is a surprise," he boomed as we stepped out of the car. "We were just having dinner."

"Looks like your guest couldn't wait to leave. I hope we didn't intrude," Faduma countered as we walked over.

Antonelli smiled. "Some people don't like surprises as much as I do. Although I am annoyed."

"Why's that?" I asked.

"If you two can find me, so can my better-resourced competitors."

"Don't you mean enemies?" I suggested.

He shrugged. "It is what it is. I will have the men increase the frequency of their patrols and hope my competitors are not as effective as you two. Would you like to join Luna and me? There's plenty of food."

I glanced at Luna, who nodded and smiled at me.

"What do you think?" I asked Faduma. "Hungry?"

"Sure," she replied, so we followed Luna and Antonelli inside.

CHAPTER 48

ANTONELLI LED US through his family home. The interior seemed simpler than the house I had previously visited. This one seemed more comfortable, decorated to be lived in, rather than to impress with conspicuous displays of wealth. We walked through a sitting room filled with old furniture, including a couple of large well-worn couches that looked perfect for a lazy Sunday afternoon with a novel.

We went through a doorway into a stone-flagged dining room that contained an eighteen-place oak table and chairs. A couple of landscape paintings hung on one wall, and opposite them French doors opened onto a terrace overlooking the hillside.

A manservant was already setting another two places. As he finished and began to clear away the cutlery and plates from what I guessed must have been Trotta's place, Elia Antonelli gestured to us.

"Please, have a seat."

He took the chair at the head of the table, and Faduma and I sat at the newly laid places to his right while Luna returned to her seat to his left.

The servant offered us warm rolls from a basket on the serving table. We drizzled olive oil from a tiny silver jug onto our side plates and tore the rolls into pieces for dipping. I sprinkled mine with a little rock salt and glanced at Antonelli as I took a bite. He seemed deflated and distracted tonight, in stark contrast to the larger-than-life personality I'd first encountered.

"Are these made from your own wheat?" I asked, finishing my roll, which had tasted delicious and made me hungry for more.

"Of course," he replied, growing animated for a moment before slumping slightly in his seat as though remembering his woes.

Luna reached across the table and squeezed his hand tenderly.

"What brings you out here, Mr. Morgan?" she asked me.

"Another priest has been murdered in Rome," I replied, watching Antonelli carefully.

He glanced at Luna with unmistakable concern as he replied, "Yes, Father Carlos Diaz."

"We heard about that on the news," Luna said.

"But you don't know anything about why he was killed?" Faduma asked.

The servant returned with a tray of dishes that he set on a serving table. Everyone fell silent. He served small plates of ravioli, and I thanked him when he set mine down. It smelt rich yet fresh, and the tomato sauce covering the plump parcels looked delicious.

"Why would we know about that?" Luna asked, after the waiter had withdrawn.

"Because the priest died with your father's name on his lips," I replied. "Your name, Signor Antonelli. He told me you were responsible for the murders of all the priests who've died recently. And that you also ordered Filippo Lombardi's death."

Antonelli glanced at Luna, his face like thunder, then his anger dissipated and he looked crestfallen. He turned to face me and I couldn't help but hope a confession was imminent. It would save us all so much effort and trouble.

Instead, our host broke into a broad grin and laughed.

"I'm very sorry about this latest priest but I certainly didn't kill him."

I glanced at Luna and saw she was taken aback by the suggestion that he might be responsible.

"This is why you're here, Mr. Morgan? To accuse me of the murder of a man I have no interest in killing?"

Antonelli laughed again, only this time it sounded hollow.

"You have wasted your time," he said, spearing a forkful of ravioli. "If I wanted to kill a priest, I would not send in a hit squad. Eat, Mr. Morgan, Ms. Salah. You will need all your energy."

I picked at my food and Faduma did likewise. It tasted wonderful, but my keen appetite of only minutes ago had been blunted by the racing of my mind.

"Someone killed this Father Carlos to make it look as though I wanted him dead," Antonelli said. "Instead of paying unannounced visits, you should be trying to identify the real culprits."

I tried to find a hint of duplicity in the man's demeanor and tone, but everything about him spoke to his innocence. Of this crime at least. Someone was playing me, but I couldn't be sure it was him.

"Did he say anything else?" Antonelli asked.

I nodded. "*Proditio. Mendacium. Quia precium sanguinis est.*"

Antonelli laughed yet again. "You understand the significance of these words?"

Faduma was blank-faced and I shook my head.

"It is a reference to Judas Iscariot. Betrayal. Lies. This is the price of blood," Antonelli revealed. "The price of blood is a reference to the thirty pieces of silver paid for the betrayal of Christ."

I had translated the Latin but not set it in any wider context.

"It tells me Father Carlos knew he had been betrayed," Antonelli continued, "and that the killer, like Judas, was likely a fellow disciple of the Church."

CHAPTER 49

"YOU'RE CONVINCING," I said, "but the problem I have is that Father Brambilla told Matteo Ricci you wanted him and Luna warned off the Lombardi investigation. You didn't want your daughter and her partner looking into the death of a Rome prosecutor."

Antonelli's smile faded. Now even Luna eyed him with suspicion.

"Why?" I asked. "Why wouldn't you want them looking into Lombardi's death?"

Antonelli stared me straight in the eye and held my gaze for a moment.

"What do you see when you look at me?" he asked.

"Someone who's grown rich from the misery of others," Faduma replied.

Antonelli's eyes narrowed and a thin smile pinched his lips, but he said nothing as the servant returned, carrying another tray of food. The man cleared away our *primi* and then served plates of braised meat, chipped potatoes and steamed broccoli.

"Lamb shoulder," he said before departing with the used dishes.

Antonelli's thin smile hadn't wavered and he stared at Faduma while the *secondi* were served. She held her own and eyeballed him back.

"I have acquired such wealth as I possess by giving people what they want," Antonelli replied. He turned in my direction. "When you look at me with my daughter, what do you see, Mr. Morgan?"

Antonelli's gaze softened as his eyes fell on Luna.

"A father," I replied. "With love in his heart."

He nodded. "I loved her mother very much and I love Luna more than words can say. I asked Father Brambilla to advise his old seminary student to back off the investigation only because I knew it would be dangerous for the police officers involved—mostly because my daughter is even more stubborn than I am."

Luna shook her head to deny this and spoke volubly to her father.

"But you are, my darling," Antonelli said. "You would never listen to me if I told you danger lay ahead of you. You would only become more suspicious and inclined to dig in your heels."

"True," Luna conceded grudgingly.

"So I sent a man I knew Inspector Ricci trusted, to warn him off," Antonelli confessed. "Mostly to protect my daughter."

"Why?" I asked. "And protect her from what?"

"Whatever got Lombardi killed," Antonelli replied.

"Do you know why he was run off that road?" Faduma asked.

Antonelli shook his head.

"Then why warn them off?" I remarked.

"If you have played this game as long as I have, you learn to spot the signs. Murdered priests, a dead prosecutor, rumblings in the high places of Rome . . . someone is making a play for more of the power that tantalizes so many in this city."

"But not you?" Faduma asked.

"This is my land. I am a farmer at heart. It keeps me grounded."

"And even with your network and resources, you still have no idea who is behind all this?" I said.

He shook his head again. "I have moved here to the security of my family's ancestral home in order to protect my daughter. The attempt on Matteo's life demonstrates that whoever is behind this wants all the loose ends dealt with."

"But why not take the battle to whoever that is?" I asked.

"Perhaps when we know their identity that will be possible, but in times of uncertainty, self-defense is the prudent course," Antonelli replied.

I glanced at Faduma, who shared my skepticism about this measured response.

"I may not agree with my daughter's career choice, but I honor it," Antonelli continued. "I would never disrespect her role as a police officer by commissioning the assassination of a priest, and certainly wouldn't order an attempt on her police partner's life."

Luna's expression softened and she looked at her father with something approaching tenderness.

"You can still surprise me sometimes, Papà," she remarked.

"Love can do that, my dear," he replied. "I value nothing higher than your happiness and safety. Mr. Morgan, you have been manipulated by someone who does not know me into believing I would harm my daughter's career, destroy what little trust she has in me, and make her an accomplice to the murder of innocents."

He let his words sink in.

"So I ask you again, what do you see when you look at me?"

He took Luna's hand and held it fondly.

For a moment I studied the man and his daughter before replying in the only way I could: "A loving father. One who is devoted to his child."

CHAPTER 50

WE FINISHED THE meal with an *affogato*, a double shot of espresso over homemade ice cream, and the conversation turned to Antonelli's experiences as a child, growing up on this farm. If I hadn't known better, I could have believed I was listening to a fifth-generation Roman farmer with no passion other than nurturing the finest produce possible from his patch of earth. I kept catching Faduma's eye. Her suspicion of earlier was clearly gone. She seemed to be enjoying the evening, smiling and asking questions about our host's early life.

After the dessert we thanked Antonelli and Luna for their generosity. He even invited us to visit again, which made me wonder whether it was lonely being at the top of one of Rome's most notorious criminal organizations.

"What do you think?" I asked Faduma once we were back in her Volkswagen and on our way into the city.

"I think he was telling the truth," she replied as she followed the winding road.

Asphalt materialized out of the night and we headed back to the bright lights of Rome. We would glimpse the shining city whenever there was a gap in the creases and folds of the hills. The urban sprawl looked like a magnificent beacon, its ambient glow reaching up toward the stars. I tried to imagine what it would have been like to see it for the first time during the age of empire as a traveler arriving from a simple provincial village. The sheer spectacle of the imperial city must have been breathtaking.

"Video or no video," Faduma remarked, referring to my gambit earlier tonight to get us into the estate, "if he wanted us dead, we'd be dead by now."

She checked the rear-view mirror, and I glanced back to see there was nothing trailing us through the darkness.

"I think he was right about Father Carlos's last words," I said. "The priest knew his killer."

"If not Antonelli, then who?" Faduma asked.

"I want to know more about Milan Verde," I replied. "Father Carlos's death was exactly the kind of noisy statement the Dark Fates live to make."

Faduma nodded. "Maybe he's been using priests to transport money for him?"

"Maybe."

We followed the snaking road down the side of the valley and soon joined the highway heading into the city. It took us over an hour to cross Rome, reaching Ostia shortly after 1 a.m.

"You didn't have to drive me," I told her. "I could have caught a cab in the city."

"I'd like to take a look at what you've got on Milan Verde if that's okay with you?" Faduma replied.

"So the ride was less of a favor, more a favor for a favor," I remarked. "If we're going to work this together, information has to go both ways. You share with me whatever you've got."

"Deal," she said.

She parked a block from the cell-phone store and we walked the busy streets.

"Exciting neighborhood," she observed. "Very lively."

"It suits me," I replied. "As long as no one else traces me here."

We walked through the alleyway to the yard behind the terrace and climbed the metal steps up to the apartment. When I reached the door, I sensed something was wrong. I was struck by the feeling that something here was out of place, like when a favorite photo is moved from its usual position or a painting hangs crooked. I realized the grubby welcome mat was not set flush against the bottom of the door frame anymore.

I signaled to Faduma to be silent and crept forward, sliding my key into the lock. I felt the tiny teeth run along the tumbler mechanism. Once they were fast, I turned it gently and slowly pushed the door open.

I moved inside and crept along the corridor, taking great care not to make a sound. I heard people in the living room and sidestepped into the kitchen to slide a carving knife out of the block.

Faduma's eyes widened. I signaled for her to stay back.

I held the knife ready and pushed the living-room door open.

"Jeez, Jack!" Mo-bot yelled. "What the hell are you doing, wandering around like you're in a slasher movie?"

I breathed easy and grinned at the welcome sight of Mo-bot, Sci and Justine. The three of them smiled right back at me.

CHAPTER 51

JUSTINE LEAPT TO her feet, crossed the room and threw her arms around me. As we hugged I felt the tension ebb out of her.

"Jack," she said. "I missed you."

"I missed you too," I replied.

Faduma cleared her throat awkwardly. Justine and I parted reluctantly.

"Faduma Salah, this is my colleague and partner Justine Smith," I said, and she stepped forward and offered her hand.

"Pleased to meet you," she said.

"Likewise," Faduma responded.

"And this is Maureen Roth," I continued.

"Everyone calls me Mo-bot," she told Faduma with a wave. "Or Mo."

"And Seymour Kloppenberg," I added.

He also waved. "Call me Sci."

"Nice to meet you all," Faduma said.

"How did you find me?" I asked.

"Your phone," Mo-bot replied. "I tracked your location, looked at where you spent the night."

It wouldn't have been much of a challenge for Mo-bot, who was one of the world's leading computer and digital surveillance experts. She didn't look it now though, wearing a sensible cool white linen dress that was crumpled from the journey.

Sci was in his customary biker boots, T-shirt and jeans, busy reviewing the files I'd obtained on the various players in this investigation.

"Have you been working together?" Justine asked, returning to her spot on the couch next to him.

Like Sci, she'd been examining a stack of files, and I knew she'd be trying to build psychological pictures of all the key players. I was most interested in her insight into Milan Verde but sensed there was more to her question than simple curiosity. Was she jealous?

"Not really," I replied. "We've just been out to see Elia Antonelli together, and Faduma wanted to check the information we have on Milan Verde."

Justine smiled and nodded, but I wasn't sure she was entirely happy. We'd had our problems in the past, and she had even become convinced I was involved with Dinara Orlova, the head of our Moscow operation. Faduma was a beautiful woman but I was devoted to Justine, who looked magnificent tonight in a long Pucci-print dress. I couldn't imagine she had travelled in it. Had she put it on in anticipation of my arrival? Was her frustration due to the fact that we weren't alone?

I didn't have the time to indulge myself in such thoughts. Instead I briefed the three of them on what we'd learnt from Antonelli. I also brought them up to speed on the death of Father Carlos and everything that had happened since.

They listened transfixed, incredulous in places, and when I was finished, Mo-bot said, "I'm beginning to regret our decision to come here. Rome sounds dangerous."

CHAPTER 52

JUSTINE AND I finally kissed and it felt great to hold her in my arms again. We were in the small bedroom that had become my temporary home, light from the neon signs outside bleeding around the edges of the threadbare drapes, lending the room an eerie orange glow. The old shabby furniture and peeling wallpaper made it one of the least romantic venues we'd ever experienced, but I didn't care. I was just grateful to have her with me.

"Jack," she said. "Don't leave me like that again."

I smiled. "I missed you so much," I said, kissing her.

"I know it's selfish but I need you with me," she replied. "Every time you leave, you take my heart with you."

"I know."

I pulled her close. We were alone in the room but Sci and Mo-bot were just outside, sorting through gear and checking the files I'd put together on the key players. Faduma had left a few minutes before Justine and I had moved into the bedroom. Even though I longed for her, this didn't feel like a relaxed environment where we could be uninhibited and free. One of the pitfalls of dating my beautiful, smart, talented colleague was the blurred, sometimes confusing, line between personal and professional. This was one of those blurry moments, but it didn't last long.

There was a knock at the door and Mo-bot entered almost immediately. Justine cleared her throat and stepped back, making a show of looking around the room as though searching for something.

Mo-bot registered the awkwardness of the scene. "I'm sorry. I keep forgetting you two are an item." She smiled and I wondered whether that was true or if she was just being mischievous.

"It's okay," I assured her. "We're here on business."

"Good," Mo-bot said, stepping forward. She had a small device in her hand. "I wouldn't want to intrude. Sci and I have been running inventory. We can mount a full-scale surveillance operation and we think we should target the Dark Fates."

She drifted out to the living room and I followed, to see rows of mini-drones, listening devices and video cameras arranged on the floor by the window.

"We can get all this installed tomorrow, have eyes and ears on everything they do, with special focus on Milan Verde."

"Sounds good," I replied.

Sci was rearranging his holdall. "If they're behind all these murders, we'll find out. And we'll get to the bottom of why."

Satisfied with the rearrangement of his gear, he stood, slung the bag over his shoulder and walked toward my bedroom.

"I'll bunk in with you," he said. "I can take the floor. Mo-bot and Justine can have the other bedroom. Girls together."

"Girls?" Mo-bot replied icily.

"Or whatever," he said.

"Or whatever?" she countered. "You know you're just making it worse now? You're rude, Seymour Kloppenberg. As well as a dinosaur."

"Not extinct yet though," he said with a smile, before heading into the bedroom.

I glanced at Justine and saw disappointment writ large on her face. I shared it but couldn't object. This was the best arrangement for all of us as professionals, even though it was frustrating for Justine and me personally.

"Let's get a good night's sleep," I said to Mo-bot. "We start work on the Dark Fates first thing tomorrow."

CHAPTER 53

I WOKE EARLY the following day. I'd given Sci the bed, despite his protests, and had slept on the floor, which was luxury in comparison to some of the quarters I'd had to endure while serving in the Marine Corps.

He was still asleep, breathing deeply, so I eased the door open and went into the living room where I found Mo-bot and Justine, dressed and ready, running through final gear checks.

"There are pastries on the table in the kitchen," Justine said.

"Thanks," I replied, rubbing my hand over my face.

"Thank Mo-bot," Justine responded.

"I was up early and wanted something to do," she remarked.

"Earlier than this?" I said.

Mo-bot glanced at her watch. "It's six-forty-six. That's not really early. Especially when your body clock is fried from jetlag."

"What's the plan?" Justine asked.

"He needs to put some clothes on," Mo-bot replied.

I had slept in shorts and a T-shirt.

"Then we go to the Inferno Bar?" I suggested.

Mo-bot shook her head. "I don't think we need the numbers. It will just draw attention. I'll handle it with Sci. We thought you and Justine could visit our client."

"I'd like to meet Joseph Stadler's executive assistant, Christian Altmer," Justine added, pointing to one of my files. "You said you thought he might be hiding something. I'd like to check him out."

I nodded. It made sense to see what an expert could pick up from the guy who had roused my suspicions. "Okay. I'll get dressed when the old man is awake."

"Who are you calling an old man?" Sci asked, and I turned to see him looking every inch the gnarly biker: Metallica T-shirt, denim vest, jeans and heavy boots. "I'm ready to go catch some bad guys. You?"

"Point taken," I said, and I headed into the bedroom to get dressed.

Three hours later, Justine and I were walking along Via Sant'Anna, heading for the headquarters of the Vatican Bank. I'd emailed Altmer and secured a 10 a.m. appointment with Joseph Stadler, knowing his executive assistant would join us.

"This is so beautiful," Justine said, taking in our surroundings.

I saw the Eternal City through her eyes and had to admit it was stunning. The dome of St Peter's loomed to our left, the white stone walls striking against a cloudless sky. The Papal residence was ahead of us behind the bank, and the street was lined on both sides by delightful old buildings that exuded character.

"I'd like to come back here as tourists one day," Justine said. "For a visit. No crime. No danger."

I looked at her and smiled. "Deal," I responded, and she smiled back at me.

Within minutes, Altmer had taken us through security and we were on our way up to the Chief Operating Officer's suite. Stadler's right-hand man seemed more somber than during my last visit and said very little.

We passed through the assistants' office, and I saw Justine taking in the grandeur of the building and the opulence of the interior.

Altmer led us into Stadler's room. The powerful executive was seated on a couch, reviewing a bundle of papers.

"Mr. Morgan," he declared, rising politely as we entered.

"This is my colleague Justine Smith," I said, and he shook hands with us.

"Very pleased to meet you. Do sit."

Justine and I took the couch opposite his. Altmer sat in the armchair between us.

"Christian says you wanted to see me about something," Stadler began.

I nodded and delivered my lie. "We have reason to believe Elia Antonelli is behind what's happening."

"What reason?" Altmer asked.

"We can't say," Justine replied. I could tell she was studying the young man closely, though in all probability he could not. "But the information checks out."

"Antonelli?" Stadler said. "What does he have to do with dead priests?"

"That's what we're trying to figure out," I replied. "We thought you might be able to help, with all your contacts."

"Does this have anything to do with the priest who was shot?" Altmer asked. "Father Carlos."

Justine and I exchanged a look. Even I knew he had just revealed too much about himself.

"It might do," I conceded. "We just don't know how at this stage." I turned to Stadler. "Are you aware of any links between Antonelli and the Church?"

He shook his head. "Nothing that is known to me personally, but I can ask around. It is possible he has links he does not publicize. I only know about the bank's business."

"I'd appreciate it if you could treat it as a matter of urgency," I said.

"Of course," Stadler replied. "Is there anything else we can help with?"

I looked at Justine, who was studying Altmer. She caught my eye and shook her head.

"I think we're done here," she replied.

CHAPTER 54

"HE WAS REALLY uncomfortable," Justine said to me as we left the headquarters of the Vatican Bank.

"I got that," I agreed.

"Did you see the way he was looking at his boss?" she asked. We started along Via Sant'Anna, heading for the North Colonnade.

I shook my head. I hadn't picked up on any interplay there.

"There's something he doesn't want Stadler to know. Something he's concealing from his superior," Justine said.

"Interesting," I replied. "Could signify he's involved in this in some way. And doing it behind the boss's back."

"That's what I was thinking. Or it could be nothing at all. A task he hasn't completed for work," Justine said. "I doubt it though. It seemed like it was weighing on his mind."

She stopped and looked around at St Peter's, the North

Colonnade and Via Sant'Anna, stretching to our west. "This is really beautiful. Can we stay a while, take a walk?"

I nodded. "Sure."

We turned back the way we'd come and took a snaking cut through from Via Sant'Anna to Via delle Fondamenta, passing the Sistine Chapel and the Papal Residence. Soon we were behind St Peter's, walking alongside the gardens in front of the Governor's Palace, a large four-story structure with wings built either side of a central office block. We wandered on and ended up at Campo Santo Teutonico, unofficially known as the Garden of Secret Confession.

"Is this the place you told me about?" Justine asked.

I nodded.

"What an unbelievable tradition," she observed, walking around the beautifully landscaped space.

"Mr. Morgan," a voice said, and I turned to see Father Vito, the priest I'd first met here, entering the garden. "So good to run into you again."

"Father Vito, this is my friend and colleague Justine Smith."

He nodded to her. "Pleased to meet you, Ms. Smith."

"My pleasure, father," she replied.

"Were you telling Ms. Smith about the garden?" he asked me.

"Yes," I replied. "Well, I'd already mentioned it to her."

"I'm fascinated by the story of this place," Justine said. "The idea that priests would have sins they would be ashamed to confess to God."

"Human beings can be fallible," Father Vito said. "Including some of the most devout. Well, I must attend to my duties. Lovely to see you both."

He turned to leave.

"Father," Justine said. "Could we trouble you for something?"

He hesitated before nodding assent. I wondered what Justine was doing but stayed quiet.

"Do you know what this symbol means?" she asked, producing her phone from her purse.

She caught me looking at her in puzzlement.

"What?" she said. "It's a religious symbol. We should ask a man of God."

I shrugged and she opened the photo folder on her phone, scrolling to a drawing of the Jerusalem Cross tattoo I'd found on the body of the dead assassin.

Father Vito studied the image for a while before exhaling loud and slow.

"You don't want to know this," he said.

"We do," Justine assured him. "We really do."

He looked to me for confirmation and I nodded.

There was suddenly a weariness about him. "It is the mark of Propaganda Tre, a secret society here in Rome," he replied. "They are extremely dangerous. Do you understand? They bring the touch of death with them wherever they go."

CHAPTER 55

"WHAT IS PROPAGANDA Tre?" I asked, grateful for Justine's presence of mind.

"During the Second World War, a group of powerful Italians formed a secret chapter of the Freemasons. It was originally intended to be an anti-communist network if Italy ever fell to the left," Father Vito revealed. "These men were supposed to occupy positions of power—political, financial, criminal, religious—and act against communism if it ever took root. A state within a state to protect the values these people held dear. But communism never came to Italy, so Propaganda Due lost its focus and morphed into a renegade group. It was expelled from the Masonic order and focused on financing right-wing governments around the world, funding this activity by laundering money for organized crime. It was finally dismantled in the early

1980s, after a reign of terror blighting Italian politics and society for almost forty years."

I vaguely recalled reading a review of a book about the group some years ago.

"*Due* means two, *tre* means three. Propaganda Tre is the original group's successor," Father Vito said. "Or at least, that's the rumor. No one really knows much about it."

"But you recognized the symbol?" Justine asked.

"I am a student of Rome. I make it my business to know what goes on in the city. The Jerusalem Cross represents the crusader knights, and the three fleur-de-lys are the three orders of Propaganda, the most recent incarnation symbolized here on the head of the cross."

"Knowledge is power," I suggested.

"Knowledge is knowledge," Father Vito responded without hesitation. "I leave power to the Almighty."

He smiled and I almost envied him his boundless faith in an all-powerful God.

"Well, if you'll excuse me, I have a busy day ahead," he said. "I hope you find what you are looking for."

"Thank you," Justine said.

"Yes, thank you," I told him.

Father Vito left us and we walked on through the Garden of Secret Confession.

"That was a smart move," I said to Justine.

"I figured a priest might recognize the symbol, or at least give us some historical background. I wasn't expecting him to know what it was being used for now."

"I don't think there are many genuine secrets in Rome," I replied. "Too many hidden passages, peep holes, spies, priests, assassins. Too much power flowing through the streets. I think the secrets seep out."

Justine looked at the monuments to God surrounding us. "How can a city so holy be so corrupt?" she asked.

"It's human nature. We're weak," I replied. "Look at this garden. A place for priests to confess sins they wanted to keep hidden from God. Why would this exist if we truly were a strongly pious species?"

"You sound disappointed," Justine remarked.

"I am," I responded. "There was a time I believed humans were closer to the divine than the material."

"And now?"

"Now, I've seen too much of the world."

"I never realized how important all this is to you," she said.

"I didn't realize it myself. It's been a long time since I've thought about these things, but being here in the beating heart of my faith has brought it all back."

"I hope it's not too troubling," she said.

"Troubling? No. More puzzling than anything else. I don't know what to do with it. It's reminded me how far I've drifted . . . how far adrift we all are," I replied.

I took her hand and pulled her to me.

"But you always make me feel better," I said, and she leant closer and we kissed.

"I love you, Jack Morgan," she said before kissing me again. For the briefest moment I had no worries at all.

CHAPTER 56

MO-BOT HAD RENTED a metallic-red Renault Duster. The unremarkable mid-size SUV was equipped with basic comforts such as air conditioning, which fought the worst of Rome's oven-dry heat, but what had interested her most about the vehicle was the large trunk, which she'd filled with newly acquired flight cases that contained the surveillance gear they'd brought with them from Los Angeles.

She was frustrated not to have access to the full equipment store of a local Private office, but Rome wasn't properly open yet. She and Sci would have to make do with the gear they'd brought with them, which was enough to run a decent operation against a single target.

And that target was the Inferno Bar, nerve centre of the merciless Dark Fates.

Mo-bot could see the bar now, both from the observation

vehicle, parked two blocks away on Via Filippo Turati, and on the remote-control screen she was holding, which enabled her to pilot a mini-drone that was currently nearing the building. As before, there was a crowd gathered in the street outside, seemingly unconcerned by the fact that it was barely lunchtime and their alcohol consumption was already veering out of control.

Mo-bot flew the device up higher and took it through an open window on the second floor, into an office furnished with a desk and a row of filing cabinets. She piloted the device, which was not much bigger than a butterfly, into one corner of the room and brought it down on a cabinet, next to an in-tray that would conceal it from all but the most determined observer. She checked the microphone and camera and was satisfied it would give us eyes on the office for at least four days before the batteries ran dry.

"We're all good," Mo-bot said to Sci, who was lying in the fully reclined passenger seat. "Eight micro-drones deployed around the building. You're up."

Sci had unclipped the straps on his boots, so he could recline in comfort. Now he fastened them. He looked every inch the renegade old biker. Sometimes Mo-bot had to remind herself this grizzled road warrior was in fact one of the world's foremost forensics experts.

"Tell me what I'm doing again," he said, using a lever to bring the seat up.

Mo-bot rolled her eyes.

"I'm just kidding," he confessed with a smile.

They climbed out of the Renault and went to the trunk. Mo-bot opened it and took out a heavily worn satchel.

"You have twelve audio and eight audio-visual devices," she said. "Your target is the main bar and public areas."

Drones would have been noticed flying around the bar, so they needed a human asset to install the devices that would complete their surveillance of the Dark Fates.

"Sink a few drinks and catch up with my new biker buddies," Sci suggested. "That sound about right?"

Mo-bot elbowed him. "When are you going to grow up?"

"When someone makes me," he replied, setting off toward the bar.

CHAPTER 57

SCI'S HEART STARTED thumping as he left Mo-bot and walked along Via Filippo Turati toward the Inferno Bar. When he reached the corner with Via Mamiani he turned right and went along the rundown side street, heading for the crowd gathered outside the target. Sci had been in law enforcement long enough to be accustomed to danger and knew a little fear was healthy, just enough to give a person an edge.

This wasn't even in his top ten most dangerous assignments. He was being asked to play himself; a veteran biker, a role that didn't require him to stretch his acting ability. Anyone who knew him was familiar with his love of motorcycles, a passion of his since his early teens. He loved the sense of freedom he gained from being on two wheels, not to mention the speed and acceleration offered by even the most mundane bikes.

When he got about half a block from the Inferno, he relaxed

a little. Like so many biker bars the world over, it was rowdy and attracted big personalities, loud drinkers who didn't adhere to social norms. As if to prove his point, one of the men out front punched his neighbor and the two big guys set to brawling.

Sci held the messenger bag more tightly and wove around the crowd, which surged toward the scuffle. He opened the door and stepped inside the bar, which was the source of the loud heavy metal music that filled the street. The patrons here looked lackluster and depressed, but a couple of them did manage to muster the enthusiasm to go to the windows and doorway to watch the fight.

Sci walked over to the bar and was greeted by a sour-faced bartender.

"Sì?"

"Beer," he replied. "Peroni."

The bartender nodded and grabbed a bottle from the fridge, which he served without a glass.

"Grazie," Sci said.

The bartender asked for five euros, which Sci paid, surreptitiously slipping an audio device under the lip of the counter as he handed over the note.

As the fight outside took people's attention, Sci carried his drink and moved to a booth in the middle of the bar. He slid across the bench seat and placed a bug under the table.

He sat silently drinking his beer for a while before going to the rear of the bar and placing audio-visual devices in the men's room, corridor and outside the kitchen.

Satisfied with his work, Sci returned to the main saloon and his booth only to find a man waiting for him there. He had short gray-flecked hair, evil eyes, a scarred face and a broken nose. Sci recognized him as Milan Verde.

"I've not seen you here before," the man said. "And I know everyone."

"I'm visiting Rome and I read about how great this place is for bikers," Sci replied.

Milan sneered. "Tourist? That's nice. But this isn't really a place for out-of-town visitors."

Sci looked around. "Seems nice enough to me."

Milan pursed his lips before breaking into a thin smile. "I'm going to need to see what's in your bag."

Sci remained impassive.

"New faces are rare in here," Milan continued. "You understand."

Sci slung the old leather satchel off his shoulder and pushed it across the table.

"My girl left me a couple of months back. I forgot her birthday," he said. "I'm getting back on two wheels and into the scene again after years of being with someone who hated bikes, but if that's not something I'm allowed to do here, you just let me know."

Milan opened the bag and peered inside. He frowned and pulled out a bottle of peach schnapps and a Rome guidebook. Sci hoped he didn't delve any deeper and discover the secret compartment beneath the false bottom, where the AV devices were hidden.

"Schnapps?" Milan scoffed.

"My girl switched me onto it," Sci said. He believed cover stories had to have an absurd quality to feel authentic, reflect the absurdity of life. "It's the only good thing she left me with."

Milan returned the bottle and book to the bag. "What do you ride?"

"A Fat Boy, but I have half a dozen other bikes, including an original 1941 Indian Scout.

Milan whistled. "Nice bike."

"Don't I know it."

Milan stared at Sci, holding his gaze with eyes that exuded darkness. Finally, he spoke.

"You can come here whenever you're in Rome."

Sci drained his beer.

"Thanks. It's been fun," he said, standing. "You run a tight place here."

He felt Milan's eyes burning into his back as he walked toward the exit, eager to leave before he did or said something that renewed the man's suspicions.

He didn't feel truly safe until he climbed into the passenger seat of the Renault Duster. Mo-bot had been busy and was cycling through the various surveillance devices, listening to and watching the feeds coming from the Inferno on a small handheld LCD screen.

"Everything okay?" she asked.

"Yeah," Sci said, breathing a sigh of relief. "Everything's fine."

Their gamble had paid off. Soon they would know everything there was to know about Milan Verde and the Dark Fates.

CHAPTER 58

JUSTINE AND I left Vatican City and took stock at the Ristrot San Pietro, a café and restaurant with seats on the sidewalk that offered a stunning view of the dome of St Peter's across Via di Porta Cavalleggeri. The south side of the street where we were sitting was lined with modern apartment blocks, and the north side, across the wide four-lane road, featured buildings influenced by French colonial architecture and the imposing dome of the grand church.

The café was busy with tourists, but we managed to get a table out front. Rather than being an irritation, the busy road beside us was a reminder that we were at the beating heart of one of the most vibrant cities on earth.

"So, we have an assassin connected to a street gang that's tied in with a powerful secret society?" Justine asked.

I nodded.

"And they've been killing priests?" she went on. "A Rome

prosecutor, the first victim we were aware of, Father Brambilla, and they tried to kill Matteo Ricci while he was being held in jail?"

I nodded again. "And in each of those instances they made the deaths look like an accident or from natural causes."

"Apart from Fathers Brambilla and Carlos, who were shot," Justine noted. "So, they are the odd ones out. Their deaths mean something different."

"Yes," I agreed, sipping from my rich roasted double espresso. "Here's the thing—Matteo said someone tried to kill him. In a police station. Well, police headquarters in fact."

"Which means it was someone with access to his cell," Justine remarked. "Or someone with the connections to gain access."

"Exactly," I said. "Come on."

I waved for a waiter, paid the bill, and hailed a cab heading east along Via di Porta Cavalleggeri.

"Via di San Vitale," I told the driver as Justine and I settled on the back seat.

"If Father Vito is right and the Jerusalem Cross marks the rise of a successor to Propaganda Due, we can't trust anyone," she said, as we crossed Ponte Principe Amedeo Savoia Aosta over the Tiber. "Propaganda Due infiltrated every section of Italian society. Its successor will almost certainly have done the same."

I nodded. We'd both done some initial research into the post-war group and it was indeed a powerful underground network. Any organization modelled on it would be extremely dangerous. Propaganda Due had counted government ministers, police chiefs, mob bosses, financiers, press barons and industrialists among its members. A similar group in today's social and political landscape, with a mix of wealth and power plus the ability to manipulate the media offered by new technology, would be formidable.

The taxi deposited us outside police headquarters fifteen minutes later. Justine and I went inside and asked to speak to Mia Esposito. We were told to wait and sat down in the busy lobby, watching the comings and goings of Roman justice.

Tourists and locals came in to file complaints, suspects presented themselves for interview, and harried lawyers bustled in and out of the building, barely seeming to pause for breath as they chatted rapid-fire into their phones.

When Esposito finally came out to see us, she looked just as harassed as one of the defense lawyers we'd been watching.

"I can't give you much time, Mr. Morgan," she said. "My superiors are concerned your colleague may attempt to take his own life again. They want him moved somewhere more secure, but his attorney is challenging our authority."

"Matteo didn't—" Justine began, but I interrupted her.

"We won't take much of your time, Inspector," I assured her. "In fact, we just want to know who the duty officer was when Matteo was found in his cell. We'd like to ask him or her a few questions about the events leading up to the discovery."

"Bernardo Baggio was the duty officer," Esposito replied.

"Can we talk to him?"

Esposito shook her head. "He isn't in today. He must be ill or something."

"Ispettrice Esposito," one of the officers behind the desk called out, beckoning her over.

"Excuse me," Esposito said before walking toward him.

"Jack," Justine said, nudging me.

I followed her eyeline and saw four uniformed police officers come through the door that led to the interview rooms and back offices. The cops' interest in me was unmistakable; they fixed me with gazes that ranged from hostile to predatory. Despite their feigned nonchalance it was clear they were fanning out, trying to block my path to the door.

I looked over at the reception desk to see Esposito conferring with one of the duty officers. He was watching me with narrowed, suspicious eyes.

"I don't like this," I told Justine.

"Neither do I," she agreed. "Let's go."

"Mr. Morgan," Esposito said, turning to us. "I need to talk to you."

The shift in her demeanor was unmissable. Harried cop had been replaced by hunter.

"Come on," Justine said, grabbing my arm and pulling me toward the exit.

"Mr. Morgan," Esposito yelled, and when it was clear we weren't going to listen, she shouted: "Stop! *Arrestate quell'uomo.*"

I didn't need to understand Italian to know she had just ordered my arrest because all four cops sprang toward me, barking out commands.

"Run," Justine yelled, pushing me toward the exit while she stayed behind to slow down my pursuers. "Go, Jack! Run!"

Bewildered, heart pounding, fearful of what might happen to me if I was taken into custody, I did exactly as she said.

I ran.

CHAPTER 59

I BURST OUT of the main doors and immediately collided with two officers coming through the arch. I reacted instinctively, pushing one into the wall opposite. I knocked him out by slamming his head against the stone. The other tried to grab me but I ducked and slipped free from his grasp, delivering a jab and right cross that knocked him flat on his behind.

I heard shouts behind me and the sound of heavy footsteps. I ran on, leaving the injured officers in my wake. Outside I dodged a passing car as I sprinted across the street, hearing shouts behind me as more police officers joined the chase.

I glanced over my shoulder. A group of four, led by Mia Esposito, were racing after me. I ran past the dilapidated buildings opposite police headquarters before turning left and sprinting south along Via Genova. There was more traffic here but the sidewalk was quiet. I made good progress to the next intersection. I burst onto Via Nazionale beside a Guess store and found myself surrounded by pedestrians strolling in the afternoon sun. I had to dodge and weave around them as I turned left and headed east along the busy street.

My pursuers were forced to do the same, but there were more of them and they caused consternation and chaos as they chased me.

I ran across the street, picking my way through a line of traffic heading west, and sprinted along the sidewalk before turning right down Via Venezia.

There was a mother and baby store on the corner of this narrow cobbled street lined with apartment buildings. Just beyond the store was a stone feature, set into the front of the neighboring block, a façade that decorated the first floor. The stones were about a foot tall and stacked like an asymmetric ladder. I realized it would be an easy climb to an open window visible on the second floor and sprinted to the foot of the column.

I grabbed the first stone, which had been hewn from some kind of volcanic rock. It was rough and solid, great for climbing, and whoever had designed the building had left a gap between the first stone column and the rising arch that curved over the adjacent window, so I was able to apply lateral pressure with my left foot, to make me more secure and accelerate my climb. I made it to the windowsill on the second floor as the cops ran into the mouth of the street. They yelled as I thrust myself in at the open window.

I didn't know why they wanted me, but I wasn't going to make the mistake of finding out. I fell into a small kitchen where an old lady was warming milk on a stove. She cried out and said something very fast, but I didn't stop and ran through her apartment to the front door. I opened it and raced into the corridor beyond. My lungs were burning, my arms aching from the climb and my legs were sore, but I kept going.

The corridor beyond was laid with cheap gray carpet and the walls covered by peeling floral paper. I ran past a dozen apartments before I reached the stairwell at the end. When I burst through the door, I heard commotion below me and looked over the guardrail to see Mia Esposito leading her squad of officers in pursuit of me.

"Mr. Morgan! Stay where you are!"

No chance, I thought, as I bounded up the stairs to the next floor.

I ran through the stairwell door into a corridor much like the one below. I sprinted along the old carpet, past a dozen apartments to the door at the end. I burst through to find a twin corridor, the common area of the second wing of this apartment block.

I rushed for an elevator lobby, aware of pounding footsteps and shouts behind me, and turned left through a door marked *Scala* next to an image of stairs. I ran into a stairwell and started down, jumping three or four at a time. I raced down two flights to the ground floor, and when I burst through into the lobby, saw two uniformed officers coming toward me, batons in hand.

Without breaking stride, I grabbed an ancient dust-covered bronze pillar ashtray and swung it at one of the officers, who didn't react in time and took the full force of the blow. It knocked him down.

The second cop tried to parry the blow with his baton, but the pillar caught him with enough force to drive the weapon into his face, knocking him out.

I dropped the ashtray and flew through the lobby, reaching the street as Esposito led her team of cops through the stairwell door.

"Stop!" she yelled, surveying the men I'd incapacitated. "You're only making it worse for yourself."

I doubted that somehow. My colleague had ended up in hospital after being taken into police custody, and there was no way I was giving whoever was behind this the chance to reach me in the same manner.

I ran into the street and tried to flag down a car, but it didn't stop. I sprinted south to the corner of Via Palermo where I saw a motorcyclist getting on his dirt bike. I raced toward him.

The surprised man caught sight of me too late. I yanked him off his vehicle, jumped on, started the ignition, and when the engine roared to life, kicked into first gear and shot away, narrowly avoiding the grasping hands of Esposito and her colleagues.

Her cries for me to stop rang in my ears until they were lost against the sound of the speeding bike and the clamor of the city.

CHAPTER 60

I DESTROYED MY SIM card and dropped my cell phone in a drain on Via Napoli, a few blocks away from police headquarters. Five minutes later, I ditched the motorbike in an alleyway behind Via Urbana. I couldn't run the risk of keeping my phone with me. Even switched off and with the counter surveillance Mo-bot had installed, she'd always said there was still a chance a savvy hacker or law-enforcement agency would be able to use it to find me. And that was a risk I couldn't afford to take. It could put my life in danger, and not just mine, but those of the people I cared for.

This situation was one of the reasons I hadn't wanted Justine, Sci and Mo-bot to come to Rome. They were on the frontline now and were very much at risk.

I moved through the city on foot and bought a pair of mirrored sunglasses and a 'Roma' baseball cap from a souvenir shop.

Looking every inch the tourist, I walked the streets, taking a winding route to the Colosseum. The surrounding streets were full of restaurants and bars heaving with people. The groups spilling out of these places onto the street, and the tourists taking in the sights, gave me plenty of cover and I wasn't worried about any of these good-time folk turning me in to the law. Even if my details had been publicized, these people were the least likely in the city to pay attention to the news.

After wandering around for a while, considering my next move, I found a computer store on Via dei Capocci where there were a couple of Internet terminals for rent by the hour. The sales assistant, a twenty-something woman with long curly dark hair and an uneven smile that suggested she saw tragedy in every joke and comedy in every disaster, showed me to one of the old terminals in the back of the store. They were dusty and didn't look as though they'd been used in a while, which wasn't surprising in the age of cell phones and ubiquitous Wi-Fi.

The assistant returned to the counter at the front of the store and left me to sit through fifteen minutes of software installations and upgrades when I switched on the machine. Finally, with the air in the street outside cooling to the early evening's gentle warmth, I was able to log into Private's secure virtual network and safely access our comms server.

I sent an instant message to Justine, Mo-bot and Sci, and it was Mo-bot who answered first.

Mo-bot: *Where are you?*

Me: *I don't want to say. It could compromise you. Why are the police trying to arrest me?*

Mo-bot: *They say there's new video evidence that implicates you in the death of Father Diaz.*

Me: *That explains it. Is Justine okay? I left her at the station.*

Here Justine joined the chat.

Justine: *I'm fine. The cops held me for an hour, but I cooperated and pointed out I wasn't even in Rome when Father Carlos was killed, so Gianna Bianchi forced them to release me.*

Me: *Good. I'm going to have to stay hidden until this blows over. I'm a risk to you all. Aiding and abetting won't help anyone.*

Justine: *Do you have money?*

Me: *A little under two thousand bucks. Enough for a hotel for a few nights.*

Justine: *Gianna Bianchi is putting pressure on Esposito to reveal the evidence the police claim to have on you. I was thinking of involving the embassy.*

Me: *Good idea. Let me know if you learn anything.*

Justine: *Will do.*

Mo-bot: *Stay safe.*

Justine: *Love you.*

Me: *Love you too.*

Sci entered the chat.

Sci: *Love you too.*

Me: *I'm taken. I'll be in touch as soon as I can.*

Sci sent a smiley face emoji before I logged off. I wiped the computer's history and shut down the machine before leaving to find somewhere safe to spend the night.

CHAPTER 61

JUSTINE SLIPPED HER phone into her purse and tucked it into the gap between the table and the bed. Mo-bot and Sci were in the living room of the grungy little apartment above the cellphone store, watching surveillance footage of the Inferno Bar, but Justine hadn't been able to concentrate since Jack's disappearance.

She had been taken into police custody for a while, not arrested but assisting with their inquiries, and once she'd been released, had spent her time checking the secure message server, praying Jack would get in touch.

Contact had been brief, but it gave her the most important thing of all: reassurance that he was safe. She'd known why he'd run. Matteo Ricci was in hospital after spending time in police custody, and given what they already knew about this investigation, they couldn't trust anyone—including the cops.

Justine checked herself in the mirror. Her red floral-patterned dress was lightweight, perfect for the warm Rome evening. She hadn't been crying, but the color had drained from her face under the strain of the situation. She looked distressed but not distraught, and in any case, had no reason to be embarrassed. Her colleagues in the other room know her better than anyone other than Jack. She couldn't hide anything from them even if she wanted to.

She stepped into the living room and found Mo-bot on the couch with her laptop on her knees. Sci was at the small dining table in front of his machine.

"Good news about Jack," Mo-bot observed, and Justine nodded.

"I don't know," Sci said. "I'm kind of sad he doesn't love me back."

Justine smiled. "You never were any good at reading the room. Do you think now is the appropriate time for humor?"

"He's in forensics. You should hear his dead-body jokes," Mo-bot said.

Sci's smile fell and he lowered his head in contrition. "I'm sorry, Justine. Just trying to lighten the mood."

She scowled at him and then broke into a smile. "Like I'm going to bust your chops over that. You're a sucker, Seymour Kloppenberg."

"Damn!" Sci grinned. "You got me."

"You going to reach out to the embassy?" Mo-bot asked.

Justine nodded. "I'm going to call in a favor from a friend. You got a burner I can use?"

She was referring to a disposable phone that hadn't been used before and was untraceable.

Mo-bot nodded and got to her feet. She walked to one of the flight cases near the kitchen and rooted around.

"How's the surveillance going?" Justine asked.

"Nothing yet," Sci replied, twisting his screen so she could see the video program cycling through feeds from various cameras they'd placed in the Inferno. "Just a bunch of metal heads spending their whole time getting drunk."

"Try this one," Mo-bot said, tossing Justine a cell phone.

She activated the phone's keypad and dialed a number she'd committed to memory.

"Yes," a voice said. It sounded small and distant.

"The secretary, please," Justine responded. "It's Justine Smith."

"Hello, Ms. Smith," a familiar voice said a moment later. Justine recognized the speaker as Eli Carver, US Secretary of Defense. He was a fan of Private and owed Jack a few favors. "I'm in the middle of something."

"Golf?" she asked.

"NATO summit," he replied coolly, "but I'd rather be golfing. How can I help?"

"We're in Rome. Jack is in trouble."

"Mr. Morgan sure does get around," Carver remarked. "And he has a knack for getting in trouble with all the wrong people. What can I do to help him get back on the straight and narrow?"

"I need to talk to the ambassador here. See if we can access evidence the cops claim to have against Jack."

"Rome is Emily Carter," Carver remarked. "I'll make an intro. One of my people will contact you when it's done."

"You can reach me at—" Justine began, but Carver cut her off.

"We know how to reach you, Ms. Smith. We know how to reach everyone."

He hesitated.

"I'm sorry. I didn't mean that to come out as sinister as it sounded. We'll contact you, Ms. Smith. Say hi to Jack for me."

Carver hung up.

"All good?" Mo-bot asked.

Justine nodded.

CHAPTER 62

I SPENT THE night in a dive hotel that was one notch above derelict. There were rodent droppings in the corridor, damp and mold on the walls and rot everywhere, but it was the kind of place that took cash, didn't ask for ID, and couldn't afford to probe too deeply into the backgrounds of its motley clientele. I was sharing the building with drug dealers and sex workers and a selection of street criminals.

The room was shabby but the bed wasn't too bad. I managed to get a decent night's sleep despite my worries. I woke soon after dawn, dressed in new clothes I'd bought the previous evening: jeans and a Rome T-shirt. My shades and baseball cap completed my enthusiastic tourist look.

I was on the street at 6:15 a.m., walking along Via di Porta Maggiore, an ugly road situated between the railway tracks and an old industrial park. I passed other low-cost hotels and hostels, the rundown buildings that housed them all covered in graffiti.

The neighborhood was still in the process of waking up and I didn't have to avoid too many people as I headed south.

An hour later, I was outside the headquarters of *La Repubblica* on Via Cristoforo Colombo. The newspaper was located in a business district south of the city center, where broad avenues and parkland combined to create a sense of space. Via Cristoforo Colombo was a wide road lined with low-rise office blocks, open-air parking and mature trees. I stood on a grassy square in the shadow of a tall fir and watched the entrance of the building opposite. I had no idea whether Faduma would show, but I was prepared to wait until lunchtime. If she didn't come into the office by then, I would track her down offsite.

Thankfully, I saw her drive her Volkswagen into the lot in front of the building a little after 8 a.m. She stepped out of the car, wearing white linen trousers and a red blouse. I hurried toward her as she wove her way through the parked cars and walked over to the newspaper building. There was a security guard in the lobby and other staff filing through the entrance.

"Don't overreact," I whispered as I took her arm.

She glanced at me and spoke through gritted teeth. "Are you crazy? Do you have a death wish, coming here?"

"Why?"

We kept walking south, past the entrance to the building, and she took her phone from her purse.

She held the device in front of me and I saw my own face on-screen.

"This footage was released this morning. Authorities say it implicates you in the murder of Father Carlos Diaz."

My stomach wrapped itself in knots as I watched a video clip of me, taken from inside Chiesa Santa Maria dei Miracoli, the twin church we'd fled to through the secret tunnel. The footage must have been shot by a security camera and in fact showed me trying to help Father Carlos.

In the absence of context, though, it did look as though I might be trying to kill him.

"You know I didn't hurt him," I said, suddenly aware of all the faces around us. I studied them for flashes of recognition. "It's a set-up."

"Of course," Faduma replied. "But you come to Rome's best newspaper when your face is plastered all over the front page? Someone is going to recognize you."

"I didn't know," I said, feeling very exposed.

"Then if you didn't know, why are you here?" she asked. "If it's not about Father Carlos's murder, what do you want?"

"I need to find the cop who was on duty the night Matteo was supposed to have tried to take his own life," I said. "His name is Bernardo Baggio. I need to speak to him."

"At police headquarters?" Faduma asked in disbelief.

"Of course not," I replied, ignoring her mischievous smile. "Not in the circumstances. And besides, last time we checked, he hadn't shown up for his shift."

"I'll see what I can do. There's a little café around the corner, next left, about two hundred meters along. Wait for me there."

I nodded and she left me. I watched her head into the newspaper building, hoping I was right to trust her.

CHAPTER 63

AMBASSADOR EMILY CARTER had a large office on the top floor of the US Embassy in Rome, a beautiful imperial-style building, located in immaculately manicured gardens dotted with high palm trees. It was on the Via Veneto near the Villa Borghese Park. It was a magnificent setting in which to work. Justine admired the gardens and surrounding buildings through the floor-to-ceiling windows that spanned one side of Carter's office.

Justine sat on a severe contemporary leather couch next to Mo-bot and both of them kept shifting position, unable to get comfortable. Justine could see her colleague squirming and couldn't resist a smile.

"What?" Mo-bot asked indignantly. "Who designed this thing? And who even buys something like this?"

"That would be me," Emily Carter said.

She was standing in the doorway leading to her executive assistant's office, and neither Justine nor Mo-bot had noticed her enter.

"Sorry," Mo-bot said. "It's been a difficult night."

"Don't apologize," Carter replied. "I was kidding. It came with the office, probably chosen by my predecessor as a statement piece. I hate it, but I've been so busy I haven't got round to remodeling."

Justine took an instant shine to the fifty-one-year-old former technology executive who'd agreed to lead the President's diplomatic mission in Rome. Emily Carter was charming, polished, funny and intelligent. Her lightweight green tea dress would have been regarded by some as too casual for an ambassador, but to Justine it spoke of having enough self-confidence to ensure her own comfort over outdated convention.

Carter took a seat in an armchair that matched the couch.

"Sorry I was late," she said. "Local situation briefing."

"Intelligence? Maybe a background briefing on us?" Mo-bot remarked, and Carter smiled.

"Maureen Roth and Justine Smith of Private," she said. "What can I do for you?"

"Our colleague Jack Morgan—" Justine began, but Carter interrupted her.

"Hero of Moscow and Beijing. Got himself into trouble here in Rome from what I've seen."

"Yes," Justine replied. "He didn't do what the police are accusing him of."

"Kill a priest?" Carter suggested.

Justine hesitated. "Are you trying to test us, Ambassador? Because this doesn't feel like a friendly welcome."

Carter smiled. "Does either of you sail? I do. The best way to get to know a crew is to sail with them in difficult conditions. Fair weather doesn't show you a person's character. Choppy waters reveal the truth."

"Conditions here are already tough without any extra games," Mo-bot said.

"And I've already learnt so much," Carter replied. "So, tell me what I can do for you?"

"We'd like to know what the police have on Jack. We've seen the footage released to the media, and knowing him as we do, it's clear he was trying to save the man's life," Justine said. "They must have something else on him."

Carter thought for a moment. "That's a reasonable request for any American citizen. Justice and due process. I'd make representations for anyone, but for Jack Morgan, I'll make them at the highest level. Eli Carver speaks well of him. We'll challenge the narrative—see if we can get hold of whatever they've got. Cast Rome police onto those choppy waters."

Justine sat back and breathed a sigh of relief. It seemed her first instincts had been good and Emily Carter was someone she could trust to do the right thing.

CHAPTER 64

FADUMA FOUND ME an hour after we'd parted. I waited in a pedestrianized strip that ran down the center of the avenue opposite the little café she'd suggested as a meeting place, loitering in the shade of an old plane tree. It wasn't that I didn't trust Faduma, but I was being careful and had no idea who she might inadvertently talk to or if she was being watched.

I saw her walk along the sidewalk past shops, restaurants and bars, and she went into the café. I checked the street behind her to ensure she wasn't being followed and moved through the narrow strip of parkland, crossing the road to meet her as she came out.

"Being careful?" she asked.

"Wouldn't you be?" I countered.

"I probably would have left Rome by now," she confessed.

"Someone is making a play to either put you out of commission or get you somewhere they can reach you."

"To put me out of commission permanently," I suggested.

She nodded slowly.

"I'm not easily intimidated," I said.

"I can see that," she replied. "I found Bernardo Baggio's address. He lives at Balduina. It's a suburb in the north-west, about a forty-minute drive from here."

We hurried back to the parking lot around the corner, got in Faduma's Volkswagen, and started our journey through the city. She kept us away from the center and took us on a route that swung west through Gianicolense. She was quiet throughout, clearly uneasy, and every time we stopped at an intersection her eyes darted busily around. I guessed she was scanning our surroundings to make sure no one recognized me. I was in my cap and shades, but my face was all over the news, so I remained equally alert.

We arrived at Via Eutropio just after 10 a.m. The neighborhood featured a mix of contemporary apartment blocks of varying architectural styles, all set back from the road in private gardens that were full of mature trees. Ivy covered the exterior walls and a number of residents had garden balconies, adding to the impression of greenery. The area looked like a lovely place to live.

Bernardo Baggio's building was a five-story contemporary block set behind a high wall and a stand of mature trees. The apartments all had large balconies that overlooked the gardens. Faduma parked in front of the main gate, and we got out of the car and walked toward the entrance.

"How do you want to do this?" Faduma asked.

"You happy to say you're doing a story on Matteo?" I asked. "That you've been told it was a suicide staged by someone who had access to the cell?"

She nodded.

"Then let's play it straight, see how well he copes under pressure," I suggested as we went inside.

CHAPTER 65

BERNARDO BAGGIO'S BUILDING looked to be twenty or thirty years old. Modern, but with enough time elapsed since its construction to have acquired some character. The lobby had a marble tile floor, painted plaster walls and an art deco staircase that ran through the heart of the building, creating an atrium topped by a glass roof. Everything was clean and well maintained and the indoor garden of potted plants added to the impression that the residents took pride in their building. There was a sign for an elevator toward the back of the building, but Faduma and I took the stairs.

"You know we're going to see a cop?" I asked as we climbed. She looked blank.

"Aren't you worried about being caught with a fugitive?"

"I'll just tell them you took me hostage," she said with a mischievous grin.

I chuckled as we reached the second-floor landing.

We walked through a set of ornately decorated doors into a small lobby with corridors running off it in both directions. A sign informed us apartment 23 was to our right. We walked along the carpeted corridor past apartment doors embellished with wooden details of leaves and branches, complementing the decorative cornicing. Modern buildings didn't generally expend much effort on decorative touches like these, but here they added a sense of style.

We found apartment 23 and Faduma rang the bell. I noticed the door wasn't fully in the frame and kicked it gently. It swung open.

"Hello?" I said.

There was no reply, just the stillness of an empty home.

I looked at Faduma, who nodded.

I went first, senses heightened, alert, and she followed. The birds chirping in the trees and cars passing in the street below were audible through the large sash windows, but there was no other sound in the apartment.

The building's fine finish was evident here too as we walked along a corridor with high ceilings. The walls were half wood panel, half painted plaster, with molded reliefs adorning them here and there. The kitchen lay to our left and was tidy apart from some dishes in the sink. Opposite was a dining room with a long table and eight chairs, all of which looked unused. Further to our right was a sitting room, comfortably furnished with two couches before a television that stood in front of the windows overlooking the street.

Further along on the left was a bathroom, and then at the end of the corridor two bedrooms arranged opposite each other.

I took the one on the right and Faduma went into the room on the left.

There was a king-size bed, a dresser, bureau and a built-in closet with mirrored doors. I caught my reflection and removed the cap and opaque shades to reveal a mop of messy hair and tired eyes. I needed a break when this was over and promised myself I'd go somewhere with Justine.

I moved toward the closet and opened one of the sliding doors. I had seen some grotesque things in my life, but nothing could prevent the gasp of shock I released and the shiver of dismay I experienced when confronted with the body of the man I presumed to be Bernardo Baggio. It was hanging from an electrical cable rigged to a clothes rail. He wasn't even off the ground. His knees were simply bent so that his neck took the full strain of his own weight. If he'd been conscious when he'd died, he could have stood up at any moment and chosen life.

"Faduma, I've found him and it's not good. If you come in here, prepare yourself," I said. Moments later she hurried in and joined me.

"Oh my God," she exclaimed. "Poor man."

"We need to call—" I began, but cut myself off when I noticed a red target marker appear on the back of her head.

"Down!" I yelled, grabbing her and pushing her to the floor.

CHAPTER 66

THERE WAS THE quietest of cracks and the tinkling of shattering glass. The bullet hit one of the mirrored closet doors roughly where Faduma had been standing the instant before. The glass shattered into a spider's web of broken pieces.

"Is someone shooting at us?" she asked in disbelief.

"Stay here," I said, before crawling round the bed that gave us both cover.

I pulled myself along on my forearms, just as I had many years before, crawling through mud during my Marine Corps training, and reached the window. I glanced over the lip of the sill and saw the unmistakable shape of a suppressed sniper's rifle in the hands of a man leaning over the balustrade on the roof of the building opposite. He was scouring the windows of the apartment for any sign of us. He spotted me and let fly a couple rounds. The bullets punched holes in the window as I ducked down. They thudded into the side of the bed.

"Count to fifty and then stand up," I said to Faduma. "And immediately duck down again."

She glanced over the bed at me and nodded before disappearing from view.

I crawled out of the bedroom. When I was safely in the corridor, out of sight, I got to my feet and started running.

I sprinted through the front door, along the corridor, and bounded down the stairs. I flew through the lobby and burst into the street just in time to see two flashes above me as the shooter took aim at Faduma and opened fire.

With his attention on her, I ran across the street to the entrance of the building opposite; a modern cream-rendered block. The main entrance was locked, so I pressed all the buzzers. When someone answered, I said, "DHL," and was buzzed in.

I ran across a black-and-white marble checkerboard floor to a bank of three elevators and pressed the call button. The doors of the car on my left slid open and I raced inside and pushed the button for the top floor, number four.

The elevator rose too slowly for someone hunting their would-be killer, but I took the opportunity to steady my breath and was ready the moment the doors opened. I ran into a corridor, headed for the fire door on my right and burst into a concrete stairwell. I sprinted up, taking the steps three at a time, and reached the roof in moments.

Breathing heavily, I paused to listen at the door. Based on my rough grasp of the building's layout, I had worked out that access opened to the rear of the roof. I pushed the bar and eased the door wide, before stepping carefully through the gap.

I closed the door silently behind me and edged round the stairwell structure until I reached the corner. I craned my neck to see the shooter leaning over the balustrade at the front of the building. He had his back to me and was some forty feet away. Not far, but a huge gulf for an unarmed man to cross. My only hope was surprise, and that I'd get sufficiently close to make the long-bareled gun impossible to use.

I crept forward and made it halfway across when the sound of gravel grinding beneath my feet gave me away.

He turned and I recognized him as one of the many hostile bikers I'd escaped from at the Inferno Bar. He was undoubtedly a member of the Dark Fates, sent by Milan Verde to kill us. He had a scar over one eye that ran down his left cheek, close-cut black hair and a scowl that would have made the devil blush.

I sprinted toward him as the shock of seeing me faded and he swung the rifle round.

I dodged the first shot and made it to within striking distance. I parried the gun, sending the second shot wide, and moved in, hurling punches at him. He staggered back, reeling, but quickly recovered. As I came in again, he drove the stock of the rifle into my face, dazing me. I lashed out instinctively and connected with something soft, his neck maybe.

I heard a clatter and as my vision returned, saw the rifle abandoned on the rooftop. I glanced over at the stairwell to see the shooter sprint out of sight.

With my adrenalin reaching fever level, I raced after him.

CHAPTER 67

THE SHOOTER WAS a blur of black jeans and dark gray T-shirt as he ran down the stairs. I followed him, bounding and bouncing off the walls, closing the gap, but saw him fumbling with his waistband and pressed back away from the guardrail when I realized he had a pistol. He waved it in my direction and fired two shots that sounded like thundercracks in the enclosed stairwell.

Being at the wrong end of a gun slowed me down. I hugged the wall as I followed him. He reached the ground floor, ran through the stairwell door and I followed, only to be confronted by the barrel of his gun.

He'd ambushed me.

I knew the advantage would play to him if I lost momentum, so I ducked as he fired, ignored the loud gunshot and the ringing in my ears, grabbed his outstretched arm and twisted it up and inwards, applying enough pressure to break it. He reacted before the bone cracked, cried out, dropped the gun, kneed me in the gut and wriggled free. Winded, I picked up the pistol and sucked in breath as I ran after him.

He sprinted onto the street and waved down a car, which screeched to a halt as he stepped in front of it. He pulled the unwitting driver, a terrified woman in her fifties, from her seat and jumped into the Alfa Romeo Giulia.

I reached the street as he accelerated away and brandished the gun at the driver of a BMW 3-Series that had been forced to stop behind the Alfa. The driver, a man in his thirties, came out scowling, but stepped back as I jumped in.

I gunned the engine and the car roared like an animal as I set off after the shooter.

He was reckless, racing along Via Eutropio, past parked cars on either side, before performing a screeching handbrake turn onto Via Appiano, a wider street that was flanked by smaller, more tightly packed apartment blocks. The gunman accelerated, weaving around slower- moving cars, mounting the sidewalk, blasting his horn to urge people to jump clear. He shot beneath a bridge and raced downhill, weaving around a delivery truck. I followed more cautiously, eager not to hurt anyone but keen to keep within striking distance.

The tires screeched as I swerved around a Mercedes, the shocked face of the driver receding apace in my rear-view mirror as the BMW surged forward, chasing the shooter onto Piazza Giovenale, a small square with a playground at its heart. He went round the square the wrong way, dodging oncoming vehicles, and turned left on Via Ugo de Carolis.

I heard a bone-crunching crash and slowed as I approached the intersection. I saw the crumpled wreck of the Alfa concertinaed against the back of a garbage truck.

The shooter, dazed and disoriented, bleeding from a gash on his head, was tamping down the driver's airbag and struggling to get free of the vehicle.

I stopped the BMW, unclipped my seat belt and jumped out. The sight of me approaching spurred him on and he got to his feet, staggered a few steps and started running along the street, ignoring the shouts of the garbage workers who were understandably upset by the crash.

I followed, pushing through the gang of uniformed men and onlookers, and raced after the shooter. I tucked the pistol in my waistband. There was no way I'd even threaten to use the weapon as an attempt at intimidation when there were so many innocent people around.

The shooter was limping and I was closing the gap between us. He kept glancing back and looked increasingly dismayed and agitated to see me gaining on him.

We were approaching the intersection with Via Filippo Nicolai, and a crowd of pedestrians was gathered on this side of the street, poised to go south.

The shooter pushed his way through the crowd until he was at the very edge of the crosswalk. He glanced back at me and, very deliberately, stepped off the sidewalk into the path of a speeding dump truck.

CHAPTER 68

I STOOD IN silence for a moment, reeling at what I'd just seen, while people all around me screamed and backed away from the horror. This was the second member of the Dark Fates to have taken his own life rather than risk being captured. Whatever indoctrination these men had undergone was sufficiently powerful to subvert the most basic human instincts. Survival is at the heart of who we are, and to see a core trait so hideously twisted was deeply troubling to me. Could my own belief system ever be subverted like that?

I pulled myself together and in the moment of calm that followed the scattering of the shocked crowd, and the bewilderment of the truck driver and motorists who'd ground to a halt either side of the macabre scene, I ran forward. Under the pretext of checking whether the shooter was alive, I took his wallet and phone from the bloody remains.

"He's dead," I yelled as I stood. "Someone call an ambulance."

I could already hear sirens and knew that was my cue to leave. I pressed through the crowd reconvening on the sidewalk some distance from the crushed body, and when I broke the edge of the cluster of people, jogged along the street and then retraced my steps to Bernardo Baggio's building, pulling the cap and mirrored sunglasses from my pocket and putting them on.

I found Faduma loitering outside, looking lost and uncertain. She brightened when she saw me.

"What happened?"

"I almost caught him, but he jumped in front of a truck," I replied.

"Like the last guy," Faduma remarked.

I nodded. "Whatever this group is, they've got a real hold on the minds of these men."

"What now?" she asked.

"I need to contact Mo-bot. I've got the guy's personal possessions."

I produced his wallet and phone. "I need them analyzed. See if we can find out who was giving him orders."

"Milan Verde, surely?"

"I'd like to be certain," I told her. "Where is the nearest Internet café?"

Faduma shook her head. "Are you from the nineties? Use this."

She produced a Silent Circle Blackphone. I was familiar with the model. Mo-bot said they weren't completely reliable at preventing tracking and data theft, but combined with Private's secure network, it would suffice in the circumstances.

I used the phone to log into Private's virtual network and accessed the messaging platform.

Me: *I need to meet.*

Justine: *Where?*

"Where should we meet?" I asked Faduma. "Somewhere public with lots of people."

"Centro Commerciale Aura," she replied. "It's a shopping mall not far from here."

Me: *Centro Commerciale Aura. Food court. One hour.*

Justine: *Okay.*

I disconnected, cleared the cache as an extra precaution, and returned the phone to Faduma.

"Thanks," I said.

"No problem," she replied. "When are we meeting them?"

"In one hour. The mall should give us plenty of cover."

One hour later, as Faduma and I walked through the beautiful glass and lattice metalwork entrance to the mall on Viale di Valle Aurelia, I started to regret my decision. There were so many people around, it was impossible to secure early warning of a threat. But I told myself the throng of people would work in my favor too, masking Faduma and me, giving us cover from prying eyes.

We followed the mass of pedestrians heading along the

walkway between the luxury stores, high-end clothing boutiques, and fragrance shops that filled the air with the sweetest scents.

Adrenalin flooded my body, heightening my perception as we took the escalator up to the next level. I scanned the eyes of the people around me, particularly those riding the down escalator, but there wasn't the slightest flicker of recognition from anyone.

Faduma and I made it to the food court and saw Sci, Mo-bot and Justine seated at a large round table next to a luxury bakery and sandwich bar. There was a fire exit behind them. I couldn't imagine the choice of table was accidental. The green door offered a quick escape route.

I saw Justine register our arrival and draw Mo-bot's and Sci's attention to us. Looking back on that moment, I'm not sure whether that was the trigger or whether the cops had simply picked us up as we arrived, but when we got within a few feet of the table, the food court was swarmed by police officers, most of them not in uniform, who had been seated at adjacent tables. They ran at us, shouting, weapons raised.

Mo-bot got to her feet and walked toward them, saying, "What the heck is this? What do you guys want?"

She was roughly manhandled and handcuffed, but the distraction bought us a heartbeat's reprieve. I grabbed Faduma and pulled her through the fire door.

I ignored the commands to stop. When I glanced over my shoulder, I saw Sci and Justine, face-down against their table, being handcuffed.

Every fiber in me wanted to go to Justine's aid, but Faduma pulled me away.

"Come on!" she said. "You can't help her if you're dead."

I nodded and ran after her as she raced down the stairs. Above us, I heard the hammer of footsteps, but we had a decent head start and reached the ground floor quickly.

We burst through the fire door, startling two cops who had obviously been given what they thought was the light duty of standing guard by an emergency exit.

I grabbed the larger of the two and slammed his head against the door, dazing him. As he fell to his knees, I unclipped his pistol and drew it on his colleague.

Faduma spoke in Italian and clearly told the men to lie down because that's what they did.

I heard shouts coming from the stairwell and looked around urgently. I caught sight of an elderly couple walking to their car, a classic sky-blue Peugeot 505, parked in a disabled space.

"Come on," I said to Faduma, and we ran over to the man and woman.

I grabbed the car keys from the man's hand and Faduma and I jumped in the beautifully maintained old car before the guy had really registered what had happened.

He started yelling as I turned the ignition, and the prone cops got to their feet and staggered toward us just as the pursuing officers burst out of the fire exit and ran our way.

I put the Peugeot in gear, floored the accelerator and we shot to safety, leaving a dozen angry people yelling in our wake.

CHAPTER 69

FADUMA AND I abandoned the Peugeot a couple blocks away. Other than the engine enduring a bit of a workout, the car was unscathed, thank goodness. I didn't feel great about the theft, but sometimes doing the right thing under intense pressure involves breaking a few rules.

We cut across the grounds of a school, hopped a fence and saw the number 31 bus heading south along the Via Anastasio II.

"That will take us west out of the city," Faduma said, flagging down the vehicle as she ran toward the stop.

We climbed aboard, paid the fare and settled into seats near the back as the bus rolled on. We saw heightened police activity everywhere, patrol cars speeding in the opposite direction, beat officers being mustered to checkpoints, and a helicopter in the sky.

We had just driven through an underpass when Faduma's cell phone rang. She pulled it from her purse.

"Unknown number," she said, before answering.

She listened for a moment.

"Police," she whispered. "They want to know if I'm okay."

I reached over and took her phone.

"Faduma Salah is my hostage. I will only release her when my demands are met. I will be in contact soon," I said before hanging up.

I slid the phone down the side of my seat and stood.

"Come on," I said.

"My phone," she protested.

"I'll buy you a new one."

I pressed the bell and walked to the exit as the bus slowed. Faduma followed grudgingly.

"Did you really have to do that?" she asked.

"Which bit? The hostage? Or leaving your phone?"

"Both," she said as the doors lurched open with a pneumatic hiss.

"You gave me the idea," I said. "It absolves you of any wrong-doing. And you know I couldn't let you keep your phone. No matter how secure it's supposed to be."

She nodded and sighed as we left the bus.

"What now?" she asked while the vehicle rumbled away.

"I need to get the surveillance gear from the apartment," I said. "No one is watching Milan Verde and the Dark Fates. We have no idea what they're doing. If I can review the footage, I might be able to see who sent that man to kill us at Baggio's apartment."

"I'm guessing the cops followed your friends after Justine was released from custody," Faduma remarked. "So, the apartment is probably being watched."

I nodded. "We'll just have to be careful. And maybe a little cunning."

"You're dangerous, Jack Morgan."

"Hold that thought," I responded, hurrying toward a payphone beside a petrol station.

I stepped into the booth, swiped a credit card through the slot and dialed the operator.

An automated announcement played in Italian and I handed Faduma the receiver. She listened and then spoke in Italian.

"Who do you want?" she asked me.

"Gianna Bianchi," I replied. "The attorney."

I heard Faduma repeat the name along with some instructions in Italian. After a short pause she handed the receiver back to me.

There was a ringing tone and a woman's voice said, "*Bianchi avvocatessa.*"

"Gianna Bianchi, please. Tell her it's Jack Morgan."

I was connected almost immediately.

"Jack, what's going on? The things they're saying on the news—"

"They're not true," I interrupted Gianna. "Someone has done a great job of setting me up. Listen, I need you to do me a favor. My colleagues Seymour Kloppenberg, Maureen Roth and Justine Smith have just been arrested at Centro Commerciale Aura. Do whatever you can to get them released. They've done nothing wrong."

"Of course," Gianna said.

"And you should probably let the cops know one of their own is dead. Bernardo Baggio is hanging in his closet. I think it's murder staged to look like suicide."

"Why?" Gianna asked.

"He was on duty the night Matteo is supposed to have tried to kill himself."

I could sense her putting the pieces together.

"I'll inform the authorities," she assured me. "What about you? Come in. We'll challenge the accusations."

"Not yet," I replied. "I can't risk what happened to Matteo and Baggio happening to me. I need to take care of a few things."

She hesitated.

"I understand. But I have to advise you to turn yourself in."

"You've done that. Now do whatever you can to get my friends out. I'll be in touch."

"Be careful," she advised before I hung up.

I turned to Faduma.

"Everything okay?" she asked.

I nodded, my mind whirring, my body still charged with adrenalin.

"Just trying to figure out how we get inside an apartment that is probably under tight police surveillance."

CHAPTER 70

I TRIED TO encourage Faduma to leave me but she refused to listen, saying she would never bail on a story like this. I couldn't help feeling there was more to it, that there was a sense of honor guiding her, compelling her not to abandon me. It was a sentiment I shared. I'd never abandoned a case.

She took me to a tiny basement bar in Poggio del Torrino, a neighborhood that lay between the center of Rome and Ostia, and we passed the evening there with a handful of heavy drinkers who spent enough on alcohol to keep the place going. The bar was called Il Tucano and was set beneath a modern apartment block. It was the kind of watering hole where people drank alone and purposefully, determined to achieve oblivion. While I'd hesitate to label strangers alcoholics or problem drinkers, these folk certainly weren't fair-weather.

Faduma and I sat in a booth in a back corner of the bar,

nursing a steady stream of Cokes, coffees and water to ensure the taciturn old barman, who looked as though he'd soaked up many lifetimes of misery, didn't kick us out.

No one paid us any mind and for a while I was able to forget I was a wanted man whose face had been beamed across the airwaves and the Internet.

"You don't have to do this," I said to Faduma.

"You keep telling me that, and I keep telling you I want to be here."

"You're risking so much," I responded.

"And you?" she asked. "Why do you have to be here?"

I hesitated.

"I don't," I conceded. "But if I wasn't here, who would find the truth? Who would protect Matteo from wrongful conviction? I can't stand by if there's a chance an innocent man might be jailed."

She nodded slowly. "Do you know what it's like to come to a country as a refugee? To be spat on? Told you're inferior? To be abused? Ridiculed? Told you aren't welcome? That you have no worth?"

I shook my head. I couldn't imagine experiencing any of those things and was suddenly conscious of the privilege life had granted me.

"It can break a person," Faduma said, and I couldn't be sure in the low light of the bar but I thought her eyes were glistening. "Or it can build strength. It can teach you to know when the crowd is wrong and when those less fortunate than you need help. Rome is hunting you, Mr. Morgan, and for someone who grew up being marginalized by Rome, that is reason enough for me to stay."

We remained in our booth until the last of the swaying customers staggered out and the barman finally presented us with the bill shortly after 1 a.m. We stepped onto Viale degli Astri, a wide avenue lined with palm trees and modern apartment blocks, and the warm air hit us along with the echoes of drinkers and diners making their way home along the otherwise quiet streets. We walked through a small park that lay to our east and caught a taxi from an office set in the foot of an apartment block on Viale Don Pasquino Borghi.

About five minutes into our journey, as we reached the open highway that would take us to the coast, I noticed the driver, a short, stocky man with stubble and the hungry expression of a hyena, kept glancing at me in the rear-view mirror and every so often his gaze would linger. I could see my face in the mirror, lit up now and again by the headlamps of vehicles coming along the carriageway on the other side of the median.

"Five hundred," the driver said at last.

"*Mi scusi?*" Faduma responded.

"For a safe journey," he explained. "It seems a fair price for your friend."

And there it was. His eyes were on me not because he was a conscientious citizen thinking of turning me in, but because he was calculating how much he could extort for his silence.

Faduma said something in Italian. She sounded angry, but I interrupted her.

"That's a fair price," I said. "I'm assuming it buys your silence forever."

"That's another five hundred," the greedy man replied.

I nodded. "Okay."

Fifteen minutes later, he pulled to a halt on Via Ottavio, a quiet residential street in Ostia.

"One thousand," he said, turning with his hand held out expectantly.

"The meter says thirty euros," I remarked.

He scowled and waved his phone menacingly. "Police."

"You know why they're hunting me," I said, leaning forward so my face was inches from his. "They say I killed a priest. Go ahead and make the call, Paolo Sachetto." I gestured at his license displayed on the dash. "My friends and I will know exactly where to find you."

His bravado crumbled. I handed him fifty euros.

"A generous tip for such a comfortable ride," I said, before getting out.

"Remind me never to cross you," Faduma said as she joined me on the sidewalk.

We waited for the taxi to leave before heading for Via Orazio, ten minutes away. We walked on arm-in-arm, playing the part of lovers coming home from a date.

As we got closer to the cell-phone store, we feigned chit-chat but were in fact pointing out potential risks to one another.

"Van, twenty feet from the store," Faduma said, touching my arm as though she was telling me how much she loved me.

"I see it," I replied, and we crossed the street and walked behind the empty market stalls opposite the terrace where the store was located.

Faduma was nearest the van and kept her head turned toward me, providing me with good cover so I wasn't easy to see from the vehicle. But by leaning around her briefly, I caught a glimpse of two men in the cab, their faces lit by the glow of the gaudy lights in the store window.

"It's not the cops," I said, surprised by the fact I recognized the men. "I know these two. They were at the Inferno. They're members of the Dark Fates."

We walked more quickly and took a left down Via Stefano Cansacchi.

"Why aren't the police watching the apartment? Why is it being staked out by gangsters?" Faduma asked.

"My guess is the Rome police force is even more compromised than we thought," I replied. "Someone high up must have told the cops to back off in order to give these guys a clear run."

We stopped and turned to look back at the bright lights of the cell-phone store.

"They're going to have at least one pair of eyes on the rear of the building too," I said. "So I'm going to need you to create a distraction."

CHAPTER 71

FADUMA WAS ABLE to buy almost everything we needed from the cell-phone store. She got the two-liter bottle of soda from a mini-mart down the street, emptied the contents into a drain, and followed the instructions I'd given her. Phone-cleaning cloths soaked in lighter fluid, fused lithium cell-phone batteries stuck in the bottle with its top cut off, and matches were all it took to create the distraction.

I watched her approach the van from the rear, strike a match and set the device on fire. The cleaning cloths caught instantly and she shoved the device under the rear wheel, beneath the fuel cap, and ran.

The guy in the passenger seat noticed the flames first and alerted his companion. Both men jumped out of the vehicle and ran to the burning device, which wasn't what I'd had in mind because the batteries would be unstable and could explode at any moment.

But I took advantage of the distraction and hurried across the street and down the alleyway that led to the metal stairs behind the building. As I glanced over at the van, I saw the passenger hurl the flaming device across the street. It exploded in mid-air, knocking both men down, shattering nearby car windows and setting alarms ringing.

I raced into the darkness of the alley and encountered a man coming the other way. I had no doubt it was a Dark Fates lookout drawn to the explosion. He almost ran into me, but I saw his silhouette against the light beyond the alleyway and swung at him. My fist connected with tremendous force, his own momentum carrying him into the punch, and he groaned and fell instantly.

I stepped over him and ran on, reaching the rear of the building. There was no one else around, so I climbed the stairs carefully and found the front door of the apartment ajar.

I took a moment to catch my breath and compose myself before creeping inside. The hallway was dark but there was low light coming from the living room. I moved cautiously and silently toward it.

I could hear the sound of chaos rising from the street, car alarms, people shouting, and in the distance approaching sirens.

I didn't have long.

When I craned my head round the door frame, I saw the silhouette of a man at the window, watching the street outside. Sci's and Mo-bot's computers were on the table and had been connected to a hard drive. I could see status bars on both screens showing the progress of data being downloaded.

I moved toward the man at the window, noting the fleur-de-lys tattoo on his forearm that marked him out as a member of Propaganda Tre. He must have sensed me because he turned and tried to pull a gun from his waistband.

I rushed forward, blocked his draw and headbutted him. As he staggered back I kicked his knee, causing him to hunch over, and drove an uppercut into his chin with so much power his head snapped up and his eyes rolled back, before he fell in a heap.

I looked out the window to see flashing blue lights rising above the buildings a few streets away.

I grabbed Sci's holdall from the bedroom, put the laptops inside along with the hard drive, and then stuffed the bag with all the surveillance gear I could fit inside, before slinging it over my shoulder and racing out of the apartment.

I ran along the alleyway, avoiding the fallen gang member, and emerged onto the street as the first police car rounded the corner.

I went the other way, heading west, and passed the two Dark Fates members who were lying on their backs in the road, trying to come to their senses.

I walked on as tires screeched behind me. I saw the cop car pull to a halt and the two officers jump out. Behind them came more cars, and locals who had been watching from their windows drifted into the street as the area became a major crime scene.

"Jack," Faduma whispered.

I saw her hiding in the shadows of a doorway near the intersection with Via Stefano Cansacchi.

She joined me as I passed and together we marched to the corner.

"Everything okay?" she asked, glancing back.

I nodded.

"I got what we came for," I said as we hurried into the night.

CHAPTER 72

"I'VE NEVER KNOWN anyone need a second safehouse so quickly," Valentina said. "You're quite a celebrity here in Rome."

I shifted awkwardly as we waited for the Italian hacker's friend Amr Badawi to unlock the roll shutter of the warehouse that was to be my new temporary home.

"The clever stray is the one who isn't seen," Amr added, and I tried not to take offense at him comparing me to a dog.

"Yes," I conceded. "My notoriety is less than ideal. And I'm sorry about your other place."

"Don't worry about it," Amr replied, working the rusty lock. "The police haven't linked anything to the apartment. They think the Dark Fates were planning a hit on someone, and if there was police involvement in letting the gang conduct surveillance, whoever was behind it is not going to come forward with the truth."

Amr managed to force the lock and opened the smaller of two roll shutters at the front of this seemingly deserted warehouse. It was just big enough for people to enter the building, while the larger twenty-foot-wide shutter next to it was clearly designed for freight.

Amr switched on the lights as we stepped inside and illuminated a 60 x 100-foot space filled with boxes of LCD screens and other electronics.

"One of the places I keep stock," he explained. "Please don't damage anything."

Faduma gave me a disapproving look as I raised my hands in mock deference.

"I won't do anything," I said.

"There's an apartment upstairs. Three bedrooms, living room, kitchen," Amr said. He handed me the key. "The lock sticks, but you'll get the hang of it."

"Thank you," I replied.

"As I said before, it's a business arrangement, Mr. Morgan," he responded. "There is no need for thanks. You are a profitable guest. Trouble, but profitable."

Valentina nudged him. "Don't let Amr fool you with his hard-nosed persona. He likes helping people, particularly people he likes. He has a big heart."

Amr smiled bashfully. "Don't listen to her lies about the size of my heart. But I do hope you'll be safer here, Mr. Morgan."

"Thank you," I told them both.

"I'd do anything for Mo-bot," Valentina said. "I owe her."

"She's in Rome," I revealed. "In police custody, I think."

"Why? What for?"

"Knowing me," I replied.

"I hope she's okay," Valentina said. "I'll ask around. See if I can find out where she is. Come on, Amr, let's get out of here before he gets us busted."

They left the warehouse and I closed the shutter, sealing myself and Faduma inside. We were in another part of Ostia, this neighborhood even more rundown than the first, and I didn't want to invite any trouble, particularly as the entrance could be seen from the road. The warehouse was located on Via dell'Idroscalo, a road that ran through the estuary marshes to the north of Ostia center, and the building and surrounding industrial estate backed onto the River Tiber.

Twenty minutes later, Faduma and I were in the living room of a musty apartment above the offices at the back of the warehouse. We had a view of the estuary from here and could see the bright lights of buildings on the other side of the river.

Faduma sat beside me on a frayed old couch, the floral pattern bleached by the sun. I'd set up Mo-bot's and Sci's computers and was analyzing the hard drive that had been connected up to them. The guy I'd knocked down had been trying to steal data from the machines and was copying the hard drives of both computers, clearly intending to mine them for everything and anything useful. He had a disk-wipe program set up and ready to execute. I was relieved he had prioritized the theft otherwise we'd have lost the surveillance footage being recorded from the devices planted around the Inferno Bar.

As it was, the footage seemed intact, right up to the moment

Milan Verde discovered and destroyed the bugs. There were multiple final shots of angry, hostile members of the Dark Fates finding the cameras, snarling into the lenses and cursing before reaching up to send the transmission dark for the very last time.

"So, they found the cameras," Faduma remarked.

I nodded. "And the listening devices. Thankfully the guy wasn't able to wipe the hard drives, so we can see what was recorded while Sci, Mo-bot and Justine have been in custody."

I set up multiple windows so we could view simultaneous feeds from most of the cameras and started scrubbing back through the footage.

It was painstaking work, and my eyes were heavy with tiredness that only pulled at me more as the adrenalin of the night ebbed away. I could sense Faduma's fatigue, but like me she fought through it.

"There," she said, and I followed her pointing finger to see a man in a suit enter the bar.

I paused the videos. The timecode showed he'd arrived at 2:13 p.m. He looked uncomfortable and out of place.

I pressed play and the videos ran forward simultaneously. It wasn't until the awkward-looking man approached the bar that I saw his face.

It was Christian Altmer, Joseph Stadler's executive assistant, the man Justine had flagged as having something to hide. My mind raced, wondering what a respectable banker was doing in the lair of one of the most dangerous gangs in Rome.

CHAPTER 73

WHATEVER ALTMER WAS doing at the Inferno Bar, neither he nor Milan Verde wanted anyone to know about it. The brutal gang leader came in a couple of minutes after Altmer arrived, greeted him like an old friend, put an arm around his shoulders and shepherded him outside.

Milan returned fifteen minutes later, alone.

There was nothing else in the footage, and for a while Faduma and I puzzled over the incident with Altmer.

"You think they're laundering funds through the Vatican Bank?" she asked.

"That's a step up for a street gang," I replied.

"Or a step down for a bank," she countered. "Some institutions are desperate for liquidity though."

"I don't know," I said. "But what I do find interesting is that this meeting took place after Mo-bot, Sci and Justine were taken into custody. Did they know they were being watched at this point? Were they counting on being able to delete the footage before Justine and the others were released?"

Faduma shrugged, but I couldn't help feeling the heat of anger building within me. I considered the prospect that someone working for a client might have set us up for arrest or worse.

Faduma stretched. "I'm going to sleep," she said. "My place is probably too dangerous, so I'll take a bedroom if that's okay?"

I nodded. "Of course."

She got to her feet and headed along the corridor toward the bedrooms. I stared at the image of Altmer, puzzling over the man and his intentions until finally, in the early hours, bereft of answers, my anger smoldering, I fell asleep.

The following morning, I woke on the couch, the computer in sleep mode, the rising sun shining brilliantly through the large windows, the river shimmering beyond.

I stood, stretched and walked along the corridor to the bedrooms. The doors were all open and there was no sign of Faduma, although the bed clothes in the middle room looked to have been slept in.

I heard a noise coming from behind me and crept into the living room to discover her coming in from the main warehouse. She was holding a large paper bag packed with groceries.

"I got some breakfast," she said, placing the bag on the table.

She started pulling out juice cartons, pastries and spreads.

"I was thinking about Christian Altmer," she said. "How would you like the chance to talk to him?"

CHAPTER 74

ROME IS FULL of mysteries that extend beyond the metaphysical into the physical. How did the emperors and senators flee from a siege and escape to their homes in the provinces? Or the old Renaissance families hide from civil unrest?

Secret tunnels like the one linking Basilica di Santa Maria in Montesanto and Chiesa Santa Maria dei Miracoli, the church where Father Carlos had died, run beneath the city like veins, a physical manifestation of the intrigue and mystery that has been the city's lifeblood for centuries.

Faduma and I took a taxi from Ostia to Via Angelo Emo, a busy street a few blocks from the western edge of Vatican City. She led me past shops and offices until we reached the mouth of Via Giovanni Secchi, a narrow sidestreet that bent sharply before running east. We followed it past a line of modern five-story apartment blocks until we came to a dead end. The street was fringed by thick greenery; bushes and trees packed tightly together beneath the ancient Fornaci Viaduct, a tall, multi-arched brick causeway that ran toward Vatican City.

Faduma guided me through the thick mass of undergrowth and I thought I could discern the faintest of paths as we pushed on. Suddenly we came to a clearing beneath the viaduct, a stretch of stone under one of the arches. It looked like a storm drain and followed the line of the viaduct above us. Faduma turned into it, heading toward the brick column that formed one side of the arch we were standing in. When we got closer, I realized it was a freestanding wall, designed to look like part of the arch, and that there was in fact a one-foot gap between the wall and the viaduct structure. As we edged into the gap, I saw granite steps leading into the ground, beyond the line of the viaduct, past the foundations. When we reached the bottom of the steps, we found an ancient cobblestone well capped with a manhole cover.

We were about sixteen feet below ground level, and the area around the well was cool, damp and shaded. Moss grew on the walls and the stone beneath our feet was wet. Faduma knelt down and brushed away some drifts of leaves to reveal cobblestones interspersed between the big flagstones. She counted three stones across and one up, then applied pressure to it. The stone gave under her touch. As it dropped, the manhole cover rose and I realized it was on a runner. I pulled it round, revealing a spiral staircase.

Faduma went down it and found a light switch. I followed, closing the manhole cover as she brought a row of lights to life.

When I reached the bottom of the stairs, I peered along a narrow gray stone tunnel that felt as old as the city itself.

"How did you know about this?" I asked.

"I've been smuggled into the Vatican in the past," she replied. "When the Church wanted a favorable view of the restitution it made to victims of abuse. I didn't give them the puff piece they were looking for, but the route they used to smuggle me in is something I've never forgotten."

I shrank inside a little at this mention of one of the great crimes of history, and one of the reasons my faith had waned.

"They did not want to be seen consorting with someone who had been so outspoken in criticizing the Church, which was why they brought me this way."

"Why didn't you write what they wanted?" I asked as we moved along the tunnel.

Faduma's nose crinkled as she thought about this.

"The Vatican is where the temporal is supposed to touch the divine. The Holy Father is God's appointed representative on earth, but he is still bound to the same soil as the rest of us. All clergy are, and if we are fallible so are they. Crimes are to be expected in any human population," she said. "Where the Church went wrong was in failing to honor the victims and give them the justice that is at the heart of Christianity. Instead, some members of the clergy at the highest level tried to cover up the abuse and sweep the victims under the rug."

I nodded. Humans are fallible and some are evil, but the Church is meant to embody all that is best in us and protect those too weak to protect themselves. In that respect it had been a major disappointment to me.

We walked along the tunnel and climbed three flights of steps that tracked the slope of the hill beneath Vatican City. The stairs were steep and long, the ceiling low, so that we almost felt the weight of the city pressing down on us.

Finally, we reached a dogleg in the tunnel, which was now blocked by an ancient metal grille.

"This brings us out near the Gallery of the Candelabra, not far from the bank," Faduma said, running her fingers along the wall until she found a particular stone, which she pressed to unlock the barrier.

She swung it open and we stepped out into a narrow alleyway between two red-brick walls. I followed her along this until we reached the end and emerged from the narrow alleyway to see the Gallery of the Candelabra, a long gray building famed for the paintings it housed. We saw a couple priests walking together, chatting, and when they had moved out of sight, we took the deserted lane that would lead us to the headquarters of the Vatican Bank.

We passed under an archway that led us into one of the Vatican's car parks and joined Via Sant'Anna near the bank. We walked around the semi-circular building and found a stairwell in the adjacent block leading to a basement. Here we stood a few steps down, so we could watch the bank entrance without being seen ourselves.

We waited there for an hour, hardly talking, to minimize the risk of giving away our location. The Swiss Guard and Vatican police each conducted one routine sweep of the courtyard ahead of us and the streets nearby, but we ducked into the stairwell on both occasions and remained undisturbed in our hiding place until 8.15 a.m. when Christian Altmer walked through the courtyard in front of us on his way to the bank.

I left our hiding place immediately and headed straight for him. He turned when I was almost within touching distance, face contorting in shock as he registered me and then Faduma, a few paces behind.

"What are you doing here?" he asked. "Are you crazy?"

"I want the truth," I said. "I know you're working with the Dark Fates. Are you a member of Propaganda Tre?"

"I can't talk about these things. Not here," Altmer protested. "You have to leave."

"Not until you tell us the truth," I responded.

"Hey!" a man yelled, and I turned to see the Vatican police officers who'd swept the courtyard, approaching from Via Sant'Anna.

"You have to go. For your own safety," Altmer said, as the men started running toward us. "I'll meet you at the Basilica di San Giovanni in Laterano tonight at ten. Now go!"

I hesitated.

"Run!"

"Listen to him, Jack," Faduma implored. "Go! I'll try and slow them down. Just go!"

I took her advice and started running.

CHAPTER 75

I SPRINTED SOUTH, across the courtyard, away from the police officers and through a small parking lot toward a high wall and the San Pellegrino Gate, which opened onto the North Colonnade and St Peter's Square. When I glanced over my shoulder, I saw Faduma intercepting the two Vatican police officers, hands raised, arms outstretched, yelling in Italian. Christian Altmer retreated inside the Vatican Bank Headquarters.

The border officers at the San Pellegrino Gate noticed me, and their colleagues pushed past Faduma and yelled at them in Italian. The gate officers started moving toward me as their colleagues resumed pursuit, so I veered east toward the wall. I jumped onto the hood of a delivery wagon, stepped onto its roof and leapt up to grab the lip of the high wall that marked the perimeter of St Peter's Square.

I ran along the top, ignoring the shouts of my pursuers, and clambered onto a battlement, before jumping down into a concrete yard on the other side.

My path was blocked by high walls that ran around three sides of the 20 x 60-foot paved yard. The fourth side was occupied by a building. It looked like some kind of residence. I saw what had to be the back entrance a few yards away from me. I ran over to it and peered through the partly glazed door to see a corridor that connected the rear entrance to the front of the house. On the other side of the far door was Via Sant'Anna.

I tried the black iron handle and was surprised when it gave under my touch. Inside four interior doors led off the central corridor: a well-equipped kitchen, dining room with twelve tables, sitting room with lots of couches, and a library well stocked with books. To my left the staircase wall was lined with photographs of former pontiffs.

I was almost at the front door when I glanced over my shoulder and saw three Vatican police officers sprint into view in the yard. Their leader was a forty-something man with gray hair and hungry eyes. He caught sight of me through the door.

He yelled a command.

I swerved left and sprinted upstairs as the cops ran into the corridor behind me. More shouts, which I ignored.

By the time I reached the next floor up, the sound of my thundering steps and the cries of the officers behind me had drawn priests to doorways set close together either side of a long corridor. Two lines of faces surveyed me fearfully.

I rounded the landing and bounded up the next flight of stairs, lungs burning, legs aching, and was soon on the next floor, which had fewer doors. I could hear the cries and shouts of the Vatican police behind me and the hammering of their shoes against the wooden stairs. There was another flight and I started toward it, but stopped in my tracks when a door opened ahead of me.

Father Vito appeared in the doorway. Once he got over the shock of seeing me, breathless and harried, he beckoned me over.

"Come, my son," he said. "I will give you sanctuary."

CHAPTER 76

I RAN TOWARD the kindly priest. He stepped aside to allow me to pass before closing the door. He had simple but comfortable lodgings—a small living room overlooking the courtyard, a bedroom off to the right with its own bathroom, and a kitchen of sorts tucked behind a three-fold floral screen in one corner of the living room.

"Please sit," he said, indicating an armchair away from the window.

It faced a couch across a low table covered in old newspapers. There was a stovetop coffee maker steaming on a burner in the kitchen area.

"I've just made coffee if you would like some," Father Vito remarked.

I didn't answer. I couldn't. My heart was racing, I was trying to catch my breath and my attention was focused on the sound of Vatican police officers hammering on doors further down the corridor.

"Fate will decide what happens to you," Father Vito said.

He wore black trousers and a white T-shirt, which robbed him of some of his gravitas. It was fascinating to see the difference the black robe made. He seemed less divine, more human somehow.

"Fate? Or God?" I asked.

"I used the word I knew you'd be more comfortable with," he replied with a smile. "You look as though you already have enough on your mind without having to wrestle with questions of faith."

There was a loud knock on the door, and whoever was on the other side tried the handle. Thankfully, Father Vito had locked it.

"Quick," he whispered. "Into the bedroom."

I nodded and hurried into the next room, shutting the door behind me. I took a moment to settle, pressed my ear against a panel and heard Father Vito working the locks. There was a creak as the sitting-room door swung open, followed by a voluble exchange of words. Father Vito sounded calm and considered; whoever he was talking to, angry and imperious. I held my breath and listened to the movements on the other side of the door.

I looked around the room for somewhere to hide, but it was little more than a cell with a small window, a low single bed and a wooden closet. There was a bathroom about half the size of the bedroom, and I edged into it now.

I steeled myself for inevitable discovery. With no means of escape I'd have to fight my way out, and these cops would be well equipped, possibly armed. I hated making enemies of the cops, but I couldn't risk being taken into custody.

I heard movement beyond the bedroom door, and then the handle turned. I readied myself to charge at whoever came through. I took a step before registering it was Father Vito and that he was alone.

"Would you like that coffee now?" he asked, and I smiled at him and nodded.

"How did you get rid of them?" I asked, following him out.

"I told them about the sanctity of my chamber and said I would complain to their superiors if they doubted my word that I hadn't seen you," he said, pouring me a cup of coffee from the aluminum stove-top pot.

"You lied?" I asked.

"A small transgression to prevent a greater one," he replied, handing me my coffee.

It was just the right temperature. I took a sip before sinking into an armchair. He sat on the couch opposite.

"This is good," I said, over my cup.

"Thank the coffee growers of Colombia."

"Why would you lie for me?" I asked, changing the subject.

"Because you're a good man. I see it in you," he replied. "I've also read about you on the Internet. We are not totally backward here."

"If honesty doesn't have to be absolute, how do you know when you can lie?" I asked.

"Sometimes it is hard to tell. Sometimes it is easy. Today was easy."

"It seems so much of faith is subject to human interpretation," I remarked. "It can be used for good or evil, depending on who wields it."

"Like a gun," Father Vito counted. "But unlike a gun, there is a book that gives us the key principles. Follow it and life becomes easier to decipher, because that's what we're all trying to do here: read the signs that allow us to find our way."

"And the Bible is our map?" I suggested.

He nodded. "Exactly. It is a guide. The closer you stay to it, the better your life will be—here and in the hereafter. But of course you can stray. The good stray only when necessary, the bad whenever they feel like it."

"And if you follow its tenets without being a believer?" I asked.

"That's okay too," he replied. "Substance is much better than form. Whatever path you find to God, the important thing is that you take it."

I heard commotion in the yard outside and rose to see the Vatican police leaving. I drained my cup.

"Thank you for helping me," I said. "And for the coffee."

"You're welcome," Father Vito replied. "I hope you find peace, Mr. Morgan."

"So do I," I said, before I moved to the door. "So do I."

"Mr. Morgan, there is a side exit through the kitchen," Father Vito told me. "You might find it useful for a quiet departure."

"Thank you again," I said, before I opened the door to the deserted corridor and stepped out.

CHAPTER 77

I MOVED SWIFTLY through the old building. I went to the front door and checked Via Sant'Anna where I saw a squad of Vatican police officers. I moved down the hallway to the kitchen, where I found the side entrance Father Vito had told me about. A covered walkway led between the bank and the papal residence. I followed this to an arch that brought me out at the car park a short distance from the Gallery of the Candelabra.

When I was halfway across the car park, I saw two men in suits heading in my direction. I was ready to retaliate if they attempted to stop me but they paid no attention to me. I went to the narrow alleyway beside the gallery and found the metal grille over the entrance to the secret tunnel.

I sensed movement nearby and tensed, ready for a fight.

Faduma stepped out of an alcove further along the alley, and I grinned with relief.

"You made it then?" she asked.

"I made it," I replied. "You weren't arrested?"

"I just told them I was your hostage," she replied. "That you'd grabbed me in the street and forced me to go with you. By shouting and pretending to panic, I managed to slow them down a little."

"Thank you," I said.

"And you?" she asked, as we headed toward the grille.

"There's a priest," I said. "He's been a friend to me a couple times now. He hid me from the cops."

"Wow," she replied. "Someone is looking out for you. It's useful to have those kinds of friends."

"I think he believes he can bring me back to the faith," I said.

"Oh. Ulterior motive," Faduma remarked, reaching toward the grille.

She put her hand through a four-inch square that had been cut into the metal and felt around for the catch.

A moment later, it clicked open and she pushed the grille wide open.

"If this priest is bringing us good luck," Faduma said, "then long may it continue, whatever his motives."

I smiled and followed her into the tunnel. I closed the grille behind us and we set off at a jog, heading back the way we'd come, returning to the secular side of Rome.

CHAPTER 78

JUSTINE HAD SPENT far too long in the cell. She tried to keep track of time, but night had fallen and eventually she drifted off to sleep lying on an uncomfortable molded fiberglass bunk. She had woken early to the sounds of other people being moved in and out of custody. Could she hear Mo-bot or Sci being marched around police headquarters? She had no way of knowing if they were even in the same building. They'd been separated since their arrest at the mall and taken away in different vehicles.

Justine had no idea on what charge or charges she was being held. Everything had happened so quickly, and the translator had done a perfunctory job.

She had been taken to the holding cells and locked behind a steel door with nothing but a grubby fiberglass toilet and basin to keep her company. There had been a packaged sandwich for dinner, and after dawn a shrink-wrapped pastry that tasted mealy and months old. Despite her own ordeal, Justine was most worried about Jack and had spent hours worrying about whether he'd got away.

After the morning hubbub had died down and the block had settled into a calmer rhythm, Justine heard footsteps outside her cell. There was an electronic buzz and the door clicked open. A uniformed officer pulled it wide and a woman dressed in a navy blue trouser suit stepped inside.

"Ms. Smith, my name is Inspector Mia Esposito. I'm leading the investigation into the deaths of Father Arturo Brambilla and Inspector Bernardo Baggio."

"You'll forgive me if I don't get up," Justine said from her bunk. "It's been a rough night."

"I'm also leading the hunt for Jack Morgan."

Justine stiffened at the inspector's words, fearing the worst.

"You don't happen to know where he is?"

Justine's heart soared. So they didn't have him.

"I don't," she replied. "I didn't even know he was going to be at the mall. He must have followed us there."

Esposito eyed her coolly.

"That's what your attorney says," she admitted at last. "Which is why we can't hold you any longer."

Justine's mood brightened, but she didn't show it.

"Pretty lousy move, trying to pump someone for information when they wrongly think they're still under arrest," she said, getting to her feet.

Esposito shrugged. "We all have to play the game to win."

"This isn't a game," Justine countered, squaring up to the investigator.

They eyed each other for a moment before Esposito stood aside and allowed her to pass.

Twenty minutes later, she'd been reunited with her possessions and signed out of custody. She left the booking room and entered the busy lobby at police headquarters where she found Mo-bot, Sci and a woman in a smart gray skirt and white blouse waiting for her.

Mo-bot and Sci clustered round like a couple of surrogate parents.

"Are you okay, honey?" Mo-bot asked.

"Can you believe how they treated us?" Sci remarked.

"Ms. Smith, my name is Gianna Bianchi. I represent Private's interests in Rome. Mr. Morgan asked me to do what I could to secure your release."

Gianna Bianchi looked intelligent and resolved, the type of dogged lawyer who'd never give up.

"Thank you," Justine said, shaking her hand.

"I had some help," Gianna revealed. "Your embassy protested about your treatment, which created the right kind of pressure."

Justine guessed she and Mo-bot had made a good impression on Emily Carter. "Any word on Jack?"

Mo-bot and Sci shook their heads.

"I've made arrangements for your new accommodation," Gianna said. "There was a police operation at your former residence last night."

Mo-bot leant in closer. "Intruder alarms were tripped, but I only saw the alerts on my phone when I was released about thirty minutes ago," she whispered. "Someone was in the apartment. Someone who wasn't Jack."

"I checked with my police contacts at Ms Roth's suggestion," Gianna said, "and there was an explosion and two arrests made there yesterday."

Justine's heart sank.

"It's not Mr. Morgan," Gianna went on. "Apparently it was a couple of gang members found outside the building."

"Dark Fates?" Justine asked.

Mo-bot nodded. "But no news on Jack, so we have to assume he's okay."

"Secure messenger?" Justine asked.

"I haven't checked yet. Good chance we've picked up some additional company while we were inside. Friends listening to our calls, keyloggers checking passwords, spyware monitoring our browsing and location," Mo-bot revealed.

It hadn't even occurred to Justine their phones might be bugged by the police.

"We're going to need to make a stop on our way to the new place," Mo-bot said, before turning to Gianna. "We're ready whenever you are. I've had enough of this dive."

CHAPTER 79

GIANNA BIANCHI'S LATE-MODEL Audi Q7 seemed an impractical car for Rome, but Justine was glad not to be in one of the many tiny Fiats that whizzed fearlessly around the city. She looked out of the window at the sun-kissed buildings and pedestrians walking in the heat, the packed pavement cafés and air-conditioned stores, and wondered where Jack was and what had happened to him after their arrest.

Mo-bot had made a call as they'd walked to the lawyer's car and had spoken to whoever replied in code. After the call, she told Gianna to head for the Fontana di Venere near the Gianicolo, one of the tallest hills in Rome.

Gianna knew exactly where it was, though it took them thirty minutes of fighting through heavy traffic to reach the lush green park with its grand fountain and formal gardens.

"Can you wait here?" Mo-bot asked her when she pulled into

a space in the nearest parking lot. "My contact is a little skittish."

The lawyer nodded. "It's better if I stay away. Particularly if there is any illegality involved."

"Oh, we won't be doing anything illegal," Mo-bot assured her. "The opposite in fact, if my hunch is right."

Justine was intrigued, but she knew better than to quiz Mo-bot, who was obviously concealing something from the lawyer.

"Bring everything the cops took from you," Mo-bot told her associates.

They followed her through the parking lot and along a tree-lined path beside a walled garden. They tracked the wall to its end and went through a doorway into a less cultivated area. Justine noticed a woman sitting on a bench set back from the path. She beamed as Mo-bot approached and rose to make a beeline for them. The woman had short brown hair, piercings in her ears, nose and eyebrows, and tattoos covering her arms and legs, where they were exposed by a black T-shirt and pair of matching shorts.

"Justine, Sci, this is Valentina," Mo-bot said, before embracing the younger woman. "She's a formidable digital warrior."

"A hacker?" Sci asked.

Valentina rolled her eyes.

"Don't mind him," Mo-bot told her. "He's a dinosaur."

"Are you the one who helped Jack?" Justine asked.

Valentina nodded, but before she could say anything, Mo-bot cut in.

"Why don't we check out the gear? Did you bring the kit?"

"Yes, it's over here," Valentina said, walking to the bench by the walled garden.

Justine, Sci and Mo-bot followed, and joined Valentina as she was opening a Peli flight case that contained a trove of electronic equipment. Justine recognized some of the gear as counter-surveillance devices.

"Give me everything the cops took from you," Mo-bot said.

Justine and Sci complied, handing over a wallet, purse, phones, passports and belts. Mo-bot ran a scanner over everything and found two tracking devices: one embedded in Sci's phone and the other sewn into Justine's purse.

After scanning each item with a wand that detected electronic signals, Mo-bot passed the item to Valentina, who examined it further. She connected Sci's and Justine's phones to a tiny computer and analyzed the installed apps.

"Software tracker, using the phone's GPS to send its location to a remote server," Valentina revealed. "It's on both devices. And there's a keylogger sending the same server everything typed on these devices. All your messages can be read remotely."

"They hacked us," Sci remarked.

"I do wish you'd stop using that word," Mo-bot replied. "But yes, they hacked us. That's probably why they held us for so long—so they could install all this junk. What about my phone?" she asked, handing over her device.

Valentina connected it to the computer and examined the file directory. She nodded.

"Same."

"Can you clean them?" Mo-bot asked.

"Sure," Valentina replied. "No problem."

"No listening devices?"

Valentina shook her head. "Location and text only."

"Good," Mo-bot said. "Then we can speak freely." She turned to Justine. "You wanted to ask about Jack."

"Yes. Have you heard from him?"

"Of course," Valentina said. "I found another safe place for him and his friend. I'll take you as soon as we're finished here."

CHAPTER 80

FADUMA AND I rode buses to return to the warehouse by the river. I wanted to be able to see if anyone was following us. Hopping on and off the crowded vehicles provided us with plenty of cover, hiding among the tourists in central Rome and then commuters as we moved toward the suburbs.

"Are you going to meet Altmer tonight?" Faduma asked as we stepped off the number 5 bus at a remote stop a short distance from the warehouse.

I could smell salt in the air blowing in on a west wind.

"What choice do I have?" I asked. "We went to the Vatican this morning in search of answers. We didn't find any, so I have to try again. I don't understand why he was concerned for our safety."

"Maybe it was a ruse to give himself enough time to set a trap," Faduma remarked as we walked along the lane leading to the riverside warehouses. "To destroy evidence or warn collaborators."

"Well, we know he's involved somehow, and the Dark Fates obviously play a role, and that there is a powerful conspiracy at work—let's try and put the pieces together from what we have," I suggested. "We should review everything again. Go back to the beginning."

Faduma nodded and we hurried into the warehouse. We went up to the apartment and I made us some strong coffee using the supplies she had purchased earlier that morning.

Armed with the black jet fuel we sat at Mo-bot's computer and reviewed the copious amounts of evidence we'd amassed: the surveillance footage of the Inferno Bar and the background files on Altmer and Milan Verde. We worked for over an hour without success until Faduma accessed her files on *La Repubblica*'s cloud server. She reviewed the dossier she'd amassed on the mysterious deaths Filippo Lombardi had begun investigating. She had started a file on Father Brambilla and was swiping through some archive photos the newspaper had of him at Vatican functions.

"Wait," I said. "Go back."

I'd seen a face I recognized at a fundraiser being held at the Vatican for the Orphans of Rome, a city charity. Faduma scrolled back and there in the image, standing next to Christian Altmer and Father Brambilla, was Father Vito, but he wasn't wearing the priest's cassock I was familiar with. He wore the deep purple of a cardinal.

"That's Father Vito," I said. "The priest who helped me."

Faduma shook her head. "That's Cardinal Vito Peralta, one of the most powerful princes of the Church."

I thought back to our first meeting at the Garden of Secret Confession. What had he been doing there? Could he have been involved in what had happened? Had I been taken in by his simple piety?

"Why is he posing as a priest?" I asked.

"He is known as an ascetic. He believes in the purity of simplicity and thinks the ceremonial trappings and ceremony of the Church are a distraction from true worship," Faduma replied. "He is a divisive figure, for that and other reasons."

"Such as?"

"He is one of the directors of the Vatican Bank. He believes the Church should be more interventionist in the way it uses its assets. That it should tie investments to religious aims and political objectives."

I realized I had misjudged the man, taking him for a junior priest because of his plain clothes and approachable manner.

"His supporters whisper his name whenever there is talk of who will become the next Pope," Faduma revealed.

As I studied the photo of the man who had twice offered help and advice, I wondered if concern for my soul had motivated him to take an interest in me, or whether all along he had sought to manipulate and misdirect.

CHAPTER 81

I STARTED TO replay my encounters with Father Vito but didn't get far in my trawl because there was the loud and unmistakable sound of someone hitting the warehouse shutters.

Faduma and I were on our feet instantly and left the apartment. We crept downstairs into the disused and empty offices and I moved ahead into the warehouse itself, picked my way around the stacks of boxes, and climbed a loading platform that gave me access to the high letterbox windows overlooking the main entrance.

My thundering heartbeat eased and the tension melted away when I saw Justine, Sci and Mo-bot standing outside with Valentina.

"Let them in," I said to Faduma, and she hurried over to the small roll shutter, unlocked it and opened it.

My colleagues stepped inside, their relief to see me palpable. Valentina followed them and closed the shutter behind her.

I jumped off the loading platform and went over to Justine, who threw her arms around me. We kissed and I didn't care that we had company. I was just so relieved to see her and hold her in my arms again, I was reluctant to let go.

"Okay. That's enough," Mo-bot said. "We'll cut you love birds some slack, but this is a professional outfit and we've got work to do."

Justine and I parted, and I saw Faduma and Valentina grinning at Mo-bot's intervention.

"It's so good to see you," I told Justine before turning to Mo-bot and Sci. "All of you. Let's go upstairs."

I took them into the apartment above the offices. Mo-bot squeaked with delight when she saw her laptop.

"I thought I'd lost my baby," she said, as though speaking to a cherished pet.

"You nearly did. A member of Propaganda Tre was in the apartment downloading the hard drives. He had a program set up to wipe them, but I managed to stop him."

"I owe you, Jack," Mo-bot said, sitting at her machine.

Sci crouched to check the contents of the holdall I'd managed to retrieve.

"You got our gear," he said. "Well, most of it anyway. Good work, boss."

He had a way of saying "boss" that made it sound as though he was praising a junior.

"We've lost all the feeds," Mo-bot said, retrieving the surveillance footage that showed Milan Verde and the other members of the Dark Fates destroying the concealed cameras. "They must have swept the place to discover them all, which makes them more sophisticated than your average street gang."

"We have enough gear left to get eyes and ears on them again," Sci responded, gesturing at the holdall. "I want to know what they're hiding."

"A meeting with Christian Altmer for one thing," I revealed. "It's on the surveillance footage about four hours before they destroyed the cameras. We'd never have known if they'd succeeded in wiping the machines."

"Altmer again," Justine remarked.

"Looks like you were right about him," I replied. "I'm meeting him later."

"And walking into a trap," Faduma said unhelpfully.

Justine flashed me a look of concern.

"When? Why?" she asked.

"To find out what he knows, why he's consorting with a street gang," I said. "I want you, Sci and Mo-bot to re-establish surveillance on the Inferno. We need to know what else the Dark Fates are hiding."

I wanted us to have eyes and ears on the gang, but a large part of the reason I asked Justine to go to the bar in Esquilino was to keep her away from my meeting with Altmer. I knew I would be walking into danger and didn't want our personal relationship to complicate a potentially volatile situation.

"No way," she said. "I'm coming with you. I can help you

with Altmer, read the situation, watch for danger. Have your back."

"And I can get you out of danger," Mo-bot said.

"Sci can't handle the Inferno on his own," I responded.

"Not after last time," he conceded. "They'll have guessed I was the one who planted the devices. And if their man reviewed the footage, he'll have seen me walking away from them after I put them in position."

"I'll go, Jack," Faduma said. "I'll help Sci. Then the others can go with you. Keep you safe."

I couldn't think of any reason to object.

"Thank you, Ms Salah," Mo-bot said. "It's nice to meet someone else who's brimming with common sense."

"I'd like to help too," Valentina said, speaking up at last. She seemed a little starstruck and looked at Mo-bot with unmistakable awe. "It would be an honor to work with you in the real world."

"Don't overdo it, Valentina," Mo-bot said. "I might develop a God complex or something. If it's okay with the boss, I think we'll take all the help we can get."

I nodded. Mo-bot was right; we were facing a network of powerful interests and weren't in any position to turn away offers of assistance from people with special talents.

"It's fine with me," I said, and Valentina smiled.

CHAPTER 82

VALENTINA GAVE SCI and Faduma her car, a two-year-old black Maserati Levante. Faduma drove it through the busy streets of Rome, more crowded than usual thanks to Roma's match against Inter Milan, which was due to start at 7 p.m. It took them over two hours to get from Ostia to Esquilino.

"Do you do this much?" Faduma asked.

Sci shook his head. "Normally I get to hang out with dead bodies and crime scenes. Forensic investigation is my specialism, but when Jack gets himself in a jam, we all have to improvise. You?"

"More than I would like," Faduma replied, steering the car around a crowd of Inter fans, who were chanting boisterously as they crossed the road. "It's getting harder and harder to hold the rich and powerful to account. Often it requires exceptional measures."

"Exceptional measures," Sci responded. "I like that."

"Does Jack get in many of these jams?"

Sci sighed. "Too many to count. Trouble follows him like a loyal dog, and he's got too much decency and honor to shoo it away."

"Yes," Faduma replied. "He seems like a good man."

"He is," Sci said, and they drove on in silence for a while.

The streets shed any semblance of wealth, comfort, and much of their beauty as they entered Esquilino.

"Next right," Sci said as they approached Via Mamiani.

Faduma nodded and took the turn. She saw the brightly lit symbol of a flame and the similarly illuminated word "Inferno" over the entrance to the bar.

She pulled into a space about fifty yards from the corner. Most of the stores around them were closed either permanently or for the match, their drawn shutters daubed with graffiti. Further along the street, a takeaway, café and another bar were open, but none had many customers. The Inferno Bar was the liveliest place on Via Mamiani, blasting music into the early-evening air.

There were a few smokers gathered outside who looked to Faduma angry and degenerate. The kind of ignorant men and women who had given her such a hostile reception when she'd first arrived in Italy.

"What now?" she asked Sci, but he was already rooting around in the holdall on the back seat. After a moment he turned back to face her with a tiny device and a remote control in his hand. The device looked like a wasp and was about the same size.

"Micro-drone," he said. "It will give us eyes and ears very quickly."

He switched on both devices and wound his window down to allow the miniature drone to fly out.

Faduma watched him use the screen on the remote control to pilot the small aircraft, which broadcast a live feed from a camera attached to its nose.

"This would be really useful," Faduma said. "How can I get one?"

"Military grade," Sci remarked, before cracking a smile. "Just kidding. We have a supplier who specializes in building them for law-enforcement and intelligence agencies around the world. I'm sure I can talk Jack into loaning you a couple if we have any left at the end of this."

He turned his full attention to the screen as the drone approached the bar. He tried the windows first, but they were all closed.

"Let's see about the air conditioning," he said, piloting the drone toward an AC intake. The vents had been covered with a micromesh and the resin fixing it looked fresh.

"This wasn't here before," Sci remarked.

The same mesh covered every pipe and inlet leading into the building.

"Then it's going to have to be the front door," Sci said, steering the drone around the group of smokers.

The front door swung wide and another member of the Dark Fates stepped out to join the smokers, which gave Sci the opportunity to pilot the drone inside the bar.

Suddenly, the image became a jumble of shapes and the remote control turned unresponsive. Moments later the screen cut to sudden static.

"Jeez," he said, reviewing the last few seconds of footage. "They've put an air curtain above the door. Someone has helped them bolster their physical security."

"What do we do?" Faduma asked, but she already knew the answer. "One of us needs to go inside, right? And it can't be you."

CHAPTER 83

"IF THEY RECOGNIZE you—" Sci began, but Faduma cut him off.

"I'll run. I just need to get one of those drones inside, don't I?"

Sci nodded. "I can put it in Milan Verde's office. Provided it doesn't fly too much, we'll get two days out of the batteries."

"Then it's worth doing," Faduma said, taking a deep breath.

The Dark Fates were dangerous, but she had faced danger before. She'd crossed the Mediterranean in a tiny boat, seeing people in her flotilla die; she'd been up close to catastrophic loss, and it had forever changed her perspective on life, making her simultaneously more appreciative and less cautious. She cherished life, but she also knew there were times one had to risk sacrifice because it was the right thing to do.

Sci handed her another drone from the holdall and checked it was connected to the remote.

He nodded. "You're good to go."

Faduma smiled wanly and stepped out of the car.

The warm afternoon air combined with her nervousness to make her feel a little queasy, but she fought the rising nausea and forced her feet to move one step at a time toward the Inferno Bar. She could hear the sound of the television build up to the Roma–Inter Milan football match coming through the windows of nearby apartments. As she got closer to the bar, the sound of football was lost beneath thunderous music. She saw far-right insignia among the tattoos on the arms of some of the smokers on the pavement. She'd met many racists in her life, but was conscious of her increased personal risk in this situation. She didn't need to be recognized as a journalist. One of these angry men or women just had to take a dislike to the color of her skin. She heard them talking, discussing some show on Netflix.

They fell silent as she drew near and she was suddenly very aware of her smart white linen trousers and red blouse, which were at odds with the biker/rock band roadie vibe of the place. She couldn't have stood out more if she'd tried.

"This is a private bar," the man closest to her said, drawing on a cigarette. "Foreigners aren't welcome."

The men and women around him chuckled.

"I don't see a sign," Faduma replied in Italian. "And I'm not a foreigner."

"Well, you don't look Italian."

"You don't look intelligent, but we shouldn't judge others on their appearance," Faduma responded, finding the reserves of courage that had never yet failed her.

The reply played well with the man's companions and drew a louder chuckle, but on finding himself the butt of the joke, the smoker scowled and lumbered closer to her. He sported a gray T-shirt bearing the image of a screaming white skull and wore his loose jeans hitched low.

"It's a private bar," he said, reaching out and putting an intimidating ham-sized hand on her shoulder.

She looked at his fat, scarred fingers as they squeezed.

"That's assault," Faduma said calmly. She produced a stun gun from her purse, drove it into the man's ribs and pulled the trigger.

He fell to the ground, convulsing, and she stepped clear and addressed his companions.

"I just want a drink and to use the ladies' room."

Their chuckles and smiles had vanished. A couple of them hurried over to help their fallen companion, but no one did anything to stop Faduma entering the bar.

She felt the powerful air blanket on the top of her head and walked on, sensing the stir her arrival had caused. As she moved toward the counter, conversation stopped and soon the only sound was the angry screeching of death metal blaring through the bar's sound system. A muted television hanging on the wall showed the kickoff of the Roma–Inter match.

"I'd like a beer," Faduma said to the unfriendly barman. "And the ladies' room."

He stared at her for a moment before nodding toward a corridor to her right.

She put twenty euros on the counter and walked in the

direction he'd indicated. When she reached the corridor, she slipped her hand into her purse and took out the drone, which flew away silently. She reached for the ladies' room door handle, but it was opened from the inside and Faduma was confronted by a woman wearing too much eyeliner and mascara, and a vintage Led Zeppelin T-shirt. She looked taken aback for a moment.

"Who the hell are you? You're not coming in here. This is a private bathroom. Move."

The woman pushed Faduma, who this time didn't react. She'd done what she needed to do and allowed herself to be marched through the bar by the angry, over-made-up rocker. A man held the door open, gave a mocking bow, and the whole bar erupted in cheers as Faduma was thrown out.

Even though she'd acquiesced in this treatment, she walked away full of anger and thoughts of vengeance against such narrow-minded, hateful people. She could hear their raucous laughter and chatter above the pounding music.

She glanced back at the group of smokers who'd now managed to revive the man she'd stunned. Faduma moved more quickly to avoid any attempt at retribution.

Adrenalin coursing, heart pounding, she sighed with relief when she rejoined Sci in the Maserati.

"You were brilliant," he said. "So brave."

She almost teared up at his kind words, but swallowed the lump forming in her throat.

"And look," he said, gesturing at the screen on the remote control. "This is the view inside Milan Verde's office."

Faduma glanced over and saw Verde sitting on a couch. In the armchair next to him was a man she recognized: Stefano Trotta the finance minister she had briefly encountered at Elia Antonelli's farm.

"What's he saying?" Sci asked.

Faduma listened to Trotta's words.

"He's saying they have nearly achieved their goals," she replied, translating. "That their friend and patron is close to reaching his objective."

Faduma couldn't help feeling they were talking about Antonelli, and that the seasoned gangster had once again played her and Jack Morgan for fools.

She settled in to see what else the drone would reveal about these evil men.

CHAPTER 84

IT WAS ONE minute after ten when I arrived at the Basilica di San Giovanni in Laterano, a magnificent place of worship less than a mile from the Colosseum. Situated at the heart of a large piazza, the grand building, described as the Mother of All Churches, stood more than four stories high. Thick marble columns supported a portico adorned with statues of the saints.

I walked beyond the metal railings that were used for crowd control during the day and went through an open gate to access the portico. The sign by the main entrance said the church should be long closed, but the door gave under my touch. When I entered, I found the interior was illuminated by lights set into the stone cornicing halfway up the magnificently decorated walls. The floor was as beautiful as any I'd ever seen, an intricate black-and-white pearlescent tile pattern, and the ceiling was embossed with gold reliefs. Marble statues set in arched niches lined the walls. Beyond the pews, directly in line with the main entrance, stood the high altar.

I crossed the grand floor and moved down the central aisle, unable to shake the feeling I was being watched, though I saw nothing untoward as I scanned the ancient church to left and right of me. I made my way to the altar, but there was no sign of Altmer seated in the nearby pews or hidden in the shadows farther away.

When I was within a few feet of the first row, I heard a distinctive sound that chilled me. I ran forward to find him lying on his back, blood pooling on the tiled floor around him, the hilt of an old-fashioned steel dagger sticking out of his chest. He was pawing at it weakly, but his eyes shifted and focused on me when I rushed to his side.

He gasped and moaned in pain. As I checked his pulse and tried to overcome my shock at finding him this way, I realized he was trying to speak.

I'll never forget the choking, gurgling noises he made as he frantically sucked air into lungs that sounded as if they were full of fluid. Finally he managed to say, "I . . . tried . . . to . . . do . . . right . . . Matteo . . . is . . . lying."

His eyes went blank. I tried mouth-to-mouth but it was no use. He was gone.

I couldn't believe another man had died in front of me. And that, with his dying breath, he had warned me not to trust my latest Private recruit. I'd managed to convince myself of Matteo's innocence, but could I continue to do so now?

"Jack Morgan, we know you're inside. Surrender immediately!"

I recognized the voice of Inspector Mia Esposito. She was talking through a bullhorn.

I'd been completely set up and had no doubt this death would be pinned on me too. I heard movement around the church, the tramp of boots, the catch and lock of weapons being checked, radios crackling to life with terse commands.

There was no way I was fighting my way out of here or escaping unscathed.

I got to my feet and walked toward the main entrance with a sense of weary resignation.

When I opened the door, I saw Esposito had brought what looked like half of Rome's police officers with her. Many were armed and had their weapons trained on me.

They needn't have bothered. I put up no resistance when Esposito climbed the steps and turned me around.

"Jack Morgan, you are under arrest," she said as she put me in handcuffs.

CHAPTER 85

ROMA MUST HAVE won because when I was transported from the Basilica to whichever police station I was destined for, the streets were filled with loud and cheerful fans, singing and chanting.

Mia Esposito sat up front, next to the driver—a plain-clothes officer who kept giving me hate-filled looks. He was the kind of cop who took the job personally and had probably swallowed the line that I was responsible for Bernardo Baggio's death.

They exchanged words in Italian and laughed at the sight of some of the raucous celebrations. A few of the Roma fans had their shirts off and were running around, clearly very drunk.

"I didn't kill them, you know?" I said to Esposito. "Christian Altmer, Bernardo Baggio and Father Carlos Diaz. Someone has set me up."

"Then you took a risk coming to the Basilica if you're the victim of a conspiracy, Mr. Morgan," Esposito replied.

"I thought Mr. Altmer was behind whatever got all these people killed. So it seemed worth the risk to come and talk to him," I replied. "I never expected to find him the way I did, but the fact that he's been murdered tells me he was just a bit player in whatever's happening."

"And you think you are going to be left alone to sit out the rest of it, do you?" Esposito challenged me. "Not while there's a theory that you've killed anyone who might testify against your colleague, Matteo Ricci! You will remain in custody until you can prove your innocence to the satisfaction of Rome's prosecutors."

"Or I'm conveniently killed in jail," I said, and Esposito and her colleague exchanged looks.

"Did you find Bernardo Baggio?" I asked.

"We did," the hostile cop said. "And I want to know how come you knew about him."

"I don't know anything about the circumstances of his death. All I know is he was on duty the night my colleague is supposed to have tried to take his own life."

I leant forward, my arms locking against the cuffs.

"Inspector Esposito, if you can't see you're being played, you're not the cop I thought you were."

She considered my words but didn't respond.

We were in the thick of the revelry by now, and the traffic was making slow progress through cheering crowds on both sides of Via Marco Aurelio. I could see the Colosseum up ahead, the ancient monument beautifully lit against the night sky. The bars either side of the street were packed with exuberant fans spilling out onto the road. At the intersection with Via Claudia we had to wait for a herd of Roma supporters to migrate south to north over the zebra crossing. When the street finally cleared, the hostile cop at the wheel inched forward only to find our path suddenly blocked by a bus full of Roma fans that had stopped at the mouth of the intersection.

The driver cursed and hit his horn, starting a cacophony of other car horns from behind us, the sounds merging with the celebratory cheers and shouts to add to the general air of chaos. The driver had no more idea than Inspector Esposito what was about to happen, but I did, and when I saw Amr Badawi sitting near the front of the bus, I steeled myself for what was to come.

The bus doors opened and a crowd of Roma supporters spilt out of the vehicle, led by Amr. Inspector Esposito and her colleague were bemused at first, but their bewilderment quickly turned to panic as fifty fans, some of them armed with crowbars and other tools, encircled our vehicle.

Inspector Esposito glanced back at me as one of the men closest to her swung his crowbar.

"I'm still in the game," I remarked, the instant before the window shattered.

Esposito tried to draw her weapon but was quickly disarmed by men who prised the front doors open. Both cops were dragged from the vehicle and subdued, and Amr reached into the front and unlocked the rear doors. Someone I didn't recognize helped me out.

Moments later, another man found Esposito's keys and uncuffed me. I was ushered onto the bus with the men who'd helped me escape.

The whole thing had taken less than three minutes. When I glanced back, I saw Inspector Esposito and her colleague hand-cuffed to a lamppost, struggling to catch the attention of passing fans, who were so drunk they laughed and jeered at them, obviously thinking they were the victims of some kind of prank.

I walked to the front of the bus where I found Mo-bot, Justine and Valentina. We were joined by Amr.

"Thanks," I said, grateful and relieved to be reunited with them.

"No problem," he replied.

"You inspire loyalty," Mo-bot remarked. "At a price. These guys are charging for their time."

I glanced at Amr, who shrugged. "Business is business, Mr. Morgan."

I smiled and sat beside Justine as the bus rumbled north past the stunning ruins of the ancient circus.

"So Altmer is dead?" she asked.

I nodded.

"And whoever killed him tried to frame you," she observed.

"Yeah," I said.

"If we keep at them, they're going to change tactics and treat you as a more urgent threat."

I nodded again. She was right. If I wasn't already marked for death, it was only a matter of time before a target was put on my back.

CHAPTER 86

THE PLAN WITH the bus had been Valentina's idea. She knew Amr and most of his friends were die-hard Roma fans and that sheer force of numbers could overwhelm any police van or escort vehicles. As it was, Inspector Esposito had underestimated the resources at our disposal, so hadn't had an escort of any kind.

To avoid any of his friends learning where we were staying, Amr had the bus drop us off on Via delle Ancore, about twenty minutes' walk from the warehouse. He left the vehicle and joined us on the short journey to make sure we got there safely.

Justine and I walked side-by-side, and even though it didn't feel right to hold hands in these circumstances, our fingers kept brushing together. In the end, I didn't care what the others thought. I took her hand, and she smiled at me all the time we were on the dark street.

When we arrived at the warehouse, there was a young woman

inside who'd set up a table of serving dishes laden with food. She was of Middle Eastern extraction and wore tight jeans and a retro Madonna T-shirt.

"This is my sister Amina," Amr explained. "She's brought the food my aunt made for us. There's *kolkas*, a taro root stew, *koshari*, which is lentils, macaroni and rice, and *kebab hala*, a dry beef stew, plus vegetables, *baladi* bread and rice. Whatever happens, you will not starve in Rome."

"Thank you, Amr and Amina," I said, and the others concurred.

Amina gave us plates and made sure we helped ourselves to plenty of food before joining us in a makeshift dining area between the crates and boxes that formed Amr's stock.

"Thanks," I said to my colleagues and new friends.

"Anytime," Mo-bot replied.

Justine smiled.

"They say you're a wanted man, as are many of your known associates," Valentina revealed, looking up from her phone.

"Sorry," I offered.

The roll shutter rose suddenly and Sci and Faduma entered.

"What's that smell?" he asked. "It's amazing."

"Food over there," Mo-bot replied. "Courtesy of the Badawi family."

"Help yourself," Amr said.

"I will," Sci assured him.

I introduced Sci and Faduma, and when they had loaded their plates, they joined us.

"How did it go?" he asked.

"Altmer is dead. Someone tried to frame me, and they almost

succeeded. I got arrested," I replied. "But Valentina hatched a plan, and these guys sprung me."

"Standard Morgan night out," Sci replied.

"And you?" I asked.

"We were able to get a bug inside," Faduma replied.

"Only because she's got nerves of steel," Sci interjected.

Faduma waved away the praise. "We saw Milan Verde meeting with Stefano Trotta."

"The minister we saw at Elia Antonelli's house?"

Faduma nodded.

"So, Antonelli might have been lying about having no connections to the Dark Fates?" I suggested.

"Seems that way," Sci replied.

"And we've learnt the priest who befriended me isn't what he seems," I said. "And before he died, Altmer said something."

The whole group waited expectantly.

"His last words were that Matteo is lying," I revealed, and saw their expressions of shock.

Like me, they would be struggling to believe that our colleague, the man who was at the heart of this investigation, might not have been completely honest with us.

CHAPTER 87

AFTER WE'D EATEN, Amr and Amina had left and Valentina had gone with them. Sci and I bunked in one of the bedrooms, Justine and Mo-bot had taken another, and Faduma was in the third.

By 2 a.m. I had puzzled through every aspect of this investigation and the picture still wasn't any clearer. To get to the truth I needed a breakthrough and I had an idea how to get it, but it would involve a betrayal.

A small one, but a betrayal nonetheless.

I waited until I was sure Sci was asleep, his heavy breathing reverberating around the room. I grabbed my clothes and crept out.

I moved quietly through the living area until I was near the front door.

"Where are you going?" Justine whispered. I turned to see her fully dressed ready to leave.

She walked over to me and ran her fingers over my bare chest. Her touch felt good and I pulled her close for a kiss. Our lips met. For a time I forgot everything else.

"You're so predictable," she said, pulling away. "The moment you mentioned what Altmer had said, I knew where you'd go, and I knew you'd try and go alone, so as not to endanger the rest of us."

"Wow," I replied. "Am I that transparent?"

She had predicted my small betrayal: leaving my team so I could go out alone.

She nodded. "Put your shirt on," she said, pushing past me. "We can't risk waking the others."

"We?" I asked, disappointed to be getting dressed, rather than undressed.

"Yes. I'm coming with you," she replied, opening the front door.

CHAPTER 88

THE CAB DRIVER barely glanced back as he drove us into the center of Rome. Justine held my hand. We didn't speak. I didn't want to risk drawing the driver's attention, and besides there wasn't really anything to say. I was about to do something very dangerous, something that could put my liberty and possibly my life at risk. But I needed to get to the truth and was prepared to take a risk to do it. Whoever was behind this had tried to kill me and harm my colleagues. It had moved beyond proving Matteo's guilt or innocence and was now deeply personal.

We crossed the river and arrived at Isola Tiberina and Fate-benefratelli Hospital shortly after 3 a.m. We got out of the cab and Justine paid the driver.

"Are you sure you want to do this?" she asked.

I nodded. We crossed the driveway in front of the old building and went in through the main entrance.

The hospital was busy, which wasn't surprising considering how much drinking had been going on in Rome that night. Most of the people crowding the waiting area and corridors that ran off it were young men in Roma kits. A combustible mix of post-match euphoria and too much alcohol had resulted in their hospital visits.

The crowds were useful to us though. We moved through the building unnoticed by the overworked staff, climbing the stairs to the third floor where Matteo's room was located. When we emerged into an empty corridor, I heard voices in indistinct conversation and, from another direction, footsteps.

"Same plan?" Justine asked.

I nodded. While we'd waited for the cab, we'd hatched a plan to distract the cops posted outside Matteo's room, but it would require great acting on her part to pull it off. I did not doubt her ability to deliver.

We entered the ward, and I waited by the nurses' station while Justine went around the corner to get rid of the cops. There was no one else in sight and muted echoes of events taking place elsewhere made the atmosphere even more eerie. Hospitals were daunting and strange enough during the day, but at night they became positively spooky.

Justine came round the corner and waved me forward.

I frowned. This wasn't part of our plan, but she was insistent. When I joined her, I saw why.

There was a solitary cop outside Matteo's room, and he was fast asleep. Pietro, the wiry bodyguard from Primo Security, sat opposite. He nodded at us as we approached.

"No partner?" I asked quietly.

Pietro shook his head and raised his index finger, indicating a single officer was on duty.

I nodded my thanks. Justine and I moved on cautiously. When we reached Matteo's room, I opened the door and we crept inside.

He was asleep but stirred as I approached his bed. Justine kept watch through the glazed panel in the door.

"Jack," Matteo whispered.

His voice sounded a little stronger than it had during our last encounter, but he still looked weak and pale. Dark shadows ringed his eyes.

"I saw the news. I'm sorry."

"What are you sorry for?" I asked. "Lying to me?"

He didn't look shocked, just disappointed. I couldn't tell whether it was with me or himself.

"Why don't you save us both some time and tell me what you've been hiding?" I said.

"I can't," he said. "For the sake of a soul."

"Whose soul?" I asked.

I glanced at Justine and saw she shared my concern: was this man mentally competent? Had his injuries affected him psychologically? Had he really tried to take his own life?

"Brambilla's," Matteo replied.

Justine and I shared another glance, both of us perplexed.

"What do you mean, Brambilla's soul?" she asked.

"The gravest sin," Matteo replied, his eyes glistening.

"You mean suicide?" I asked.

He nodded.

"You think Father Brambilla took his own life?" Justine asked.

"When he came to the party, agitated and wanting to talk," Matteo replied, "I took him somewhere we could speak in private. After we went into the room, he knocked me unconscious. When I came to, he was dead. I must have picked up the gun instinctively when I came round and found him dead."

"And you didn't tell us because you thought you could save his soul with a lie?" I asked.

"Who would pray for such a man?" Matteo asked. "He would not receive a Christian burial."

This adherence to dogma was part of the reason I'd lost my faith. A soul in such torment was surely more worthy of absolution than a murderer, and yet someone who had knowingly taken another person's life could confess and seek forgiveness while someone who took their own could not. Dogma warped the faithfuls' perspective to such an extent that someone devout and faithful, like Matteo, trained in a seminary, believed he was protecting Brambilla's eternal soul by concealing his suicide. Faith had twisted reason. Here was Matteo trying to save the soul of someone who had caused him nothing but trouble, because he believed that telling a lie could prevent the man's eternal damnation.

"How do you know it was Brambilla who knocked you out?" I asked.

Matteo looked puzzled. "Who else could it have been? We were the only ones in the room."

I glanced at Justine, who clearly shared my frustration.

"You should have told us," I said.

"I'm sorry, Jack," Matteo responded, tears falling from his eyes. "I was trying to do the right thing for my friend. He does not deserve purgatory."

"No one does," I told him. "Especially not a good priest like Father Brambilla."

CHAPTER 89

JUSTINE AND I left the hospital and crossed the Ponte Fabricio, a cobbled, pedestrianized bridge north of the hospital. There was no one else around and for a moment I wanted to forget the danger we faced, the secrets we'd uncovered, and instead pretend we were regular people with normal lives. That we were out for a star-lit stroll in this ancient and romantic setting, and that all the wonder of Rome had been created just for us.

I stopped and pulled Justine toward me. She wrapped her arms around my neck and kissed me until I became aware of movement to my right. Two men, hospital security guards on patrol, were heading our way.

"No rest for the wicked," Justine remarked as we resumed our journey.

"Or the virtuous," I replied with a smile.

We caught a taxi on Lungotevere de' Cenci, the broad, leafy

avenue that tracked the sinuous line of the Tiber. The driver barely gave us a second glance as we got in the back, but when we said we wanted to go to Ostia, he grumbled and told us he wouldn't get a good fare on the return journey. I offered him double. That didn't quite make him smile, but it did silence his complaints.

Justine and I stayed silent, partly because I didn't want the man overhearing details of our investigation, but largely because I was still reeling from Matteo's revelation. Faith had prevented him from telling the truth. It had made him irrational. Did he really believe that by ensuring his friend and mentor received a Christian burial, he could sneak Brambilla into heaven? Surely it was the contents of a person's heart, not their actions, that defined their relationship with God. Or maybe that was just a comforting fiction I told myself.

"You okay?" Justine asked. "You seem distracted."

The cab was racing through deserted streets, chewing up the distance as we shot past stores and restaurants that were silent and shuttered.

"I'm fine," I replied. "Just thinking about Matteo and wondering whether I've made a big mistake. I hired him because he seemed honest, but he made a huge error of judgment and concealed the truth."

Justine took my hand and squeezed it gently.

"He was trying to do the right thing by his friend. It might have been misguided, but his heart was in the right place."

I nodded. Truth and justice were my guides, and sometimes I struggled to understand how other people prioritized different values.

"Do you think Brambilla took his own life?" she asked.

"He was agitated," I replied. "He badly wanted to share a secret. I don't believe he would have killed himself before doing so."

"Which leaves Matteo or someone else," Justine suggested. "And if it was someone else, it was someone at the party."

I nodded again. "Someone who got in and out of the room without being seen and was able to overpower Matteo and silence Brambilla. Sounds like a ghost, doesn't it?"

Justine frowned. "No, someone far more dangerous. You said you saw Luna Colombo that night, running away from the scene."

She let the suggestion hang. We both looked at the driver, who was nodding along to low music coming from the radio.

"No," I said, my brow furrowing. "I mean, I did, but she . . . she couldn't."

But I knew she could, and as the one person with connections to all the key players, she had to be considered a suspect.

The cab driver dropped us off near the warehouse and left with his double fare plus a generous tip. Justine and I held hands as we walked down the empty lane. When we reached our destination, she pulled me close and kissed me. I held her in my arms, squeezing her, eying her longingly.

"I've missed you," I said.

"Me too," she replied, before kissing me again.

The roll shutter rose suddenly, startling us both. We stepped back from each other. I turned to see Mo-bot in the doorway.

"If you kids are going to leave for a secret assignation, you need to let a grown-up know," she said. "I've been worried about you."

"We went to see Matteo," I revealed. "He says he was knocked unconscious before the shooting."

Mo-bot looked surprised.

"He didn't say anything because he was worried Brambilla might have taken his own life, which would deny him a Catholic burial and a proper place in the hereafter," Justine said.

"That puts everyone at the party firmly in the frame," said Mo-bot. "I mean, we'd been working on that assumption, but he just confirmed it either had to be Brambilla or one of the other guests."

I nodded. "Justine suggested Luna Colombo."

Mo-bot shrugged. "I can see why."

"We need to take another look at things," I said. "Figure out a plan of action. We'll regroup in the morning." I moved to pass her. "Right now, I'm beat."

She stood aside. Weary from the day's events, I made my way through the warehouse and up to the apartment with Justine and Mo-bot following.

I longed to be alone with Justine, but the stolen moments we'd just shared were as good as it was going to get for now.

I leant close and kissed her.

"Night," I said, and she replied in kind. Feeling professionally and personally frustrated, I retreated to the bedroom I shared with Sci. I didn't manage to fall asleep until the first fingers of dawn reached into the room.

CHAPTER 90

MY UNEASY DREAMS were a kaleidoscope of images of the dead: the priests, Lombardi, Altmer, Fathers Brambilla and Diaz careening through my mind, making me feel as though I was spinning out of control, way, way out of my depth.

I woke with a start and saw sunshine edging the drapes, and sat up to find Sci's bed was empty. I could hear low voices coming from beyond the door and the rhythmic clatter of cutlery and plates.

I pulled on a sky-blue shirt and navy trousers and went out in search of the others.

Sci, Mo-bot and Faduma were having breakfast at the kitchen table. Sci had loaded his plate with waffles and was drenching them in syrup. I eyed the stack in amazement.

"What?" he asked defensively. "Hanging around with you is going to get me killed long before anything sugary or fattening does."

Faduma and Mo-bot smiled.

"Is Justine still asleep?" I asked, and Mo-bot nodded.

"Your nocturnal adventure must have tired her out."

"What nocturnal adventure? Or shouldn't I ask?" Sci said.

"We went to see Matteo," I explained. "He told us he was knocked out. So instead of him not remembering what happened, it turns out he was actually unconscious. He thought it was Father Brambilla and didn't tell us in case the authorities declared it was suicide."

"Why the heck would that matter?" Sci asked, taking a bite.

"It's a Catholic thing," I replied.

"Morning," Justine said. She was dressed in shorts and a matching gray T-shirt. It was one of her favorite pajama sets.

"Morning," I replied, going over to kiss her.

"Waffles?" Sci asked.

"No," she replied, "but I'd love coffee."

"Scooch over," Mo-bot said to Sci, making space for Justine and me to bring our chairs up to the table.

"Morning," Faduma said. "So, if Matteo is telling the truth, someone else could have killed Father Brambilla. Someone else who was at the party."

I nodded. "Someone who was nimble enough to get in and out of that room without being noticed."

Sci poured Justine and me freshly made coffee.

"Altmer was at the party, right?" Faduma asked. "What if he kills Brambilla, and someone else takes out Altmer."

"Or it was Luna Colombo?" Justine suggested.

"Wow," Faduma replied. "Of course. Maybe."

"They have to be our prime suspects," I said. "We need to know what Altmer was doing at the bank, how he was connected to the Dark Fates. And I'm going to talk to Elia Antonelli and find out what he and his daughter have really been up to. Stefano Trotta was at their house and then turned up at the Inferno Bar. What do they know about him? What does Luna know about Brambilla's death?"

"I'd like to talk to Trotta directly, if that's okay," Mo-bot said. "See if my old friend and I can put the squeeze on him."

"Old friend?" Sci responded, still tucking into his waffle stack. "Speak for yourself. I'm a vigorous young go-getter."

"Positively teenage," Mo-bot teased.

"Sounds like a plan," I said, sipping my coffee. "You and Sci check out Trotta. Justine and Faduma, go to Vatican City and see what you can find out about Altmer. Ask Joseph Stadler to give you access to whatever records you need. And I'm going out to Antonelli's family farm to ask the old gangster and his daughter some difficult questions."

CHAPTER 91

"YOU THINK WE'LL get to do some sightseeing when this is over?" Sci asked. Mo-bot looked at him incredulously.

"Bodies piling up and you're thinking about booking tours?" she replied. "Just focus on the road."

He was driving the Maserati they'd borrowed from Valentina.

"I love Rome," Sci protested. "It's such a beautiful city."

Mo-bot rolled her eyes. Decades of working serious crime, analyzing scenes and hunting criminals, had robbed the job of some of its drama, but she still wasn't as blasé about it as Sci.

"You can go out to play when all this is over," she said in a patronizing tone.

"I'm not a child, you know," he remarked as he signaled for a right turn. "But that would be nice."

Mo-bot knew something had happened to Trotta the moment

they rounded the corner and joined Via Metronio. The wide, leafy residential avenue ran alongside the Basilica di San Giovanni a Porta Latina and the old missionary college, both buildings surrounded by ancient high brick walls. On the other side of the street stood luxury apartment blocks and grand old villas, surrounded by mature trees that reached high toward the sun.

The road was blocked by police patrol cars, vans and unmarked vehicles. There were local residents in the gardens of the neighboring mansions and apartment blocks, watching events, and a small crowd of passers-by gathered by the wall of the basilica. The high branches shaded them from the burning sun. If it hadn't been for the clear indications that something was very wrong, Mo-bot would have been focused on the beauty and architectural history of the stunning street.

Sci pulled up behind a row of parked cars.

"This probably isn't good," he said.

"I'll see what I can find out," Mo-bot replied.

"Same," he said, reaching for the holdall on the back seat. "I'll take a look inside."

Mo-bot felt stifled by the humid air the moment she left the air-conditioned car. She scanned the crime scene, centered on Stefano Trotta's house, and saw someone she recognized. Mia Esposito was talking to some plain-clothes officers.

Mo-bot walked over, but a uniformed officer at the cordon prevented her from getting too close.

"Inspector," she yelled. "Inspector Esposito."

She registered her name, glanced at Mo-bot and immediately frowned. She excused herself from her colleagues and walked over.

"What's happened here?" Mo-bot asked.

Esposito said nothing.

"Listen, I'm the one who should be upset," Mo-bot said. "You arrested me. Wrongfully."

Still nothing.

"Is Stefano Trotta dead?" Mo-bot tried.

"How would you know that?" Esposito countered.

"I don't know. That's why I'm asking you," Mo-bot replied.

"Instead of you asking me questions, I should be asking you about the whereabouts of Jack Morgan. Did he send you here?"

Whatever was in that house, it hadn't put Esposito in a good mood.

"You tried that already, remember? When you held us without charge," Mo-bot retaliated.

Esposito bristled.

"I didn't mean any discourtesy, Inspector," Mo-bot remarked, checking her own frustration. "I can see you're busy."

She backed away. Esposito scowled at her before returning to her colleagues.

When Mo-bot joined Sci on a patch of grass by the basilica wall, she saw he was piloting a tiny drone through Trotta's villa. The screen on the remote control gave them eyes on the interior. There in the living room was Stefano Trotta's body. He was seated on a large couch, gun in hand, an apparent suicide.

"Grim," Mo-bot observed.

"Not a nice way to die," Sci remarked, favoring the exit wound on the side of Trotta's head.

Mo-bot saw him frown and pilot the drone around the room. On-screen, the drone was broadcasting a view of a blank wall.

"Notice anything?" Sci asked.

Mo-bot shook her head.

"Just a wall." And then she understood. "No bullet hole to match the position of the exit wound."

Sci smiled like an indulgent teacher. "Bingo. There's a large exit wound, meaning there should be a bullet somewhere around here. The fact there isn't one suggests he was killed elsewhere. The ease with which I spotted it means this was either staged in a rush, or it's been put together by someone who knows they can rely on the police not to find the truth."

"Or doesn't care if they do," Mo-bot suggested.

"This was another murder designed to look like a suicide," Sci said.

"Do you think Esposito knows?" Mo-bot asked.

"Either she's in on it, and this is all for show," Sci replied, "or she's too junior to matter and no one cares what she thinks. I don't think she would be deploying all these people if she already knew what really happened."

"I should go over and tell her what you've found, shouldn't I? Being a Good Samaritan and all," Mo-bot said, relishing the prospect.

CHAPTER 92

JUSTINE'S PHONE RANG as she and Faduma crossed St Peter's Square on their way to the headquarters of the Vatican Bank. She saw it was Mo-bot and answered the call.

"Hey."

"Trotta is dead. Murder staged to look like suicide."

"Jeez," Justine replied. "Whatever this thing is, everyone who touches it ends up dead."

"Let's hope not everyone," Mo-bot said. "I've been trying to get hold of Jack. If you reach him before I do, let him know."

"Will do," Justine responded.

"And let me know if you get anything from the Vatican."

"Of course," Justine said, before hanging up.

"Everything okay?" Faduma asked.

"Trotta is dead. Murdered."

Faduma shook her head slowly. "What the hell is this thing? Why are all these people being killed?"

Justine was unsure what to make of the journalist next to her. Faduma was clearly whip smart, diligent and inventive, but Justine had previously had bad experiences with journalists. Most seemed to value their next story above all else and would willingly toss people into the fire of a smoking-hot headline.

They passed through the border security checkpoint, walked along Via Sant'Anna and went inside the rotunda that housed the ancient bank.

Ten minutes later they were being led to Stadler's office by a somber-faced assistant who didn't give her name. When they reached the open-plan room on the top floor, Justine saw what she guessed was Altmer's desk covered in bouquets of flowers and condolence cards. It had become a small and poignant shrine. She lowered her head as she passed, and saw Faduma do the same.

They were taken in to see Joseph Stadler, and Justine was surprised to find him with the man Jack had identified as Father Vito, who was in fact Cardinal Vito Peralta. They were seated on a couch near the window.

"Ms. Smith, Ms. Salah," Stadler said, crossing the room to greet them. "I hope you don't mind but I've asked Cardinal Peralta to join us. He would like to bring his subterfuge to an end."

"Subterfuge?" Justine asked as she and Faduma sat down opposite the men.

"I have not been completely honest," Cardinal Peralta said.

"I'm sorry for your loss by the way," Faduma interjected.

Stadler looked puzzled and Cardinal Peralta nodded sagely.

"The loss of Signor Altmer," Faduma explained. "It must be a blow."

"It is," Stadler replied. "It has been very difficult. Thank you."

"Do go on, Your Eminence," Faduma said.

Cardinal Peralta nodded.

"I was not entirely honest with Jack Morgan. I sit on the board of this bank and have suspected for some time that it is being used by someone to launder money."

"Someone?" Justine asked.

"Criminals," he replied. "I have been studying the employees and my fellow clergy who perform various functions here, looking for clues to what's happening."

"And what have you learnt?" Faduma asked.

"Christian Altmer was doing business with a man called Milan Verde," Cardinal Peralta revealed. "I believe Verde works for an organized crime figure called Elia Antonelli."

Justine shot Faduma a look of concern. Cardinal Peralta had just confirmed her worst fears about the man Jack was on his way to confront.

"After Signor Altmer died, we discovered secret records that show money being transferred to criminal and extremist groups around the world. Money that seems to have originated from Milan Verde, and ultimately, I suspect, Elia Antonelli."

"Can you show us these records?" Justine asked.

"Of course," Cardinal Peralta replied, getting to his feet. "Follow me."

CHAPTER 93

AMR BADAWI HAD rustled up a Kawasaki KX250 dirt bike painted lime green. I rode in jeans, a leather jacket and an opaque helmet so I wouldn't be recognized on the streets of Rome. I kept to the speed limit throughout the city but pushed the bike once I was in the tinder-dry hills. As I roared round the broad sweeping bends that took me toward Casape, I reflected on Antonelli and wondered whether I'd misjudged the man. A mob boss had to be a consummate liar and cheat, he had to mask his intentions and dispose of people without hesitation. Why had I been taken in by the guy?

I turned off the winding lane, onto the track that led to Antonelli's old family farm. When I reached the low stone wall that demarcated the boundary, I saw a new squad of guards who waved me down. Brandishing their weapons like a platoon of twitchy mercenaries, they made me remove my helmet and confiscated my bike, wallet, keys and phone.

My heart thundered but I didn't think they would harm me, not without Antonelli's explicit approval. My instincts proved to be right. Soon an old Land Rover Defender roared up and I was pushed onto the back seat and driven up to the farmhouse.

I was taken round the back of the old building to the grand terrace, where Luna and Antonelli sat drinking coffee. The view of rows of olive trees rolling across the valley was simply beautiful. If I'd had his resources, I'd have retired to spend the rest of my days in this very spot. But like a shark, I suspected that if Antonelli didn't keep hunting, he'd die.

"Mr. Morgan," he said, without standing. "Perhaps we should get you a room in the house?"

He smiled.

"I'm joking of course. You're very welcome. Please sit."

He gestured to the chair opposite Luna's, and it was hard not to be taken in by his genial host act. I found myself warming to the man again, despite everything I knew about him.

"What brings you out here this fine day?" he asked.

I opened my mouth to answer, but at that very moment my phone rang, vibrating in the hands of one of the men who'd brought me here.

"May I?" I asked Antonelli, and he nodded.

I took my phone and saw it was Justine calling.

"Hey," I said when I answered.

"Jack, where have you been?"

"I was on the bike," I replied. "Then I lost my phone for a while."

"Stefano Trotta is dead," she revealed. "Murder staged as suicide."

I looked at Antonelli and wondered if he'd ordered the hit.

"I understand," I said. "I'll be in touch."

I hung up. As I slid the phone onto the table, Antonelli said, "Problem?"

I thought about playing dumb, but there was nothing to be gained.

"Stefano Trotta is dead," I replied. "Murdered."

Antonelli's smile fell. Even the beige linen suit he wore seemed to darken as his face clouded over.

"You must be mistaken," he said.

I shook my head. "My people don't make mistakes about this kind of thing."

He and Luna exchanged fearful glances.

"We should leave," she said, and he nodded.

"Why? What do you have to be afraid of?" I asked.

Antonelli glared at me. "Is that why you're here? Even after all you've seen and heard, you still think I'm behind this?"

He got to his feet and issued commands to his men.

We hurried around the house to the Land Rover. The tallest of the trio of bodyguards got behind the wheel and gunned the engine.

"Switch it off," I said, as Antonelli and Luna climbed in the back.

The driver looked at Antonelli for confirmation. When his boss nodded, he killed the powerful engine.

I stood half in, half out of the car and strained to hear in the sudden silence. Then came the sound I hoped I'd imagined beneath the noise of the engine: the crack and pop of distant gunfire, likely silenced weapons. Someone was on their way to finish the old gangster, and I saw from their fearful expressions that Antonelli and Luna had heard the shooting too.

"Let's go," I said, jumping into the cab. "Now!"

The driver started the engine, stepped on the accelerator, and the powerful old SUV rolled out of the courtyard.

CHAPTER 94

WE WERE RACING along the track toward the estate boundary. The driver and another of Antonelli's men were in the front. Antonelli, Luna and a third man were in the back, and I was in the trunk space on one of the bench seats, being bounced around over every rut and pothole.

"Who's behind this?" I asked.

Antonelli turned to answer, but his breath became a gasp when dozens of bullets peppered the windshield, shattering it. I looked beyond him to see a team of men strafing the vehicle with machine-guns. They stood behind a low wall that had concealed them as we'd approached. My guess was the earlier gunshots had been the sound of them killing Antonelli's perimeter guards.

"Get down!" I yelled, pushing him and Luna toward their footwells.

They ducked, but the driver and front passenger weren't so lucky. Their bodies bucked as the windshield collapsed and they were riddled with bullets. The large SUV veered off the road and I braced for impact as a tree suddenly loomed ahead.

The Land Rover smashed into the trunk at full pelt. I was hurled against the back seat, the impact winding me.

"Is everyone okay?" I asked, the moment I could suck in a breath.

Antonelli and Luna were dazed, and so was the man beside them, but he didn't have the sense to stay in the vehicle.

"Stop!" I yelled, as he opened the door and staggered out.

I tried to grab him but he was beyond my reach. He stumbled forward, blood oozing down his face from a head wound, fumbling for a pistol in his waistband.

As he drew it, the men who'd forced the car off the road came over the brow of a rise nearby and opened fire.

The third man got one shot away before he danced to the buck and kick of each bullet that struck him.

I didn't have time to mourn the unfortunate stranger but climbed over the back seat to join the others.

"Do something!" Antonelli pleaded with me.

"If I get you out of this, you will tell me the truth. Everything you know," I said, before slamming the door shut.

"Yes. Yes!" he exclaimed, his voice almost breaking. "Anything!"

I climbed into the front of the SUV, opened the driver's door and pushed the dead man out. I jumped in his seat. Glancing in the rear-view, I saw the team of gunmen running toward us and prayed the Defender's reputation for reliability was justified.

I turned the ignition and the engine spluttered. A volley of shots hit the back door, thudding into the metal with enough force to make the vehicle tremble. I tried the key again, and this time the engine roared.

I found reverse, backed away from the tree, flipped the car into first and stepped on the gas. Dust, grass and stones were flung up by the tires as we raced forward under a hailstorm of bullets.

I drove between trees, racing across the dry earth, heading for a dip.

The car sped down the hillside. Below us, through a small olive grove, I saw a hedge and beyond it a road.

I put my foot down and we gathered speed as we bounced across the steep ground. By the time we hit the hedge we were doing fifty. As we flew through it, I stepped on the brake pedal and turned the wheel.

The heavy tires screeched and the SUV wobbled as we swerved onto the road.

Breathless, veins full of fire and thunder, I glanced over my shoulder and saw clear road behind.

I didn't relax for a full three minutes, concentrating on putting some distance between us and our attackers. When I looked back again, I saw a shaken Luna and her father had finally begun to breathe more easily.

"I think we're okay," I said to Antonelli. "Which means you're going to keep your word and tell me everything you know."

CHAPTER 95

I DROVE FOR ten kilometers before we turned off the road onto an extremely overgrown track that looked as though it hadn't been used for years. We bounced and bumped our way over long grass that grew in tufts along the median, and the suspension rattled and clattered as the wheels encountered hidden rocks and ruts. I didn't stop until we crested a rise and went down the slope on the other side. I turned off the track onto rough terrain and parked in the shade of a cluster of stone pines . I cut the engine and jumped out to ensure we couldn't be seen from the road or any buildings. There was nothing in sight except deserted countryside. I ran over to the Land Rover as Antonelli and his daughter staggered from the vehicle. I opened the passenger door and dragged the dead man out.

Antonelli came over as I set the bodyguard gently on the ground. The man's eyes were open, but he would never see the beauty of the branches above him.

"Aldo was a good man," Antonelli said, his voice faltering. "They all were."

"I'm sorry," I responded.

Luna joined us. "So, what is the truth, Papà?"

Antonelli shrank from her. "I don't know. I didn't mean—"

She interrupted him.

"You're not getting out of the deal you made. Mr. Morgan risked his life for us."

Antonelli looked ashamed. For the first time, I saw him as a tired old man rather than a powerful gangster.

"You're right of course," he said, stroking her cheek. "Like your mother always was."

He hesitated.

"I wish she was still with us. She was a good person."

"Tell him what you know, Papà," Luna insisted. "Tell me."

Antonelli smiled.

"I could never refuse my girl. I am a founding member of Propaganda Tre. It was started after the fall of the Berlin Wall to protect this country against anti-Christian socialist ideologies."

"Oh, Papà," Luna said, her disappointment so intense I could almost feel it in the air around us.

"I'm sorry, Luna. I was young. I thought I knew what was good for Italy. For Rome. For us. I found myself allied to wicked men with ambitions and plans they did not share with me. Secret plans. Dishonest plans. I thought our group would be different—not like Propaganda Due—but it wasn't. We lost our way."

His voice trailed off.

"And?" I prompted.

"We got involved with espionage, extremist groups. Like our predecessors, we laundered money, financed terror all around the world, drifting further and further toward an ideology I didn't recognize. Not left or right, but one that worships only money."

"Why didn't you tell me?" Luna asked.

"Because he was worried you'd feel it was your duty to investigate," I replied for him. "And that would have put your life in danger."

Antonelli nodded. "I swore an oath of loyalty," he said. "A blood oath. Any betrayal or attempt to leave the organization will result in death. Not just for the renegade, but for everyone they love."

"So, what's happening here in Rome? Why the power play? Why have so many died—some of them men of God?" I asked.

"I don't know," he replied. "That's the thing—I just don't know what's going on. I asked Trotta to pay Milan Verde a visit, to see if he could find out who the Dark Fates are working for. Milan is a psychopath. He's ruthless but doesn't have the ambition to play at this level, so he's working for someone higher up."

"Do you know the other members of Propaganda Tre?" I asked.

"Only the ones in my chapter," Antonelli replied. "Now Trotta is dead, so is Christian Altmer, and—"

"Altmer?" I exclaimed. "He was in Propaganda Tre?"

Antonelli nodded. "As is his boss, Joseph Stadler."

I was dumbfounded and took a moment to absorb this revelation.

"What about Cardinal Vito Peralta?" I asked when I found my voice.

"Yes. The Church is represented."

I paced around for a moment. "What if Stadler didn't hire Private to solve the case? What if he hired us in order to keep tabs on what we were doing? He knew I'd look into Father Brambilla's death and I represented a risk to the organization if I was doing things they weren't aware of. By hiring us he could share what we found, enabling him to gauge the threat of Propaganda Tre being exposed."

I hadn't had the chance to make any formal interim reports to Stadler, but I looked back on my informal meetings with our client and thought about all the useful information he would have gleaned from them. Each meeting with him had happened before an attack or an encounter with someone who'd led me into a trap. After our first meeting, Luna and I were shot at by the assassin who tried to kill us out near Poli. I hadn't made the connection before, but if Stadler was behind everything, those incidents hadn't been coincidences.

I took out the new phone Mo-bot had given me and connected to Private's secure server. I sent a message to Justine, Mo-bot and Sci.

We need to meet. Parco di Monte Ciocci, near Vatican City. Two hours.

I pocketed the phone and turned to Antonelli.

"You could have saved us a lot of time if you'd shared the truth of your involvement with this group sooner."

"I'm sorry. The oath . . . They would kill me and my daughter. I thought I could handle it. I thought I could—"

Luna cut him off. "Could what? Kill someone? Buy someone off? How can we share the same blood? These are bad things. The way you live your life, the way you make your money, the people you associate with, the things you've done . . ."

"Luna," Antonelli pleaded, but she left him nowhere to go.

"I'm sorry, Papà. I can't look away anymore. I can't pretend. Your business goes against God and man," she said. "To be under your protection is to be aligned with you. I cannot agree to live my life like that." She faced me. "Are you going back to Rome?"

I nodded.

"Will you deal with this Stadler?"

I nodded again.

"Then take me with you. I want to help. I want to see him face justice."

I admired her bravery and couldn't believe that only a short while ago I'd thought she might be in league with her father and responsible for Father Brambilla's murder.

"What about me?" Antonelli asked.

"Luigi Calio's farm is over that hill. He has always been loyal. Stay with him and his family until this is over," Luna replied.

She walked back to the Land Rover and got in the driver's side.

"Come on," she said to me.

"What about us?" Antonelli asked pathetically.

"We'll talk when this is over," his daughter told him.

He looked broken, but I didn't feel sorry for him. Luna was right: his dishonesty had cost lives.

I got in the Defender. Luna said nothing as she started the engine. She eyed her father, who seemed much diminished, standing hunched and dejected in the deserted landscape, a dead man lying close by. She kept her eyes fixed on him in the mirror as she turned the car around and we began our return to Rome.

CHAPTER 96

WE LEFT THE track and turned onto Via Roma, a winding country road that would eventually take us back to the city. Soon we were making good progress.

"You didn't know anything about your father's membership of this group?" I asked.

Luna shook her head. "He never speaks to me about his business activities. He's always said it's because he doesn't want to put me in a difficult position, but maybe it's because he felt he couldn't trust me. So there was a big blank space between us. I mean, I had my suspicions. Through my work I have been able to connect some of the dots. His low-life associates and street-level operations are known to me, places like the Pleasure Hall, but this Propaganda Tre connection was kept from me. Or it was until today."

She sounded convincing, but someone who'd been born into

the mob and had to conceal the truth from her colleagues every single day would be an accomplished liar.

"Must be difficult. You being police. Him doing what he does."

She nodded. "Very. But families are sent to test us. Love us but test us."

I smiled. Her expression didn't soften.

We headed along the valley toward Colle Merulino, a tiny village tucked behind the intersection of two highways. We would join one of them, the Autostrada Roma, and head west into the city.

The country road we were on, the Via di San Vittorino, followed a curve around the shoulder of a tree-covered hill before it narrowed to pass through a tunnel bored through a low cliff. When we emerged into dazzling sunshine, I sensed movement. As my eyes adjusted, I saw the flash of a vehicle speeding beyond some trees, coming along Via Polense toward the intersection we were approaching. It was a large dump truck traveling flat out. The driver showed no intention of slowing. In fact, he was clearly aiming to hit us.

"Luna," I yelled. "Stop!"

But it was too late. The truck collided with the Defender, mangling the front of the Land Rover, smashing through the engine block, sending us into a terrible, grinding, crashing spin. The cabin filled with smoke, diesel, the stench of burning metal, scorched rubber, and the world went round and round like a Waltzer in a giant hall of mirrors.

My head collided with the side window, which shattered. Everything went distant. I was dimly aware of us bouncing off the truck but still traveling with it, metal caught and hooked on metal as we spun wildly.

Then stillness.

Suddenly movement, hands pulling me.

Thrown onto my back. Above me, snarling unfamiliar faces, tattoos.

The Dark Fates.

A familiar face.

Milan Verde.

Above his bitter, cynical smile, hovering in the sky, was the drone they'd used to follow us from Antonelli's farmhouse.

Milan Verde lashed out with his boot, and the last thing I saw was his dirty sole filling my vision.

CHAPTER 97

I WAS TUMBLING through time and space, haunted by the dead from Afghanistan to London, Los Angeles to Moscow, time out of joint as it only is in dreams.

"*Lo incastreremo per la morte di Antonelli,*" a voice said from somewhere.

"*Attento che potrebbero sentirti,*" another responded.

"I don't care if they hear me or he understands me," the original speaker said. "In fact, I will say it in English to be sure he can. We will frame him for Antonelli's death."

I realized these speakers weren't among the many specters in my mind. The words had come from another place, the real world that I'd momentarily left behind.

I opened my eyes to blinding flashes of pain and dazzling light.

"We just need the go-ahead," the same voice said.

As my eyes adjusted, I realized the light wasn't dazzling. It was in fact quite low. I just happened to have been facing a wall-mounted spotlight when I opened my eyes. I was in a room made of stone. There were no windows, only uplighters lining the walls, and between each pair of lights was an alcove containing a stone seat. The air had a cool, still quality that made me think I was in a cellar.

I was seated on a chair in the middle of a space about the size of a tennis court. I tried to move and found that both arms and legs were bound to the chair. There were five guys in front of me. I recognized them from the Inferno Bar. Leading the pack of devils was Milan Verde, who prowled closer when he saw I was awake.

"I'm going to enjoy this," he said, slapping me. "Wake up properly, Mr. Morgan."

The sting of his palm against my face revived me further and got my heart pumping. We're predictable creatures, and pain coupled with the prospect of violence sent adrenalin coursing through my body.

My fingers searched out my bonds, and I was relieved to feel cord rather than steel. I couldn't see the knot but tracked the familiar path of a bowline with my fingertips. It wouldn't be difficult to slip. I got to work on it immediately.

"Should we kill them now?" one of Milan's associates asked.

He was looking beyond me. I glanced over my shoulder and saw Elia Antonelli and Luna Colombo, bound and gagged, fear in their eyes.

"Not yet," Milan said, pulling out his phone and making a call. He had a simple message for whoever was at the other end of the line. "He's awake."

CHAPTER 98

A FEW MINUTES later, I heard a door open directly behind me. I tried to look round but it was outside my field of view. Milan stepped forward and slapped me.

"Eyes front, American!"

I glared at him. He was the type who would feed off signs of pain.

There were footsteps behind me and Joseph Stadler walked into view. He wore a finely tailored suit, shirt and tie, and looked as though he had just come from a cocktail party.

"Mr. Morgan," he said. "Who have you told about what you know?"

I didn't respond. I focused on the knot binding my wrists and kept working it loose with the tips of my fingers.

"You and your associates here must die."

I heard muffled objections from Luna and Antonelli.

"But first I need to know how big a problem I face. Do your colleagues also need attention? Ms. Smith, for example?"

Fury must have shone in my eyes.

"She means something to you. More than the others do," Stadler said, moving closer. "Well, we can work with that. If you tell me what I need to know, if you give me assurances, I will give you her life."

I knew no deal with this man would be worth the words wasted on it.

"You killed Brambilla," I said. "When he arrived at the party, he saw you. He saw that you saw him too, and you both knew why he was there: to tell Matteo what you were doing, using the bank to launder money for criminals. For Milan Verde and Elia Antonelli and other members of your secret group Propaganda Tre. He knew you'd been killing the priests, that you'd killed Filippo Lombardi, and he wanted to do the right thing as a good man, to ease his conscience. He was going to give Matteo the whole story. So, you had to act. That's why his death was unlike the others. It was spontaneous. You killed him to prevent him talking."

Stadler smiled. "Well done, Mr. Morgan. I followed them, waited until I was sure no one could see, went into the room and used the pistol I always carry to stun Matteo."

"And then you shot Father Brambilla," I remarked. "Did you pretend to use the restroom? Join the crowd as it gathered? Or slip out of the staff entrance and come in through one of the terrace doors?"

"Staff entrance," Stadler replied. "It really wasn't difficult. Like this, being here with you. None of this is difficult for me. You know, after I'd listened to Father Brambilla beg for a while, I made him a similar deal to the one I am offering you: the truth for Matteo's life. Father Brambilla told me he hadn't shared our secret with anyone else, and he gave me that comfort so Matteo could live."

"But when I reported to you what Matteo had been investigating, you decided to have him killed in police custody," I suggested. "Because you realized he wasn't just some friend Father Brambilla had chosen to confide in, and you were worried Father Brambilla had lied to you and told him everything."

"Correct," Stadler confirmed. "Well done, Mr. Morgan. Your deductive powers came good in the end. I was worried your reputation wasn't justified."

"And the other priests?" I asked. "Why kill them?"

"Your questions are at an end, Mr. Morgan," Stadler replied. He turned to Milan Verde. "Kill him. And them." He pointed at Luna and Antonelli. "Kill them all."

CHAPTER 99

MILAN STEPPED FORWARD and drew a Beretta M9 pistol from behind his back. As he raised it toward my temple, I gave a final tug on the bowline loop binding my wrists, worked my right hand free and grabbed the gun.

He was so shocked he took a step back, but I held fast and the gun stayed in my hand.

I spun it quickly and shot him in the knee. As he went down, crying out in agony, I pointed the weapon at Stadler.

"Move and he dies," I told the five members of the Dark Fates, who were all reaching for their weapons.

I kept the gun steady on Stadler as I undid the cord at my feet and was relieved when I was finally able to stand. Milan was rolling around on the floor, groaning in pain.

"I'll ask you again," I said, stepping toward Stadler, brandishing the gun. "Why all the dead priests?"

A shot rang out and I was struck by what felt like a hammer blow to my shoulder. I fell on my back, gasping with shock, and the Beretta clattered across the stone floor.

I raised my head to see who'd shot me and was shocked when Cardinal Vito Peralta emerged from a shadowed alcove beside the heavy wooden door. He wasn't wearing his customary robe, but was instead in a dark suit and clerical collar.

"The priests were couriers we used to move money around," he said. "Each of them could have implicated Joseph and me in criminal activities. We gave them their instructions directly. They were the only witnesses to our sins who weren't criminals or members of Propaganda Tre themselves. They posed a threat to our plans."

"What plans?"

"Elevation," Cardinal Peralta said.

"To becoming Pope," I guessed. "To running the Vatican Bank," I suggested, looking at Stadler.

My initial shock was wearing off and my shoulder was burning with fiery agony.

"That's what this was about . . . Ambition? Power?" I asked, surprised by how weak my voice sounded. I caught Antonelli's eye and he gave me a knowing look. It was the ancient Roman pursuit he'd spoken of.

"God created man, Mr. Morgan," Cardinal Peralta replied. "Why would he have given us ambition if we weren't meant to use it? With eight billion of us on this planet, do we really have to worry about the loss of a handful of priests? They served a cause and fulfilled their heavenly purpose."

His words were monstrous, a betrayal of our common faith. I wondered how many warning signs had been ignored over the years. How many people had seen the hunger for power in this man's eyes and been unable to do anything about it. Unchecked evil would only grow, and these two men planned to take control of one of the oldest institutions in the world and use it to further their own warped objectives and the aims of their corrupt group. I couldn't allow that to happen.

I eyed the fallen pistol. If I could just reach it, I would take my chances with a left-handed shot.

Cardinal Peralta stepped forward.

"You wouldn't get to it in time. Your destiny was written by God before the first light flashed into existence. You will die here tonight, your reputation forever destroyed after you murdered Elia Antonelli and Luna Colombo because your organization became involved with his criminal enterprises. Your colleagues in Rome, including Ms. Smith, will all join you soon."

He raised his weapon and I held my breath. I had to move now. I pictured myself lunging for the Beretta, and tensed, ready to pounce.

The unbearable swell of expectation was punctured by the sound of my phone ringing. It was on the floor by the chair I'd been bound to. Stadler looked down at it.

"Justine," he said.

"Maybe we can convince her to tell us where they are," Cardinal Peralta said. "Or get her to come here."

"Don't!" I said, but Stadler picked up the phone and answered the call.

"Hello?" he said. "Ms. Smith?

"She wants to be on speaker," he explained shortly afterwards.

"Justine, no!" I said, but Stadler silenced me with a kick, and Cardinal Peralta pressed the barrel of his gun against Luna's temple and eyed me menacingly.

"I want to talk to Cardinal Peralta," Justine said. "I want him to hear what I have to say. Check your right lapel, Cardinal."

Peralta looked down, and as his eyes widened, I realized I'd missed something incredibly important. There, clinging to his lapel, was one of our micro-drones.

"We used Jack's phone to find him when he didn't show up for our meeting," Justine revealed. "We couldn't get the drone into the cellar until you and Mr. Stadler arrived. We flew it in with you. It has been streaming live footage to the Internet ever since you set foot in that room."

Cardinal Peralta was horrified. Horror quickly turned to rage.

I knew what was coming and sprang as he turned his gun on me.

I grabbed the Beretta, rolled over and shot the Cardinal in the gut twice before he could pull the trigger.

The wooden door exploded in a storm of splinters and I recognized some of Antonelli's men as they ran through the dust and smoke, brandishing machine-guns.

They yelled at the Dark Fates in Italian, and Milan Verde's men had the good sense to realize they were beaten.

I hauled myself to my feet and walked over to Peralta, who lay bleeding on the stone floor.

"It's over," I said. "You and your friends," I gestured at Milan Verde and Joseph Stadler, "will face justice. You will have years to consider how you've betrayed your faith."

"Jack!"

I glanced round to see Justine, Sci, Mo-bot and Faduma enter.

I hobbled over to Justine and we embraced and kissed. She felt me wince.

"Oh my God," she said. "You need a doctor."

I kissed her again.

"You have no idea how good it is to see you." I looked at Faduma, Sci and Mo-bot. "All of you. I'm already feeling so much better."

CHAPTER 100

FATE PUT ME in the same place as Matteo Ricci, in Fatebenefratelli Hospital on the Isola Tiberina, in a private room tucked away under the eaves.

Justine, Mo-bot and Sci came to visit me during my five-day stay. Cardinal Peralta had shot me in the shoulder, but the bullet had passed through muscle and bone and hadn't harmed anything vital. Although it was painful and my mobility would be impaired for a while, my prognosis was good.

I was also visited by Inspector Mia Esposito, who wanted my testimony and details of everything we'd uncovered during our investigation. No amount of power or money could save Cardinal Peralta or Joseph Stadler. In fact, Stadler was feeling so much pressure from the police there was already talk of him doing a deal with the prosecutor, giving up Propaganda Tre in exchange for a shorter prison sentence.

On my fifth day in the hospital, as the warm summer wind was blowing over the Tiber and in at my open attic window, bringing with it the glorious rich smells of the city, Dr Farid Jalili entered, a frown on his face, a chart and pen held in his hand. He made a point of studying my records, but I knew it was for show. I had taken a shine to the charismatic, funny doctor.

"It's good news, Mr. Morgan." He broke into a grin. "It looks like you're fit to go. I can discharge you."

"That's really great," I said, getting to my feet.

I hadn't been up much since my admission except for short trips to the bathroom, and it took me a moment for me to steady myself.

"Thank you, Dr Jalili, you and your team have been amazing."

"You're welcome, Mr. Morgan. Try not to get shot again."

He left the room. In the closet beside the bed I found fresh clothes Justine had brought over during a visit.

I put on a dark blue suit and white shirt, taking great care to properly fit the sling they'd given me to support my injured shoulder. The black shoes were the most difficult thing to manage, but despite working one-handed, I succeeded in the end. I made a call on the new phone Mo-bot had given me.

"Justine, it's me. Yeah, they gave me the all clear. Thanks. I'll wait for you outside."

I hung up, excited to see her and our friends.

I had originally planned to wait on the bridge in front of the hospital and watch the river go by, but after thanking the ward staff, I took the stairs down to Matteo's room.

He was lying in bed when I walked in.

"Jack," he said. "How's the shoulder?"

"I get to keep it," I replied.

He smiled, though it didn't last long. "If you want my resignation, I won't be happy to give it but I'll understand why."

I was silent for a moment.

"It's clear to me you made a couple of bad judgment calls, but none of us is perfect," I replied. "Once you're on your feet, I would like you to finish setting up the Rome office. You have the necessary skills and experience to make Private Rome exceptional."

Matteo nodded and his smile returned. "Thank you, Jack. Thank you so much."

CHAPTER 101

AFTER LEAVING MATTEO, I went outside and waited on the bridge in front of the hospital. I was relieved and happy when Sci, Mo-bot and Justine arrived in a taxi.

Justine jumped out of the vehicle and ran to me but stopped when I took a step back warily.

"I'm sorry," she said. "I almost forgot."

She embraced me on my good side, avoiding my bullet wound, and we kissed.

It felt so great to be reunited with her, and the smile on her lips told me she felt exactly the same way.

Sci and Mo-bot greeted me warmly when I joined them in the cab. The driver took us through the Eternal City to the Hassler, which had been my home when I'd first arrived in Rome.

It was a relief not to be looking over my shoulder, watching for danger at every turn. After spending the afternoon in our suite where we could finally be alone, Justine and I went to meet Sci and Mo-bot in the hotel's rooftop bar and restaurant for pre-dinner drinks.

We entered the busy space to find our colleagues sitting with Faduma Salah. The tenacious journalist had filed stories that had given her readers the inside scoop on Propaganda Tre, the Dark Fates and the role of Joseph Stadler and Cardinal Peralta in laundering money for these groups. It was proving to be one of the most sensational scandals in modern Italian history, implicating government ministers like the deceased Stefano Trotta, financiers, mob bosses and clergy.

"Hello, Mr. Morgan," Faduma said as Justine and I joined them at their table.

"You know you can call me Jack," I replied, wincing slightly as I caught myself at a bad angle while taking my seat.

"Are you okay?" Faduma and Justine said simultaneously.

"Jinx," Mo-bot teased.

"I'm fine, thanks," I replied. "Just need to get used to taking it easy."

"You did well," Faduma said. "You all did."

"So did you," Sci replied. "I see your stories being covered everywhere."

"You did great," I said. "In fact, Private is still looking for a second-in-command for the Rome office."

Faduma smiled. "That's very kind, Jack, but I'm a journalist, not a detective. I have an obligation to my readers, and quite frankly, I don't like the idea of being shot at all the time."

"It's not all the time," Sci replied. "Just on weekdays."

Everyone chuckled.

The maître d' approached. "Your table is ready, Mr. Morgan."

"If you won't join our company, at least keep us company for dinner," I said to Faduma.

She nodded. "It would be my pleasure."

CHAPTER 102

THE FOLLOWING MORNING, we packed what luggage we had and loaded it into the back of the silver Range Rover Vogue the hotel had provided as an airport shuttle.

Mo-bot sat beside the driver, an older man with thinning gray hair, a warm smile and mischievous eyes. Justine, Sci and I were in the back, and I didn't pay much attention to what was happening until I realized we weren't heading toward the airport.

"Excuse me?" I said to the driver.

"Yes?"

"Where are we going?"

"Signor Antonelli would like to show his thanks to you before you leave Rome," the driver replied as calmly as if he was giving us a weather update.

I had no idea how Antonelli had subverted a hotel driver, or how he knew about our travel plans, but he was one of the most powerful men in Rome, and for now was free from threat or worries because he had somehow been able to conceal his association with Propaganda Tre. His reach must go very high indeed.

He certainly seemed happy when I saw him standing with Luna in the car park at the end of Via Sant'Anna in Vatican City.

"I hope you don't mind," he said as we all stepped out of the SUV.

"Sorry, Mr. Morgan," Luna added as we approached. "He likes grand gestures."

"What is wrong with a grand gesture to the people who saved our lives?" he asked. "Come. There's someone I want you to meet."

He led us through the brick archway onto Via Sant'Anna and we walked along the ancient road to the Papal Palace near the Vatican Bank.

"We're going to meet the Pope, aren't we?" Mo-bot remarked.

She wasn't Catholic, but for some reason the prospect clearly excited her. I wasn't so eager to be confronted by God's representative on earth. My own feelings about my faith were unclear and hadn't been helped by the discovery that an institution like the Church had been used by evil men to spread their poison.

Thankfully, once we passed through security we were shown into the vast and opulent office of Cardinal Sala, the Pope's personal representative. Unlike Cardinal Peralta, Cardinal Sala wore the customary royal purple, but with no air of vanity or pomp. When his assistant showed us in, the cardinal rose from his desk and greeted us warmly.

"Mr. Morgan, Ms. Smith, Ms. Roth, Mr. Kloppenberg, the Church owes you a great debt. His Eminence the Holy Father has asked me to convey his gratitude."

I nodded. "You're welcome."

"The Church will of course honor your engagement and pay any bills you present in relation to this investigation."

"Thank you," I replied.

I had thought the arrest of our original client would result in this being a pro bono case, so was relieved to know the Vatican would make good.

The cardinal offered us tea, which we took on a grand balcony overlooking the Fontana dei Delfini, decorated with statues of dolphins and set in a beautiful ornamental garden. We discussed the most superficial and polite aspects of the case.

After twenty minutes, we took our leave and returned to the parking lot to find the Range Rover waiting where we had left it.

"Thank you, Mr. Morgan," Antonelli said, embracing me. "I owe you much."

He smiled at Luna. When I'd started this investigation, I could never have imagined it would end with me putting our client behind bars and being hugged and thanked by one of the biggest criminals in Rome.

"I'm going to convince him to retire," Luna said in my ear as she embraced me. "Thank you for keeping us alive."

"You're welcome," I replied. "I hope you succeed in getting him to spend more time farming olives and baking bread."

She grinned. "I'll try my best."

The two of them said farewell to Justine, Sci and Mo-bot, and we all climbed back into the climate-controlled luxury SUV.

"Ready?" the driver asked.

I looked at Mo-bot, Sci and Justine in turn, and each of them smiled and nodded.

"Ready," I replied. "Let's go home."

ACKNOWLEDGMENTS

We'd like to thank Nicole Witmer, Emily Griffin and the team at Penguin for their excellent work on this book. We'd also like to thank you, the reader, for joining Jack Morgan and the Private team on another adventure, and hope you'll return for the next one.

Adam would like to thank James Patterson for his continued guidance. Thanks too to Adam's wife, Amy, and their children, Maya, Elliot and Thomas, for their love and support. He'd also like to express his gratitude to his agent, Nicola Barr, and to Malcolm Carter, whose donation to a local school charity gave him the right to name a character after his daughter, Emily Carter.

ABOUT THE AUTHORS

JAMES PATTERSON is one of the best-known and biggest-selling writers of all time. His books have sold in excess of 400 million copies worldwide. He is the author of some of the most popular series of the past two decades – the Alex Cross, Women's Murder Club, Detective Michael Bennett and Private novels – and he has written many other number one bestsellers including stand-alone thrillers and non-fiction.

James is passionate about encouraging children to read. Inspired by his own son who was a reluctant reader, he also writes a range of books for young readers including the Middle School, Dog Diaries, Treasure Hunters and Max Einstein series. James has donated millions in grants to independent bookshops and has been the most borrowed adult author in UK libraries for the past fourteen years in a row. He lives in Florida with his family.

ADAM HAMDY is a bestselling author and screenwriter. His most recent novel, *The Other Side of Night*, has been described as ingenious, constantly surprising and deeply moving. He is the author of the Scott Pearce series of contemporary espionage thrillers, *Black 13* and *Red Wolves*, and the Pendulum trilogy. Keep up to date with his latest books and news at www.adamhamdy.com.

Have you read them all?

PRIVATE
(with Maxine Paetro)

Jack Morgan is head of Private, the world's largest investigation company with branches around the globe. When his best friend's wife is murdered, he sets out to track down her killer. But be warned: Jack doesn't play by the rules.

PRIVATE LONDON
(with Mark Pearson)

Hannah Shapiro, a young American student, has fled her country, but can't flee her past. Can Private save Hannah from the terror that has followed her to London?

PRIVATE GAMES
(with Mark Sullivan)

It's July 2012 and excitement is sky high for the Olympic Games in London. But when one of the organisers is found brutally murdered, it soon becomes clear to Private London that everyone involved is under threat.

PRIVATE: NO. 1 SUSPECT
(with Maxine Paetro)

When Jack Morgan's former lover is found murdered in his bed, Jack is instantly the number one suspect, and he quickly realises he is facing his toughest challenge yet.

PRIVATE BERLIN
(with Mark Sullivan)

Mattie Engel, one of Private Berlin's rising stars, is horrified when her former fiancé Chris is murdered. Even more so when she realises that the killer is picking off Chris's friends. Will Mattie be next?

PRIVATE DOWN UNDER
(with Michael White)

Private Sydney's glamorous launch party is cut short by a shocking discovery – the murdered son of one of Australia's richest men. Meanwhile, someone is killing the wealthy wives of the Eastern Suburbs, and the next victim could be someone close to Private.

PRIVATE L.A.
(with Mark Sullivan)

A killer is holding L.A. to ransom. On top of this, Hollywood's golden couple have been kidnapped. Can Private prove themselves once again?

PRIVATE INDIA
(with Ashwin Sanghi)

In Mumbai, someone is murdering seemingly unconnected women in a chilling ritual. As the Private team race to find the killer, an even greater threat emerges . . .

PRIVATE VEGAS
(with Maxine Paetro)

Jack Morgan's client has just confessed to murdering his wife, and his best friend is being held on a trumped-up charge that could see him locked away for a very long time. With Jack pushed to the limit, all bets are off.

PRIVATE SYDNEY
(with Kathryn Fox)

Private Sydney are investigating the disappearance of the CEO of a high-profile research company. He shouldn't be difficult to find, but why has every trace of evidence he ever existed vanished too?

PRIVATE PARIS
(with Mark Sullivan)

When several members of Paris's cultural elite are found dead, the French police turn to the Private Paris team for help tackling one of the biggest threats the city has ever faced.

THE GAMES
(with Mark Sullivan)

The eyes of the world are on Rio for the Olympic Games, and Jack is in Brazil's beautiful capital. But it's not long before he uncovers terrifying evidence that the Games could be the setting for the worst atrocity the world has ever seen.

PRIVATE DELHI
(with Ashwin Sanghi)

Private have opened a new office in Delhi, and it's not long before the agency takes on a case that could make or break them. Human remains have been found in the basement of a house in South Delhi. But this isn't just any house, this property belongs to the state government.

PRIVATE PRINCESS
(with Rees Jones)

Jack Morgan has been invited to meet Princess Caroline, third in line to the British throne, who needs his skills (and discretion) to help find her missing friend. Jack knows there is more to this case than he is being told. What is the Princess hiding?

PRIVATE MOSCOW
(with Adam Hamdy)

Jack Morgan is investigating a murder at the New York Stock Exchange and identifies another killing in Moscow that appears to be linked. So he heads to Russia, and begins to uncover a conspiracy that could have global consequences.

PRIVATE ROGUE
(with Adam Hamdy)

A wealthy businessman approaches Jack Morgan with a
desperate plea to track down his daughter and grandchildren,
who have disappeared without a trace. As Jack investigates the
disappearances, the trail leads towards Afghanistan – where
Jack's career as a US Marine ended in catastrophe . . .

PRIVATE BEIJING
(with Adam Hamdy)

After an attack on the Beijing office leaves three agents dead and
the head of the team missing, Jack Morgan immediately gets on
a plane from LA to investigate. But it's not long before another
Private office is attacked and it's clear that the entire
organisation is under threat . . .

Discover James Patterson's best new series
since the Women's Murder Club . . .

12 MONTHS TO LIVE

OUT SEPTEMBER 2023

ONE

"FOR *THE* LAST TIME," my client says to me. "I. Did. Not. Kill. Those. People."

He adds, "You have to believe me. I didn't do it."

The opposing counsel will refer to him as "the defendant." It's a way of putting him in a box, since opposing counsel absolutely believe he *did* kill all those people. The victims. The Gates family. Father. Mother. And teenage daughter. All shot in the head. Sometime in the middle of the last night of their lives. Whoever did it, and the state says my client did, had to have used a suppressor.

"Rob," I say, "I might have mentioned this before: I. Don't. Give. A. Shit."

Rob is Rob Jacobson, heir to a legendary publishing house and also owner of the biggest real estate company in the Hamptons. Life was good for Rob until he ended up in jail, but that's true for pretty much everybody, rich or poor. Guilty or innocent. I've defended both.

Me? I'm Jane. Jane Smith. It's not an assumed name, even though I might be wishing it were by the end of this trial.

There was a time when I would have been trying to keep somebody like Rob Jacobson away from the needle, back when New

York was still a death penalty state. Now it's my job to help him beat a life sentence. Starting tomorrow. Suffolk County Court, Riverhead, New York. Maybe forty-five minutes from where Rob Jacobson stands accused of shooting the Gates family dead.

That's forty-five minutes with no traffic. Good luck with that.

"I've told you this before," he says. "It's important to me that you believe me."

No surprise there. He's been conditioned his entire life to people telling him what he wants to hear. It's another perk that's come with being a Jacobson.

Until now, that is.

We are in one of the attorney rooms down the hall from the courtroom. My client and me. Long window at the other end of the room where the guard can keep an eye on us. Not for my safety, I tell myself. Rob Jacobson's. Maybe the guard can tell from my body language that I occasionally feel the urge to strangle him.

He's wearing his orange jumpsuit. I'm in the same dark-gray skirt and jacket I'll be wearing tomorrow. What I think of as my sincerity suit.

"Important to *you*," I say, "not to me. I need twelve people to believe you. And I'm not one of the twelve."

"You have to know that I'm not capable of doing something like this."

"Sure. Let's go with that."

"You sound sarcastic," he says.

"No. I *am* sarcastic."

This is our last pretrial meeting, one he's asked for and is a complete waste of time. Mine, not his. He looks for any excuse to get out of his cell at the Riverhead Correctional Facility for even an hour and has insisted on going over once more what he calls "our game plan."

Our—I run into a lot of that.

I've tried to explain to him that any lawyer who allows his or her client to run the show ought to save everybody a lot of time and effort—and a boatload of the state's money—and drive the client straight to Attica or Green Haven Correctional. But Rob Jacobson never listens. Lifelong affliction, as far as I can tell.

"Rob, you don't just want me to believe you. You want me to like you."

"Is there something so wrong with that?" he asks.

"This is a murder trial," I tell him. "Not a dating app."

Looks-wise he reminds me of George Clooney. But all good-looking guys with salt-and-pepper hair remind me of George. If I had met him several years ago and could have gotten him to stay still long enough, I might have married him.

But only if I was between marriages at the time.

"Stop me if you've heard me say this before, but I was set up."

I sigh. It's louder than I intended. "Okay. Stop."

"I *was*," he says. "Set up. Nothing else makes sense."

"Now, you stop me if you've heard this one from me before. Set up by whom? And with your DNA and fingerprints sprinkled around that house like pixie dust?"

"That's for you to find out," he says. "One of the reasons I hired you is because I was told you're as good a detective as you are a lawyer. You and your guy."

Jimmy Cunniff. Ex-NYPD, the way I'm ex-NYPD, even if I only lasted a grand total of eight months as a street cop, before lasting barely longer than that as a licensed private investigator. It was why I'd served as my own investigator for the first few years after I'd gotten my law degree. Then I'd hired Jimmy, and finally started delegating, almost as a last resort.

"Not to put too fine a point on things," I say to him, "we're not just good. We happen to be the best. Which *is* why you hired both of us."

"And why I'm counting on you to find the real killers eventually. So people will know I'm innocent."

I lean forward and smile at him.

"Rob? Do me a favor and never talk about the real killers ever again."

"I'm not O.J.," he says.

"Well, yeah, he only killed two people."

I see his face change now. See something in his eyes that I don't much like. But then I don't much like him. Something else I run into a lot.

He slowly regains his composure. And the rich-guy certainty that this is all some kind of big mistake. "Sometimes I wonder whose side you're on."

"Yours."

"So despite how much you like giving me a hard time, you do believe I'm telling you the truth."

"Who said anything about the truth?" I ask.

TWO

GREGG McCALL, NASSAU COUNTY district attorney, is wait-ing for me outside the courthouse.

Rob Jacobson has been taken back to the jail and I'm finally on my way back to my little saltbox house in Amagansett, east of East Hampton, maybe twenty miles from Montauk and land's end.

A tourist one night wandered into the tavern Jimmy Cunniff owns down at the end of Main Street in Sag Harbor, where Jimmy says it's been, in one form or another, practically since the town was a whaling port. The visitor asked what came after Montauk. He was talking to the bartender, but I happened to be on the stool next to his.

"Portugal," I said.

But now the trip home is going to have to wait because of McCall, six foot eight, former Columbia basketball player, divorced, handsome, extremely eligible by all accounts. And an honest-to-God public servant. I've always had kind of a thing for him, even when he was still married, and even though my sport at Boston College was ice hockey. Even with his decided size advantage, I figure we could make a mixed relationship like that work, with counseling.

McCall has made the drive out here from his home in Garden City, which even on a weekday can feel like a trip to Kansas if you're heading east on the Long Island Expressway.

"Are you here to give me free legal advice?" I ask. "Because I'll take whatever you got at this point, McCall."

He smiles. It only makes him better looking.

Down, girl.

"I want to hire you," he says.

"Oh, no." I smile back at him. "Did *you* shoot somebody?"

He sits down on the courthouse steps and motions for me to join him. Just the two of us out here. Tomorrow will be different. That's when the circus comes to town.

"I want to hire you and Jimmy, even though I can't officially say that I'm hiring you," he says. "And even though I'm aware that you're kind of busy right now."

"I'd only be too busy if I had a life," I say.

"You don't have one? You're great at what you do. And if I can make another observation without getting MeToo'ed, you happen to be great looking."

Down, girl.

"I keep trying to have one. A life. But somehow it never seems to take." I don't even pause before asking, "Are you going to now tell me what you want to hire me for even though you can't technically hire me, or should we order Uber Eats?"

"You get right to it, don't you?" McCall asks.

"Unless this is a billable hour. In which case, take as much time as you need."

He crosses amazingly long legs out in front of him. I notice he's wearing scuffed old loafers. Somehow they make me like him even more. I've never gotten the sense that he's trying too hard, even when I've watched him killing it a few times on Court TV.

"Remember the three people who got shot in Garden City?" he asks. "Six months before Jacobson is accused of wiping out the Gates family."

"I do. Brutal."

Three senseless deaths that time, too. Father, mother, daughter, a sophomore cheerleader at Garden City High. I don't know why I remember the cheerleader piece. But it's stayed with me. A robbery gone wrong. Gone bad and gone tragically wrong.

"Well, you probably also know that the father's mother never let it go until she finally passed," he says, "even though there was never an arrest or even a suspect worth a shit."

"I remember Grandma," I say. "There was a time when she was on TV so much I kept waiting for her to start selling steak knives."

McCall grins. "Well, it turns out Grandma was right."

"She kept saying it wasn't random, that her son's family had been targeted, even though she wouldn't come out and say why."

"She finally told me why but said that if I went public with it, she'd sue me all the way back to the Ivy League."

"But you're going to tell me."

"Her son gambled. Frequently and badly, as it turns out."

"And not with DraftKings, I take it."

"With Bobby Salvatore, who is still running the biggest book in this part of the world."

"Jimmy's mentioned him a few times in the past. Bad man, right?"

"Very."

"And you guys missed this?"

"Why do you think I'm here?"

"But upstanding district attorneys like yourself aren't allowed to hire people like Jimmy and me to run side investigations."

"We're not. But I promised Grandma," he says. "And there's an exception I believe would cover it."

"The case was never closed, I take it."

"But we'd gotten nothing new in all this time until a guy in another investigation dropped Salvatore's name on us."

"And here you are."

"Here I am."

"I don't mean to be coarse, McCall, but I gotta ask: who pays?"

"Don't worry about it," he says.

"I'm a worrier."

"Grandma liked to plan ahead," he says. "She was ready to go when we found out about the Salvatore connection. When I took it to her, she said, 'I told you so,' and wrote a check. She told me that she was willing to pay whatever it took to find out who took her family."

"This sounds like your crusade, not mine."

"Come on, think of the fun," Gregg McCall says. "While you're trying to get your guy off here, you can help me put somebody else away."

I know all about McCall by now. He's more than just a kick-ass prosecutor. He's also tough and honest. Didn't even go to Columbia on an athletic scholarship. Earned himself one for academics. Could have gone to a big basketball school. His parents were set on him being Ivy League. Worked his way to pay for the rest of college. The opposite of the golden boy I'm currently representing, all in all.

"I know we're supposed to be on opposing sides," McCall says. "But if I can make an exception..."

I finish his thought. "So can I."

"I'm asking you to help me do something we should have done at the time. Find the truth."

"You ought to know that my client just now asked me if

I thought he was telling the truth. I told him that I wasn't interested in the truth." I shrug. "But I lied."

"If you agree to do this, we'll kind of be strange bedfellows."

"You wish," I say.

Actually, *I* wish.

"I know asking you to take on something extra right now is crazy," he says.

"Kind of my thing."

THREE

ON MY WAY HOME, I call Jimmy Cunniff at the tavern. He used to get drunk there in summers when he'd get a couple of days off and need to get out of the city, day-trip to the beach and party at night. Now he owns the business, but not the building, though his landlord is not just an old friend but also someone, in Jimmy's words, who's not rent-gouging scum.

A Hamptons rarity, if you must know.

Jimmy's not just an ex-cop, having been booted out of the NYPD for what he will maintain until Jesus comes back was a righteous shooting, and killing, of a drug dealer named Angel Reyes. He's also a former Golden Gloves boxer and, back in the day, someone who had short stories published in long-gone literary magazines. The beer people should have put Jimmy out there as the most interesting man in the world.

He's also my best friend.

I tell him about Gregg McCall's visit, and his offer, and him telling me we can name our own price, within reason, because Grandma is paying.

"You think we can handle two at once?" Jimmy asks.

"We've done it before."

"Not like with these two," he says, and I know he's right about that.

"Two triple homicides," Jimmy Cunniff says. "But not twice the fun."

"Who knows, maybe solving one will show us how to solve the other. Maybe we'll even slog our way to the truth. Look at it that way."

"I don't know why you even had to ask if I was on board," Jimmy says. "You knew I'd be in as soon as you were. And you were in as soon as McCall asked you to be."

"Kind of."

"Stop here and we'll celebrate," he says.

I tell Jimmy I'll take a rain check. I have to go straight home; I need to train.

"Wait, you're still fixed on doing that crazy biathlon, even now?"

"I just informed Mr. McCall that crazy is kind of my thing," I say.

"Mine, too."

"There's that."

"Are you doing this thing for McCall because you want to or because the hunky DA is the one who asked you to?"

"What is this, a grand jury?"

"Gonna take that as a yes on the hunk."

"Hard no, actually," I say. "I couldn't do that to him."

"Do what?"

"Me," I say.

There was a little slowdown at the light in Wainscott, but now Route 27 is wide-open as I make my way east.

"For one thing," I tell Jimmy, "Gregg McCall seems so happy."

"Wait," Jimmy says. "Both your ex-husbands are happy."

"Now they are."

FOUR

MY TWO-BEDROOM SALTBOX is at the end of a cul-de-sac past the train tracks for the Long Island Railroad. North side of the highway, as we like to say Out Here. The less glamorous side, especially as close to the trains as I am.

My neighbors are mostly year-rounders. Fine with me. Summer People make me want to run back to my apartment in the West Village and hide out there until fall.

There is still enough light when I've changed into my Mets sweatshirt, the late-spring temperature down in the fifties tonight. I put on my running shoes, grab my air rifle, and get back into the car to head a few miles north and east of my house to the area known as the Springs. My favorite hiking trail runs through a rural area by Gardiners Bay.

Competing in a no-snow biathlon is the goal of my endless training. Trail running. Shooting. More running. More shooting. A perfect event for a loner like me, and one who prides herself on being a good shot. My dad taught me. He's the one who started calling me Calamity Jane when he saw what I could do at the range.

Little did he know that carrying a gun would one day

become a necessary part of my job. Just not in court. Though sometimes I wish.

I park my Prius Prime in a small, secluded lot near Three Mile Harbor and start jogging deep into the woods. I've placed small targets on trees maybe half a mile apart.

Fancy people don't go to this remote corner of the Hamptons, maybe because they can't find a party, or a photographer. The sound of the air rifle being fired won't scare the decent people out here, who don't hike or jog in the early evening. If somebody does make a call, by now just about all the local cops know it's me. Calamity Jane.

I use the stopwatch on my phone to log my times. I'm determined to enter the late-summer biathlon in Pennsylvania, an event Jimmy has sworn only I've ever heard about. Or care about. He asked why I didn't go for the real biathlon.

"If you ever see me on skis, find my real gun and shoot *me* with it."

I know I'm only competing against myself. But I've been a jock my whole life, from age ten when I beat all the boys and won Long Island's NFL Punt, Pass, and Kick contest, telling my dad I was going to be the first girl ever to quarterback the Jets. I remember him grinning and saying, "Honey, we've had plenty of those on the Jets since Joe Namath was our QB."

Later I was Hockey East Rookie of the Year at BC. That was also where I really learned how to fight. And haven't stopped since. Fighting for rich clients, not-so-rich ones, fighting when I'm doing pro bono work back in the city for victims who deserve a chance. And deserve being repped by somebody like me. Fighting with prosecutors, judges, even the cops sometimes, as much as I generally love cops, maybe because of an ex-cop like Jimmy Cunniff.

Occasionally fighting with two husbands.

Makes no difference to me.

You want to have a fight?

Let's drop the gloves and do this.

I'm feeling it even more than usual tonight, pushing myself, hitting my targets like a champion. I stop at the end of the trail, kneel, empty the gun one final time. Twelve hundred BBs fired in all.

But I'm not done. Not yet. Still feeling it. *Let's do this.* I reload. Hit all the targets on the way back, sorry I've run out of light. And BBs. What's the old line? Rage against the dying of the light? I wasn't much of a poet, but my father Jack, the Marine and career bartender, liked Dylan Thomas. Maybe because of the way the guy could drink. My mother, Mary, who spent so much of her marriage waiting for my father to come from the bar, having long ago buried her dreams of being a writer, had died of ovarian cancer when I was ten. I'd always thought I had gotten my humanity from her, my sense of fairness, of making things right. It was different with my father the Marine, who always taught me that if you weren't the one on the attack, the other guy was. His own definition of humanity, just with much harder edges. He lasted longer than our mom did, until he dropped dead of a heart attack one night on a barroom floor.

It's dark by the time I get back to the car. I'm thinking about having one cold one with Jimmy. But then I think about making the half-hour drive over to the bar in Sag Harbor and back, and how I really do need a good night's sleep, knowing I'm going to be a little busy in the morning, even before I head to court.

I drink my last bottle of water, get behind the wheel, toss the rifle onto the back seat, knowing my real gun, the Glock, is locked safely in the glove compartment. I have a second one at home. A girl can't have too many.

I feel like I used to feel in college, the night before a big game. I think about what the room will look like tomorrow. What it will feel like. Where Rob Jacobson will be and where I'll be and where the jury will be.

I've got my opening statement committed to memory. Even so, I pull up the copy stored on my phone. I slide the seat back, lean back, begin to read it over again, keep reading until I feel my eyes starting to close.

When I wake up, it's morning.

Also By James Patterson

ALEX CROSS NOVELS

Along Came a Spider • Kiss the Girls • Jack and Jill • Cat and Mouse • Pop Goes the Weasel • Roses are Red • Violets are Blue • Four Blind Mice • The Big Bad Wolf • London Bridges • Mary, Mary • Cross • Double Cross • Cross Country • Alex Cross's Trial (*with Richard DiLallo*) • I, Alex Cross • Cross Fire • Kill Alex Cross • Merry Christmas, Alex Cross • Alex Cross, Run • Cross My Heart • Hope to Die • Cross Justice • Cross the Line • The People vs. Alex Cross • Target: Alex Cross • Criss Cross • Deadly Cross • Fear No Evil • Triple Cross

THE WOMEN'S MURDER CLUB SERIES

1st to Die (*with Andrew Gross*) • 2nd Chance (*with Andrew Gross*) • 3rd Degree (*with Andrew Gross*) • 4th of July (*with Maxine Paetro*) • The 5th Horseman (*with Maxine Paetro*) • The 6th Target (*with Maxine Paetro*) • 7th Heaven (*with Maxine Paetro*) • 8th Confession (*with Maxine Paetro*) • 9th Judgement (*with Maxine Paetro*) • 10th Anniversary (*with Maxine Paetro*) • 11th Hour (*with Maxine Paetro*) • 12th of Never (*with Maxine Paetro*) • Unlucky 13 (*with Maxine Paetro*) • 14th Deadly Sin (*with Maxine Paetro*) • 15th Affair (*with Maxine Paetro*) • 16th Seduction (*with Maxine Paetro*) • 17th Suspect (*with Maxine Paetro*) • 18th Abduction (*with Maxine Paetro*) • 19th Christmas (*with Maxine Paetro*) • 20th Victim (*with Maxine Paetro*) • 21st Birthday (*with Maxine Paetro*) • 22 Seconds (*with Maxine Paetro*) • 23rd Midnight (*with Maxine Paetro*)

DETECTIVE MICHAEL BENNETT SERIES

Step on a Crack (*with Michael Ledwidge*) • Run for Your Life (*with Michael Ledwidge*) • Worst Case (*with Michael Ledwidge*) • Tick Tock (*with Michael Ledwidge*) • I, Michael Bennett (*with Michael Ledwidge*) • Gone (*with Michael Ledwidge*) • Burn (*with Michael Ledwidge*) • Alert (*with Michael Ledwidge*) • Bullseye (*with Michael Ledwidge*) • Haunted (*with James O. Born*) • Ambush (*with James O. Born*) • Blindside (*with James O. Born*) • The Russian (*with James O. Born*) • Shattered (*with James O. Born*) • Obsessed (*with James O. Born*)

PRIVATE NOVELS

Private (*with Maxine Paetro*) • Private London (*with Mark Pearson*) • Private Games (*with Mark Sullivan*) • Private: No. 1 Suspect (*with Maxine Paetro*) • Private Berlin (*with Mark Sullivan*) • Private Down Under (*with Michael White*) • Private L.A. (*with Mark Sullivan*) • Private India (*with Ashwin Sanghi*) • Private Vegas (*with Maxine Paetro*) • Private Sydney (*with Kathryn Fox*) • Private Paris (*with Mark Sullivan*) • The Games (*with Mark Sullivan*) • Private Delhi (*with Ashwin Sanghi*) • Private Princess (*with Rees Jones*) • Private Moscow (*with Adam Hamdy*) • Private Rogue (*with Adam Hamdy*) • Private Beijing (*with Adam Hamdy*)

NYPD RED SERIES

NYPD Red (*with Marshall Karp*) • NYPD Red 2 (*with Marshall Karp*) • NYPD Red 3 (*with Marshall Karp*) • NYPD Red 4 (*with Marshall Karp*) • NYPD Red 5 (*with Marshall Karp*) • NYPD Red 6 (*with Marshall Karp*)

DETECTIVE HARRIET BLUE SERIES

Never Never (*with Candice Fox*) • Fifty Fifty (*with Candice Fox*) • Liar Liar (*with Candice Fox*) • Hush Hush (*with Candice Fox*)

INSTINCT SERIES

Instinct (*with Howard Roughan, previously published as Murder Games*) • Killer Instinct (*with Howard Roughan*) • Steal (*with Howard Roughan*)

THE BLACK BOOK SERIES

The Black Book (*with David Ellis*) • The Red Book (*with David Ellis*) • Escape (*with David Ellis*)

STAND-ALONE THRILLERS

The Thomas Berryman Number • Hide and Seek • Black Market • The Midnight Club • Sail (*with Howard Roughan*) • Swimsuit (*with Maxine Paetro*) • Don't Blink (*with Howard Roughan*) • Postcard Killers (*with Liza Marklund*) • Toys (*with Neil McMahon*)

• Now You See Her (*with Michael Ledwidge*) • Kill Me If You Can (*with Marshall Karp*) • Guilty Wives (*with David Ellis*) • Zoo (*with Michael Ledwidge*) • Second Honeymoon (*with Howard Roughan*) • Mistress (*with David Ellis*) • Invisible (*with David Ellis*) • Truth or Die (*with Howard Roughan*) • Murder House (*with David Ellis*) • The Store (*with Richard DiLallo*) • Texas Ranger (*with Andrew Bourelle*) • The President is Missing (*with Bill Clinton*) • Revenge (*with Andrew Holmes*) • Juror No. 3 (*with Nancy Allen*) • The First Lady (*with Brendan DuBois*) • The Chef (*with Max DiLallo*) • Out of Sight (*with Brendan DuBois*) • Unsolved (*with David Ellis*) • The Inn (*with Candice Fox*) • Lost (*with James O. Born*) • Texas Outlaw (*with Andrew Bourelle*) • The Summer House (*with Brendan DuBois*) • 1st Case (*with Chris Tebbetts*) • Cajun Justice (*with Tucker Axum*)• The Midwife Murders (*with Richard DiLallo*) • The Coast-to-Coast Murders (*with J.D. Barker*) • Three Women Disappear (*with Shan Serafin*) • The President's Daughter (*with Bill Clinton*) • The Shadow (*with Brian Sitts*) • The Noise (*with J.D. Barker*) • 2 Sisters Detective Agency (*with Candice Fox*) • Jailhouse Lawyer (*with Nancy Allen*) • The Horsewoman (*with Mike Lupica*) • Run Rose Run (*with Dolly Parton*) • Death of the Black Widow (*with J.D. Barker*) • The Ninth Month (*with Richard DiLallo*) • The Girl in the Castle (*with Emily Raymond*) • Blowback (*with Brendan DuBois*) • The Twelve Topsy-Turvy, Very Messy Days of Christmas (*with Tad Safran*) • The Perfect Assassin (*with Brian Sitts*) • House of Wolves (*with Mike Lupica*) • Countdown (*with Brendan DuBois*) • Cross Down (*with Brendan DuBois*) • Circle of Death (*with Brian Sitts*) • Lion & Lamb (*with Duane Swierczynski*)

NON-FICTION

Torn Apart (*with Hal and Cory Friedman*) • The Murder of King Tut (*with Martin Dugard*) • All-American Murder (*with Alex Abramovich and Mike Harvkey*) • The Kennedy Curse (*with Cynthia Fagen*) • The Last Days of John Lennon (*with Casey Sherman and Dave Wedge*) • Walk in My Combat Boots (*with Matt Eversmann and Chris Mooney*) • ER Nurses (*with Matt Eversmann*) • James Patterson by James Patterson: The Stories of My Life • Diana, William and Harry (*with Chris Mooney*) • American Cops (*with Matt Eversmann*)

MURDER IS FOREVER TRUE CRIME

Murder, Interrupted (*with Alex Abramovich and Christopher Charles*) • Home Sweet Murder (*with Andrew Bourelle and Scott Slaven*) • Murder Beyond the Grave (*with Andrew Bourelle and Christopher Charles*) • Murder Thy Neighbour (*with Andrew Bourelle and Max DiLallo*) • Murder of Innocence (*with Max DiLallo and Andrew Bourelle*) • Till Murder Do Us Part (*with Andrew Bourelle and Max DiLallo*)

COLLECTIONS

Triple Threat (*with Max DiLallo and Andrew Bourelle*) • Kill or Be Killed (*with Maxine Paetro, Rees Jones, Shan Serafin and Emily Raymond*) • The Moores are Missing (*with Loren D. Estleman, Sam Hawken and Ed Chatterton*) • The Family Lawyer (*with Robert Rotstein, Christopher Charles and Rachel Howzell Hall*) • Murder in Paradise (*with Doug Allyn, Connor Hyde and Duane Swierczynski*) • The House Next Door (*with Susan DiLallo, Max DiLallo and Brendan DuBois*) • 13-Minute Murder (*with Shan Serafin, Christopher Farnsworth and Scott Slaven*) • The River Murders (*with James O. Born*) • The Palm Beach Murders (*with James O. Born, Duane Swierczynski and Tim Arnold*) • Paris Detective • 3 Days to Live

For more information about James Patterson's novels, visit www.penguin.co.uk.